PICTURE-PERFECT
CHRISTMAS

Praise for Charlotte Greene

The Wedding Setup

"Adored this story! The perfect rom-com in the perfect settings... As with all good rom-coms, there were those intense moments, the dramatic ones, and the ones of realisation that just made the whole thing magical. I really enjoyed the story and can't recommend it enough to all romance lovers."—*LESBIreviewed*

From the Woods

"[N]onstop action and vivid depictions of the wilderness keeps the pages turning...[A] satisfying diversion."—*Publishers Weekly*

"I enjoyed this one very much. I thought the cast of characters were really interesting. Anything queer, supernatural, and survival horror is going to catch my attention 100%. This kept it throughout... Action packed. Queer. Survivalist horror. It hit a lot of my marks."—*Raychel Bennet, Librarian (Bullitt County Public Library)*

"Greene is an accomplished writer and she's able to ratchet up the suspense extremely well—whether it's a slow mounting sense of danger as the heroines find more and more things 'off' or the race through the forest with god knows who or what chasing them down. This is a book that will grab you and drag you along. It was hard to put it down (at 1.00 a.m.) but I didn't want to continue reading when I was tired and miss stuff."—*To Be Read Reviews*

Legacy

"Greene does a good job of building suspense as the story unfolds. Strange things happen one by one in increasingly spooky fashion. Background information is revealed a little bit at a time and makes you want to try and solve the mystery...I recommend this to those who like to read about hauntings, nature, history, DIY home maintenance, violent husbands, scary things in the woods, and water."—*Bookvark*

"The characters are well developed, and Greene hit just the right amount of tension between them...I rarely like every character in a book, but I loved the whole group. The creepiness never let up, the tension built steadily, and...things escalated rapidly. The ending was very satisfying! Horror is definitely Greene's forte."—*Bookish Sort*

"This is a wonderfully scary paranormal novel. The setting is perfect and well described. The characters are well-drawn and likable. The romance between Jo and Andy is especially charming and fits perfectly into the tale. This is just a wonderful story, and I'm so glad I read it, even in the middle of the night. If you love a good scary story, I believe you will love it too."—*Rainbow Reflections*

"Greene likes to take her time to work up the suspense, starting with smaller and seemingly inconsequential things that build up a suitably creepy atmosphere. Placing the characters in an isolated setting ratchets things up. This isn't a gore-fest nor is it relying on jump-scares to set the atmosphere—instead it's a well paced ghost story with strongly developed characters."—*C-Spot Reviews*

"Greene does a great job of establishing a creepy atmosphere by setting a rather slow (but not overly so) pace, taking the necessary time to describe the woods, the uncared-for cabin, the ominous well from the cover, the sounds, the smells, the weather and temperatures."—*Jude in the Stars*

"Very fun horror story that just touches on the creep factor without going full blown scary. There's a lot of really good elements to the book, from the menacing spook, to the mystery, and even the relationship...Great work!"—*Colleen Corgel, Librarian, Queens Public Library*

Gnarled Hollow

"Greene has done an outstanding job of weaving in all sorts of layers; mysterious patterns in the gardens, missing rooms, odd disappearances, blandly boring journals, unknown artwork, and each mystery is eventually revealed as part of the horrific whole. Combined with intensely emotional descriptions of the fear the characters experience as they are targeted by the tortured spirit and this book is genuinely a page turner…not only could I not sleep after reading it, I didn't want to put it down."—*Lesbian Reading Room*

"*Gnarled Hollow* by Charlotte Greene is an awesome supernatural thriller that will terrify and entertain you for hours on end."—*The Lesbian Review*

"*Gnarled Hollow* is a creepy mystery story that had me gripped from the start. There was layer upon layer of mystery and plenty that I didn't see coming at all."—*Kitty Kat's Book Review Blog*

"Scared myself to death, but hauntingly beautiful! Had my heart beating at rapid speeds and my mind working overtime with this thought-provoking story. Piecing together the mystery of *Gnarled Hollow* was both fascinating and scary as hell. It takes talent to put that much suspense and thrill into words that build the picture so vividly, painting descriptions that you can imagine perfectly and see as you read."—*LESBIreviewed*

"I really enjoyed this. This is the fifth book I have read by Greene and by far my favorite. It had some good twists and kept me in suspense until the end. In fact, I was a little sad when it ended. This would be a perfect book to read around Halloween time…I would absolutely recommend this to paranormal-crime/mystery fans. I really hope Greene takes the opportunity to write more books in similar genres I would love to read them if she does. 5 stars."—*Lez Review Books*

A Palette for Love

"The relationship really works between the main characters, and the sex is steamy but not over the top."—*Amanda's Reviews*

Pride and Porters

"Have you ever wondered how *Pride and Prejudice* would work if it were two women falling in love with a brewery as a backdrop? Well, wonder no more!…All in all, I would say this is up near the top on my list of favorite *Pride and Prejudice* adaptations."—*Amanda Brill, Librarian, Rowan Public Library (North Carolina)*

"Greene's charming retelling of *Pride and Prejudice* transplants the Bennets into the world of Colorado craft beer...The story beats are comfortingly familiar, with the unusual backdrop of brewing and beer competitions, modern setting, and twists on the characters providing enough divergence to keep the reader engaged... Feminism, lesbianism, and class are all touched on in this refreshing update on a classic. (Starred review)"—*Publishers Weekly*

"*Pride and Porters* by Charlotte Greene is a contemporary take on the classic romance novel *Pride and Prejudice*, by Jane Austen. Greene works within the framework of Austen's novel and owns it with her particular blend of attraction, money, and intrigue as the women journey towards Happily-Ever-After. While the original focused on the struggles of English women to attain financial and social security through marriage, Greene shows women for whom love and partner compatibility aren't simply happy bonuses. Readers will appreciate the ratcheting drama, character chemistry, and thawing emotions in this modern-day retelling."—*Omnivore Bibliosaur*

By the Author

A Palette for Love

Love in Disaster

Canvas for Love

Pride and Porters

Gnarled Hollow

Legacy

On the Run

From the Woods

The Wedding Setup

Picture-Perfect Christmas

Visit us at www.boldstrokesbooks.com

PICTURE-PERFECT CHRISTMAS

by
Charlotte Greene

2022

Credits

Editor: Shelley Thrasher
Production Design: Stacia Seaman
Cover Design by Inkspiral Design

Acknowledgments

Special thanks to my editor, Shelley Thrasher, who clarifies and improves everything I write.

Thanks also to my family and friends, who have supported me in countless ways, promoting my work with an enthusiasm that always warms my heart.

Final thanks to my wife, who makes everything possible. Love you, hon.

CHAPTER ONE: NICOLE

"Thank God," Nicole said.

As she cleared the end of the tunnel, and the red-orange majesty of Glenwood Canyon finally opened up around her, she knew she was almost home. This stretch was one of the most startling parts of the country, connecting Denver to the Western Slope of Colorado. Canyon walls rose in stark, almost barren beauty over a thousand feet in some places above the road, the red sand and limestone dotted with pine and aspen.

Suddenly picking up a signal, her Bluetooth speakers blared to life, and she screamed, startled and swerving before getting the volume down again. Driving through the mountains, even on a major interstate like this, meant popping in and out of civilization for hours at a time.

She put her signal on for the first Glenwood Springs exit, her spirits rising at the distinct, sulfuric scent of the hot springs. The smell was so tied up with her childhood, it brought back a thousand happy memories of swimming with her family and friends.

Her mom Annette lived a few blocks behind the majestic Hotel Colorado, where she had also worked until her recent retirement. As Nicole drove past the hotel, she slowed, taking in the decorations she could make out from the street. They'd put them up last week, so they'd be here the entire month of December. At night, the hotel would be festooned with thousands of white twinkling lights, but even now, in the early afternoon, she could see an enormous Christmas tree set up in the front courtyard with decorative, oversized wrapped gifts.

Smiling, Nicole sped up, turning left past the hotel, the road now climbing into the foothills behind. She turned onto the street of her childhood home and could see her mother standing at the foot of her driveway. When she spotted Nicole's car, she started waving and jumping up and down. Nicole had to slow so her mom could get out of her way. She parked and launched herself outside. Soon they were hugging and squealing, dancing around the driveway together with their hands and forearms clasped.

Nicole calmed herself first, wiping a few tears from her eyes. Her mother's eyes were also wet, her nose red.

"Were you out here waiting for me?" Nicole asked.

"Of course! But not for long—maybe ten minutes."

"Oh, Mom. You didn't have to do that."

Annette waved a hand at her dismissively. "Oh, honey, you know me. I was too excited to wait inside. I was wearing a hole in the carpet pacing around in there, driving the dogs crazy."

The idea of her mom here alone all the time now had been weighing on Nicole since her mom's retirement last summer. Her dad had died almost three years ago, but her mom had always had work to keep her busy. She had lots of friends, and her garden and her dogs, but spending day after day by herself would be hard on anyone. Nicole visited when she could, but since she lived a few hours away, it wasn't by any means often or long.

"I can see what you're thinking, Nicole, but I'm fine! I was just excited. I haven't seen you since summer."

"I'm sorry, Mom. I tried to make Thanksgiving happen, but—"

"I said don't worry about it. I know you work hard, honey. Now come on inside. The dogs will be happy to see you."

Her mom's English bulldogs ignored her entirely as she came in, as they had their entire lives. Both had eyes only for her mom, and both were clearly ecstatic to see her, despite her short absence, their thick bodies wagging with delight. Finally, one of them gave Nicole's hand a quick, snuffling, slobbery sniff before he raced back to his favorite person.

The tiny living room was sparsely furnished—two overstuffed armchairs, a coffee table, and the big flat-screen—everything exactly as it had been when her dad was still alive. Her mom had put up a tiny Christmas tree in the only available corner—a plastic one, this year, Nicole was sad to see. It hadn't been decorated yet.

"Your room's all set up for you," Annette said, still crouched and petting the dogs. "Go ahead and get settled. Feel free to lie down for a bit while I get lunch together."

Nicole's room had been her childhood bedroom, and it wasn't a shrine, as she'd seen in some of her friends' homes after they moved out. Her parents had needed the space, and it had functioned as a guest room/craft room since she'd left for college almost twenty years ago. Very little of her own past was here.

Her mom's house was miniature—two bedrooms, one bath, and slightly under a thousand square feet, but she was lucky to have it and keep it in the current local market. Nicole and her parents had moved here from an apartment complex when she was a kid, and it had been a rental then. Her dad had managed to save enough to convince the absentee landlord to sell it to them during the housing crisis, and now, despite its miniscule size, the house was worth hundreds of thousands of dollars. Luckily her dad's life insurance policy had been enough to keep up with the taxes after his death. Glenwood Springs was not a cheap place to live.

Nicole flopped down onto the bed, too tired to go back outside and drag her luggage in. She'd had to pack a lot for this trip, so it would take several trips in and out to get it all inside. Maybe a quick nap would get her going again.

Her mom knocked a bit later, startling her upright.

"Nicole? You decent?"

How many times has she asked me that from behind that door? "Come on in!"

Her mother poked her head in, smiling. "Take a nap?"

Nicole nodded, rubbing her face. "Was I out long?"

"No. Half an hour, maybe. Come on and get up, now, and we can have some lunch."

All her luggage and equipment from the car had been set outside her bedroom door.

"Oh, Mom! Come on. You didn't have to do that."

Her mom shrugged and kept walking into the little kitchen. Somehow, in the last half hour, her mom had managed to unload her car and create a giant spread of food. Several different kinds of breads, crudité, chips, premade salads, and cheeses covered the island.

"Jeez, Mom. Feeding an army here?"

"Driving's hungry business, Nicole. Your dad always said so, anyway."

Her father had been a truck driver, and yes, he always came home ravenous. As she loaded her plate, she saw the wisdom in this claim, as her hunger woke with the sight of the food, and she served herself huge portions of several things. The dogs were watching her mother closely, waiting for the inevitable snack thrown their way, but, as always, they ignored Nicole.

She and her mom both finished their meals in relative silence, commenting once or twice on the food, but otherwise absorbed in eating. Nicole finally pushed her plate away.

"Soooo." Annette pursed her lips.

"Soooo," Nicole responded, grinning and suddenly excited.

Her mom slapped her arm playfully. "Stop teasing. You said you had a surprise for me. Do I have to wait for Christmas, or can you tell me now?"

Nicole pretended to think about it, then cracked a wide grin and grabbed her mother's hand. "I can tell you now."

"What is it?"

"Well, I'm not pregnant, if that's what you're thinking."

Her mom slapped her arm again. "Well, jeez, I know that, honey. I would be goddamned surprised, considering."

Nicole snorted. "Right?"

"Okay. Now what is it?"

"So, you know how I'm here early this year?"

"Yes. You told me you were coming twice this month—once now and once for Christmas."

"And you must have noticed all the stuff I brought with me."

"I did. I thought maybe you wanted to take some pictures while you were here."

Nicole grinned. "Well, I'm not coming twice."

"Oh?"

"Nope! I'm here until mid-January."

Annette's eyebrows shot up before she beamed at her. "What do you mean? You're going to be here all month?"

"Yes! You've got me for almost six weeks. That is, if it's okay with you. I could always get a hotel for part—"

"Oh, for God's sake, Nicole. Of course you're staying here. Do you think I've got some grand plans or something? I'm so happy, honey. How did you manage it?"

"Well, you know how I've been saying that I wanted to get some work here? So I could stay longer?"

"Yes?"

"That's what happened! The City of Glenwood hired me to do some photography for their new tourism campaign."

"Oh, wow!" Annette said, clapping. "That's so wonderful! Is it enough money?"

It wasn't—not by a long shot. Nicole normally made a great deal of money this time of year—sometimes more than a quarter of her yearly income over the next six weeks. Most of her paying photography work the rest of the year was commercial—food photography and the like—but she made an exception this time of year for what she'd started her career with: families and weddings, mostly because it paid so well during the holidays. She'd often do Christmas photos right up until the day she normally came here for a visit. And New Year's Eve was a popular wedding date. She also always had a great deal of work in early January, too, with pre-Valentine's photo packages. But she had some savings, and she'd always promised herself if she could get any kind of work here in her hometown, she'd stay longer. The pay for her job this month with the city wasn't a terrible amount of money, but she wasn't about to confess any of this to her mother.

"It's plenty, Mom," Nicole said instead, squeezing her hand.

She saw a flicker of doubt flash across her mom's face, but the next moment, Annette had pulled her into a tight hug.

When they both drew back, Annette's eyes were wet again. "I'm so happy, Nicole. It's the best gift you could have given me. All I want is to spend time with you."

"I'm glad too, Mom. I like being here with you."

They sat quietly again, both smiling, her mother occasionally wiping her eyes.

"Tell me about this job, then. What kinds of pictures do they want you to take?"

Nicole paused, trying to summarize. "All kinds, really. They want the whole shebang. They want to sell the city for vacationers, weddings, backpackers, skiers, that kind of thing. I'll be going to the usual tourist sites, but also some trails, the resorts, looking for wild animals—anything that will sell the town to someone with vacation hours to burn."

"That sounds interesting, actually."

She nodded. In fact, while Nicole was a successful photographer and made a very good living at it, the work that paid the bills could be fairly boring and repetitive. Her fine photography had been featured in galleries and museums, and her show collections often sold well, but that kind of work was always secondary to her main income stream. Getting to do a variety of shoots here in Glenwood over the next month was one more perk to this city job. Still, there was a catch, and she winced when she remembered it.

"What?" Annette asked, reading her clearly, as always.

"It's nothing," Nicole said, not wanting, in any way, to dampen her mom's joy.

"What is it? You looked like somebody goosed you."

Nicole sighed. She'd wanted to avoid this conversation altogether—the feelings, at least on her end, it would bring up, which her mom was aware of. But of course she should have known that her mother would get it out of her at the first whiff.

"There's just a small wrinkle," Nicole finally said, shrugging and not making eye contact.

"What do you mean? What kind of wrinkle?"

"I'm not working alone. The city hired two of us."

"Who's the other photographer?"

"Someone local."

"Someone local?" Annette's forehead wrinkled and then cleared. "Oh. It's Quinn, right?"

Nicole sighed. "Yes. It's Quinn."

❖

Nineteen Years Ago: December 1999

Nicole leapt into the air, slapping the huge paper banner that hung across the hallway and nearly tearing it. She landed poorly, stumbled, and almost dropped her portfolio. Her friend Kevin laughed and punched her arm.

"You're gonna get caught," he said, peering around, clearly expecting a teacher.

"So what? Who cares? Five months and we're out of here, man. What's the worst that could happen?"

Kevin shuddered. "Detention with Coach Briggs."

Nicole shuddered, too. "That's true. Sorry. I guess I'm just excited."

"About the Winter Dance?" Kevin pointed up at the banner.

Nicole rolled her eyes. "As if. No—it's this big, full-ride scholarship thing I told you about."

"Oh, yeah? Isn't that application due?"

"Yep. I have to mail everything by Friday to meet the deadline."

"How much of it do you have done?"

"The photographs are developed, but I have to get them, what do you call it, scanned and loaded or whatever. That's why I'm going to the computer lab."

Kevin paused, frowning. "Wait—you're not coming in to work?"

She and Kevin had worked at Dairy Queen together. The job had been only marginally tolerable because they both worked there and goofed around all shift eating ice cream and having food fights.

Nicole winced. "Actually, Kevin, I quit."

"What? What do you mean you quit! When the hell did that happen?"

Nicole winced further. "A few days ago?"

"What the hell, Nicole? When were you going to tell me?"

She sighed. "I'm sorry. I wanted to tell you sooner, but I chickened out. I knew you wouldn't be happy about it."

"Well, no shit, Nicole! Now what am I going to do? You know I have to work there, right? To save up for college next year? It's not like Glenwood Springs has a million jobs for teenagers or anything. I mean, isn't that why you were working there?"

"That's the thing, Kevin. If I get this scholarship, I won't *need* to work there anymore."

"That's a pretty goddamn big 'if,' though."

"But I won't even have a chance at the 'if' if I spend all my spare time making Dilly Bars."

"But you just said the application is due Friday. What are you going to do after that?"

Nicole shrugged. "Wait, I guess. Or maybe see if I can find some more scholarships to apply for. And Mom can always get me some work at the hotel, if I need some extra cash."

"You bitch," Kevin said, but with little rancor. Nicole relaxed.

They'd walked together to the computer lab, and she stopped in front of the doors, turning fully toward him.

"Tell you what—if I get this scholarship, we'll have a big blow-out celebration with some of my savings. A real, honest-to-God party at the end of the year."

Kevin seemed skeptical, his brows lowered and his lips puckered. "Yeah? Doing what? Where? Drinking Kool-Aid in your parents' two-bedroom shack?"

She smacked his arm. "Harsh, man. No—I'll rent something. It will be like an alternative prom or something, only for us freaks."

His expression brightened at once, and he beamed, showing his braces. "Yeah? That sounds cool. Good luck, in that case."

She smacked his shoulder again and waved as he left. She watched him walk toward the bus stand before she turned back to the lab doors. She'd never been in here before, and while she had several appointments booked on the computer and scanner this week, she was still anxious. Outside of the very few, infrequent computer sessions she'd had in middle school playing *Oregon Trail*, she'd never worked with computers. Her parents certainly couldn't afford one. Nicole had been meaning to take an extracurricular class to learn the basics, but she'd never found the time in her schedule. She took a deep breath and opened the door.

Quinn Zelinski looked back at her from one of the computers. Nicole froze, as always, when she caught sight of her. She and Quinn had gone all the way through school together, from kindergarten till now, their senior year. That entire time, they'd run in overlapping friend circles but were not, themselves, friends. They'd been in near contact in various classes and activities since their first day of school. They'd also attended the same parties the last couple of years, hung out with a lot of the same people. Like her, Quinn was interested in art and photography, and now in their senior year, a good portion of their day was taken up by various classes that ran as art studios. Both, without speaking about it, always sat as far away as possible in their crowded classrooms. They weren't antagonistic or hostile, by any means, but they kept their distance.

Nicole had had a massive crush on Quinn since the moment she saw her in kindergarten. Her friends teased her that this crush was blatantly obvious from the way she stared at and mooned over Quinn all the time. And Quinn seemed to know about her feelings, too, either through mutual friends or the constant dopey, dazed look on Nicole's face when she was around.

Today Quinn was wearing a cute hoodie Nicole had seen her in before—maroon with mini black skulls. She'd recently shaved one side of her head, and the hoop earrings and studs that ran up the length of her ear shone in the bright neon light. She'd brushed the rest of her blond waves over to the other side of her head and was wearing her usual palette of heavy eyeliner and dark lipstick. Her jeans were shredded and safety-pinned, her tall, black combat boots polished to a shine. She was a punk vision.

"Can I help you?" Quinn finally asked.

Nicole cleared her throat, almost choking on the sudden dryness, and stepped into the room, the heavy lab door slamming shut behind her. She flinched and gave Quinn a wry smile.

"Sorry."

Quinn shrugged. "It happens."

This was possibly the longest conversation they'd ever had, and Nicole was suddenly lost. She had no idea what to say next.

"So why are you here?" Quinn asked.

Nicole snapped back into reality. "What? Oh. I have an appointment. I'm supposed to learn how to use the scanner so I can scan some stuff and load it."

Quinn turned slightly and grabbed a nearby clipboard. She reviewed it briefly.

"I see. You have it booked all week. I'm sorry—I didn't look at this yet." She stood and gestured at a large machine in the corner. "Do you know how it works?"

"No. I was hoping Mr. Anderson could show me." Mr. Anderson was the computer and journalism teacher here at Glenwood High.

Quinn shook her head. "Mr. Anderson doesn't work here after school—he does yearbook in the fall. It's just me here till five every day. But I can show you."

Nicole's stomach dropped with excited dread, and she approached closely enough that she caught a whiff of Quinn's perfume—something floral, maybe, covering a slight hint of clove cigarettes. She watched as Quinn turned on a nearby computer. As they waited, neither of them talked, and Nicole was struck by the stunning fact that she could think of literally nothing to say.

"Okay," Quinn finally said, still in her chair. "What kind of storage device do you have?"

"What's that?"

Quinn frowned. "You know—like something to save your work on?"

Nicole lifted her shoulders. "I don't know what you mean."

Quinn's frown deepened. "You know, so you can take whatever you scan with you when you leave?"

Nicole started sweating despite the room's coolness. This was the same shame she always experienced when she ran into something she didn't know about, or had never done before, especially when that something related to her family's lack of money.

"I don't…I mean, I'm not used to working with computers. This is my first time. I don't know anything about them."

Quinn's faced cleared, and she reached out as if to touch Nicole, dropping her hand just before making contact.

"Oh. I'm sorry, Nicole. I didn't mean to—"

"It's okay," Nicole said quickly, desperate to get past their mutual embarrassment.

Quinn gave her a soft smile, the first Nicole had ever experienced directed her way, and Nicole's stomach did that funny swooping sensation again. Damn, she was cute.

"All right, so let me explain," Quinn said. "Basically, when you save something on a computer, it has to go somewhere. It can stay here on the computer's hard drive," she patted the computer's box itself, "or it can go somewhere else." She gestured vaguely at the world. "I'm assuming you need to take whatever it is with you? What do you need to scan?"

Nicole held up her portfolio. "A bunch of my photographs, and then I need to mail them out somehow."

"Ah, okay." Quinn stood up and went over to a small storage locker. She fiddled with the combination before pulling out a small, blue plastic box.

"This is called a Zip drive," she said, handing it to Nicole. "It's big enough to hold a lot of files on it but, as you can see, pretty portable, too."

"Great! Perfect! Can I have this one?"

Quinn shook her head. "That one's mine. I wanted to show it to you, so you'd know what to buy."

"Okay. So where can I get one?"

Quinn shrugged. "I had my dad order that one for me. I mean, they might have them at Kmart, but I'm pretty sure you'll have to go to Grand Junction to get one right away."

"Grand Junction? Really?" Nicole's stomach twisted. She'd taken the bus once or twice to Grand, but it was a long trip, and only a couple of busses a day ran there. She'd have to miss a day of school, and it also meant losing all day with the scanner today and probably tomorrow, too. Suddenly, Friday seemed much too soon to get this done.

Nicole groaned. "Well, shit. I guess I won't be able to do this after all."

"What do you need all these photographs scanned for?"

"I'm applying for a scholarship. The Mary Sheen? Ever heard of it?"

Quinn's expression flickered with some unreadable emotion. "Yes. I've heard of it."

"Anyway—I have to send them in with the application by Friday to be eligible."

Quinn bit her lip, gazing at the floor. Nicole's stomach started its weird dance again. Damn, she was more than cute up close like this.

Quinn's pale-blue eyes met hers, and Nicole watched a strange expression—regret? sorrow? acceptance?—pass across her face. Finally, Quinn sighed.

"Okay, Nicole—let's do this. Go ahead and use my Zip today and tomorrow. I have a pretty big hard drive at home. Then, once you have your own, we'll transfer everything over to yours."

Nicole could hardly believe it. "You'd do that for me?"

Quinn stared at her for a long beat before shrugging. "Sure. Just make sure you get your own this week, okay?"

Nicole nodded eagerly. "Thank you, thank you!"

Quinn smiled broadly this time, a light blush dusting her dimpled cheeks, and Nicole realized then that she would do about anything in her power to see that smile again.

"No problem," Quinn said, clearing her throat. "All right. So let me show you how to do this. I'll scan a couple of photographs, walk you through a couple, and then leave you to it, all right?"

"Yes. Thank you, again, Quinn. You're a lifesaver."

Quinn moved to sit down again, and Nicole grabbed a second chair to drag closer, sitting as near as she dared. Quinn was very patient, showing her each step more than the few times she'd initially suggested. Finally, on the tenth photograph or so, she turned to Nicole, indicating the scanner.

"I think you've got this now. You okay to keep working alone?"

Nicole wanted to stay here sitting next to Quinn for the rest of the day, but that was selfish. Actually, she'd grasped the whole process much sooner—three or four photos ago—and she had bumbled a couple of steps on purpose to continue the lesson. But she couldn't play stupid forever.

"I've definitely got it," she said. "Thanks for making everything so clear."

That color was back in Quinn's cheeks, and Nicole had to fight an urge to reach out and touch her, pull her closer, and kiss her senseless. Quinn's eyes widened slightly, as if she'd seen something of this longing in Nicole's expression, and she stood up, clearing her throat again, nervously.

"Okay. I'm here if you need me."

Nicole couldn't help the stab of sorrow. "Okay," she managed to say.

Quinn turned as if to move away and then stopped. Her eyes shifted to the floor again, and she bit her lip. "Oh, and Nicole?"

"Yes?"

"Your photographs are really beautiful. You're incredibly talented."

Nicole's jaw dropped and she watched, mouth still wide, as Quinn moved back across the room to her original computer. Nicole had to force herself to turn around to stop staring at her, her heart hammering. Her hands were shaking too hard to do much of anything for several minutes. *Maybe, just maybe, she likes me, too.* The happiness that followed this possibility lifted her heart for the rest of the day.

The next two days passed in a similar fashion. She would come by after school and stay until Quinn had to lock up. They would chat, very briefly, when she first got there and when they left together, and they even walked out to Quinn's car Wednesday. It almost looked like Quinn was going to offer her a ride, but Nicole made her excuses before that could happen. She could hardly be near her without making an ass of herself. Plus, she didn't want Quinn to see her house. She wasn't exactly ashamed of it, but she didn't want to see how Quinn would react. She didn't want pity.

In the meantime, Nicole was hitting up every person she knew for a ride to Grand Junction. No one was willing or able to do it, and Nicole's dad was out of town this week on a long haul. Her mom didn't drive beyond here and there to the grocery and Kmart, so asking her was out of the question. Nicole hadn't gotten her license, so she couldn't borrow her car, either. Kmart told her, when she called, that they could get one in by early January, the holidays slowing everything down.

Finally desperate on Thursday afternoon, the last day she had the scanner reserved, Nicole used her lunch break to go to the bank for a withdrawal. She took three hundred dollars with her to the lab after school. Walking into the room, she stumbled slightly, as usual, at the sight of Quinn. She was, despite the chilly weather, wearing a plaid skirt and a lacy black top—the skin above her knee-high boots exposed and terribly appealing. Once again, the heavy doors slammed behind her, making both of them jump.

Nicole grimaced. "Sorry, again."

"It's okay. I'm used to it by now."

Nicole grabbed one of the computer chairs and dragged it close to Quinn, sitting down and pulling out the envelope of cash.

"Listen. I have a big problem. I tried to get one of the Zip drive thingies, but I can't seem to get my hands on one. They're sold out all over the place because of Christmas. But I have some money here. Kmart sells theirs for two hundred dollars, so I wanted to see if you would be willing to sell me yours. For a profit, I mean. This is three hundred dollars."

Quinn stared down at the offered envelope for a long time. That earlier, troubled, unreadable emotion clouded her expression again, but after a long, awkward moment, she took the envelope.

"Okay, Nicole. But you don't have to pay me extra for it. My dad bought it for me."

Nicole grinned and stood up. "Well, think of it like a service fee. I wouldn't have anything if it weren't for you."

"I do get paid to be here, Nicole. It's my job to help you."

"You work downtown, too, right?" Nicole asked. "At that cheesy Old West photo place?"

Quinn didn't appear surprised that Nicole knew this fact. "Yes. On the weekends. My dad owns it."

Nicole winced. "Sorry. I didn't mean to call it cheesy."

Quinn shrugged. "It's okay. It is cheesy. But it's kind of fun, too."

Nicole relaxed a bit, glad her faux pas had been forgiven. "Well, then, think of the extra money like a present. A Christmas present for being…you. I mean, for how nice you are and stuff." This was as close to flirting as she'd had courage for at any point this week, and she held her breath, waiting for a rejection.

Quinn's eyes stayed on the envelope in her hands, one corner of her mouth lifting slightly, and Nicole once again had to move away from her to stop herself from doing something—hugging her (or more). They weren't like that together. Yet.

Finally, Quinn's eyes met hers. "Okay. I'll take it. College isn't free, after all."

Nicole's heart soared with joy. She'd flirted with her and offered her a gift, and both had been accepted. That was step one on her path to something more.

The next two hours passed more quickly than usual. Once she'd gotten the hang of the whole scanning thing on Monday, the work itself was tedious. Put a picture down, close the lid of the doohickey, hit the scan button, wait, check the image, replace the photo, repeat. Pretty boring, really. But today, since this was the last batch, the time seemed to slip by quickly. It helped that Quinn was busy, too. It was almost Christmas break, which meant a lot of people needed help with their final projects. Nicole could watch Quinn helping the other students that came in without censor. Normally, if they were in here alone, she had to school herself not to simply stare at her. Now, as she waited for each scan, she could turn her head Quinn's way and look at her for several seconds at a time, knowing she wouldn't be caught. A couple of Quinn's friends had come in for help today, and she was laughing with them about something, the sound more appealing than the greatest symphony on earth, her face a masterwork of angelic joy. Nicole would give anything to elicit a response like that from her.

After finishing the last of her scans and checking all her images one last time, she also finished printing the catalogue Quinn had helped her put together. Nicole was a very slow typist, which usually meant she spent most of the time her images were scanning typing the descriptions, but there had been fewer of those to write up today, too. She was wasting time when it came right down to it. She wanted to catch Quinn alone before leaving.

Finally, Quinn's friends left, and Nicole quickly grabbed everything she'd been pretending to finish. Quinn looked up at her expectantly as she approached, her eyes flickering up at the clock, apparently surprised.

"You're finished early?"

"I am. I couldn't have done any of this without you. You're a lifesaver. Thank you."

"You're welcome. I liked…" Quinn shook her head, her cheeks coloring a bit.

Nicole's heart skipped. "You liked what?"

Quinn met her gaze, confident and assured. "I liked helping you. Spending time with you."

With something like a thunderclap of recognition, Nicole realized she'd been reading this tension between them the wrong way. She'd been avoiding Quinn all these years because she had a crush on her, and now she understood that Quinn had been doing the same thing. This direct response was clear.

"Do you want...I mean would you like to..." Nicole stammered.

Quinn lifted a sculpted, pierced eyebrow. "Would I like to what?"

Nicole took a deep breath and forced it out. "Do you wanna hang out some time? Together, I mean, outside of school?"

Quinn smiled. "I'd like that a lot. What did you have in mind?"

It was on the tip of Nicole's tongue to ask her on a date. She'd been working herself up to it all week, and now, with what Quinn had said earlier, she was pretty sure she'd get the right response. She even knew where to take her—a new bistro had opened downtown that was very date-friendly. Still, her nerves betrayed her, and she blurted out the first thing she could think of.

"Oh! There's a party this weekend."

"A party?"

"At Corey Kidson's place," Nicole added.

"I know. I was planning on going."

"Oh."

Nicole desperately tried to recover the moment they'd had. Quinn looked, if anything, disappointed by this exchange. *She was expecting me to ask her on a date.* Nicole took a deep breath, willing herself to fix this, to ask her out to anything—anything at all. But she couldn't do it.

"So I'll see you there?" Quinn asked.

Nicole's shoulders sagged with regret. "Yes. I'll see you there. Maybe we can...split a beer or something."

Quinn nodded slightly and continued to stare at her, expectation obvious in her posture, and Nicole could only lamely excuse herself, nearly running for the door.

CHAPTER TWO: QUINN

Present Day

Quinn Zelinski followed the delighted Norwegians to the front door, laughing along with the occasional English they threw her way. As they walked away and up the street toward their hotel, they waved and called back to her, holding up their photos, laughing and pushing at each other well down the block. She waved one last time and went back inside, closing and locking the door before turning the *Open* sign to *Closed*. She was closing a little earlier than the official business hours posted on her door, but she was sure she wouldn't get any more customers today.

The fact that she'd had any at all on a Tuesday afternoon was something of a miracle. While ski season was in full swing at this point, the interim between Thanksgiving and Christmas meant something of a tourist lull on weekdays. The weekends were always busy, and things would pick up later in the month as people started arriving for Christmas and last through the first week of the New Year. Glenwood wasn't quite as inundated as nearby Aspen, but most of the rooms and restaurants in town would be booked, and Quinn and her seasonal helper would have their hands full here at the shop. Closing early today wasn't a problem.

She sighed and turned around, absently rubbing the tension from her neck with one hand as she surveyed the last of her day's work. The Norwegians had been friendly and enthusiastic, and they'd paid for the most expensive photo package she'd offered, but they'd left a big mess behind them. Costumes and props were strewn all over the place, dropped willy-nilly on the floor and chairs. She gathered the fake guns first, setting them back in their stand, and then grabbed some discarded hangers before shaking the wrinkles from the costume dresses, suits, and dusters.

Quinn had owned the Glenwood Springs Old Time Western Portrait Studio for about five years now. The store was a bit of a tourist trap, offering black-and-white or sepia photos. She specialized entirely in the Old West theme, which kept things simpler, but she coordinated a lot of moving parts—camera equipment, printers, and of course the costumes and props, all of which required frequent maintenance and replacement.

Among his many other businesses, her dad had owned this place before her. He'd basically given it to her when he retired, asking Quinn simply to pay the nominal owner-transfer fee with the city and a ceremonial one-dollar sales price. She'd worked here for over twenty years now, first for her dad and since she'd bought it from him.

The business was relatively successful, and, in the off-season, she had plenty of time for herself and her true passion—nature photography. Over the years, she'd managed to sell some of her animal and mountain photographs in local galleries, and she'd once had a hummingbird accepted to *Nature* magazine, but without the ability to devote herself to it full-time, her passion was always, at best, a very modest side business. People in the art world just didn't know her name. She'd taken this tourism job with the city to get her name out there more. If her photographs became known even regionally, she might be able to make her own business of it. That was her dream anyway.

She hung the last of the cowboy hats back on its peg and then went behind her sales counter to open the back door, turning off the lights as she closed and locked it behind her. Here, a small, dark, brick hallway led to the worn wooden staircase up to her apartment. Her dad had bought the space above the current studio decades ago, thinking he might expand, but he'd eventually had this upstairs room rezoned for housing instead. He put in a tiny bathroom and kitchen, and then rented it out, first to strangers and then to Quinn. She'd lived up here for over a decade now.

She unlocked her door, the winter sun blazing in through her front windows so bright she had to shield her eyes. She dropped her keys into a little dish and plopped down on her armchair, closing her eyes and leaning backward, sighing happily. She loved living here in her tiny space. Her bookcases lined every wall of the living area, she had a small gas fireplace, and when her Murphy bed was up, anyway, she had a small workspace, too.

She sat forward a few minutes later, rubbing her face. She'd been halfway dozing. She was getting together with friends for dinner tonight, but she wanted to use the rest of the afternoon to review the folder of information the city had sent her for this job. She'd had the folder for over a week without looking at it, and while the first meeting with the city's tourism commissioner wasn't until tomorrow, if she didn't look at it now, she'd never get around to it later.

First, she studied a long list of the shots she was expected to take this month. The list was somewhat formidable, featuring several different places around town, of course, including the famous hot springs and the Adventure Park and the caves near there. Restaurants, hotels, bars, and other businesses were listed, as well as several local hiking and bike trails, waterfalls, and the two nearest ski resorts. She saw a staged wedding, a New Year's Eve ball, and then a very long list of local wildlife and fauna the city hoped to capture.

She shook her head, overwhelmed. Any one of these shoots would take an entire day, and far more things were listed on the sheet than days to complete them. How on earth could they ever expect her to finish all of this on time?

"Well, shit," she muttered. She might not be able to do this after all. Her first chance in a long time to get her name out there, and she would have to back out.

As she was setting the list of photographs down, however, she noticed the next sheet of paper underneath it in the folder. She saw her CV, listing her various accomplishments and professional training. Curious, she pulled it out, wondering why they'd included a copy of what she submitted with her application, and then she caught sight of another CV beneath her own. She read the name at the top, and her stomach dropped.

"Oh, fuck," she whispered.

Nicole Steele. Nicole Goddamn Steele, of all people, had submitted a CV to the city of Glenwood Springs. If Nicole Steele's CV was in here, it could mean only one thing: Nicole was here, and they would be working together. Quinn quickly scanned the next couple of pages of instructions to confirm what she'd suspected. Nicole Steele was working on this city project, too.

"Oh, fuckity fuck," Quinn said, standing up in a panic.

She stared around the room desperately, finally spotting her cell phone resting on the charging bank on her nightstand.

"Shit, shit, shit, shit," she muttered as she made her way over there. Her fingers were shaking as she scrolled through her contacts, and when she found Molly's name, she decided to call rather than text. Molly answered after one ring.

"What's up, lady? I'm at work."

"It's an emergency," Quinn said. "It's a motherfucking emergency. Help me!"

"Whoa, whoa! Slow down! Do you need me to come get you? Were you in an accident or something?"

"No. No—it's not that kind of an emergency. It's an 'I need to see you this instant and freak out with you' emergency."

"Oh. Okay. Aren't we getting together later with—"

"It can't wait."

"Wow. Must be a big deal. The problem is, I can't leave work for a freak-out. But you can come here. It's pretty dead."

"Okay—I'll do that. See you soon." Quinn hung up, pocketed her phone, and then stood there, eyes combing the room in a panic. She finally spotted her coat, grabbed it, almost freaked again when she didn't find her keys in the pocket. Then she remembered she'd just come home. She grabbed them from the dish and rushed outside.

It was faster to walk to the brewery where Molly worked, and once inside it was blissfully cool and darkly lit and, as expected, pretty empty. Quinn spotted Molly right away behind the bar, polishing glasses and staring at something on the TV. The brewery was on the ground floor of one of the town's nicer hotels. A couple of cyclists sat at the far end of the bar, nursing beers, winded and sunburned in their bright spandex. The only other patron in here was staring up at the same TV as Molly, both watching the hockey game. Quinn walked directly to the most isolated part of the bar and sat down, waiting for Molly to notice her.

"Dang it!" Molly suddenly shouted. "I can't believe they lost!"

The solo patron laughed at her and held out a hand. "That's ten bucks, Mols."

Molly shook it and said, "You can take it out of my tip."

"I wouldn't tip you that much!" the man said, dramatically aggrieved, but he was grinning.

"Gee, thanks."

Molly spotted her then and lifted her chin slightly before addressing the man again. "You want anything else, Bob?"

"Nah. I better head back to work. A two-beer lunch is my limit on a weekday. See you tomorrow. Maybe. You better have my ten dollars!"

"In your dreams, pal."

They laughed again. As soon as he'd settled his bill, Molly finally made her way over to Quinn's end of the bar.

"Sorry about that."

Quinn waved a hand dismissively. "It's okay. You're at work. I get it."

"You want your usual? I know it's a little early, but…"

Quinn hesitated before nodding. "Special circumstances, after all."

As Molly went to get her beer, Quinn disrobed as much as possible. It was cooler in here, but she was overheated from the walk and her nerves. On the other hand, the movement and the fresh air had distracted her. Already, that panic when she read Nicole's name had faded. After all, it wasn't as if they'd be working together *directly* all the time. With so many photographs to take, they'd have to divide the list to finish on time.

Molly set a pint of Irish Red in front of Quinn, and she didn't protest the larger-than-usual size. Not only did Quinn avoid drinking during the day, but she also usually bought half-pints when she did. She took a long swallow, Molly grinning at her all the while.

"Better?" Molly asked as Quinn set her glass back down.

"Much."

Molly glanced behind her at the cyclists, but they were still nursing their beers. She rotated her hands in a "get on with it" gesture. "So? What are you freaking out about?"

Quinn sighed. "Actually…it's nothing."

Molly crossed her arms, frowning deeply. "What the hell, Quinn? After all that, you mean to tell me it wasn't important?"

"Well, I mean, it's not *nothing*, but I think I overreacted."

Molly narrowed her eyes. "Spill it, Quinn, or I'll spray you with the seltzer water."

Quinn hesitated, that strange panic suddenly spiking her heart rate again. "Okay, so you remember me talking about Nicole?"

"The girl who broke your heart in high school? The one who stole your scholarship? The one you talk about when we're alone and you get too drunk? That Nicole?"

Quinn sighed. "Yes—that Nicole. And you know how I got this great job for the next few weeks? For the city?"

"Yeeesss…"

"They hired the two of us, I guess, since there's so much work to do. Nicole is on the project for the city, too."

Molly winced. "Oh, shit."

"Right? She'll be here the whole time. I'm not sure how much we'll have to do together, but we're sure to see each other a few times, anyway."

Molly glanced around again, this time apparently checking for her boss, before she came around the edge of the bar. She gave Quinn a long hug before stepping back, hands on Quinn's shoulders.

"I'm so sorry, Quinn. That's really tough and awkward."

Quinn was more emotional than expected after this revelation, and she wiped away her sudden tears.

"I'm so stupid, Molly. I don't know why I'm so upset. It's not like I've talked to her in the last eighteen years. I'm thirty-six years old, for Christ's sake. You'd think I'd have gotten over her by now. And I am. Over her, I mean. We didn't even date. I barely even think about her at all except—"

"When you're drinking. And Quinn? Don't worry about it. First love is hard for everyone. I still remember Becky Leechman in tenth grade. I had her yearbook picture blown up, like a creep, and hung it on my wall. My mom thought she was some celebrity or something."

They both giggled, and Quinn's spirits lifted. She squeezed Molly's hand.

"Thanks, Molly."

"You bet. I need to go check in with those two bike lunatics over there, but I'll be right back. Dane and Rico should be here any time, now."

"Oh?"

"Yeah—I called them right after you called me. Said there was a Quinn emergency, and they both said they'd come as soon as they could."

Quinn, Molly, and their friends Dane and Rico had planned to have dinner and drinks later this evening. Dane and Rico worked at the ski resort in Aspen and always had strange schedules, so it wasn't a surprise that they could drop whatever they were doing if they weren't at work. Still, she was touched that they were coming, and that Molly had thought to call them.

The two men appeared after she'd finished her beer. Molly had been pulled into serving several new customers, so Quinn was sitting alone. She'd torn up several napkins waiting, leaving a small pile of cotton shreds in front of her.

Dane waved excitedly at her, pulling the smaller Rico behind him. On the outside, they made a somewhat odd couple. Dane was tall, model-handsome, with bright, almost white-blond hair, his appearance as Danish as his name. Rico was thickly muscled, shorter than either Quinn or Molly, with dark hair and skin and a finely trimmed beard. The men had met on the job, and she and Molly had encountered them here at the brewery one drunken night a couple of years ago. All four had been tight ever since.

Dane hugged her first, kissing the side of her face before sitting down and slamming a hand on the bar.

"Beer me!" he shouted at Molly.

Molly shot him a dark smile and held a middle finger up behind her back at him, out of sight of the customer she was with. Dane laughed.

Rico pushed his arm. "Don't bark at her like a dog!" He turned to Quinn before kissing her cheek and hugging her, sitting down on the other side of her from Dane. "So nice to see you, Quinn."

"You too, guys. You didn't have to come all the way down here. It's not a big deal."

Both men rolled their eyes.

Dane said, "Molly told us you said it was an emergency and a 'freak out,' if I remember correctly. It's not like her to say something and not mean it."

"What happened?" Rico asked.

Quinn opened her mouth, but Dane held up a hand. "Wait. Let's get beers first."

Rico sighed, and they waited until Molly served them, promising to join them as soon as she could. Her boss Toni had come from the back to help at this point, due to the unusual rush, and Molly was on her best behavior in front of her.

Quinn, Dane, and Rico decided to move away from the bar for more privacy, and they chose a seat near the window. The sun was still bright outside, but the light had taken on that strange, faded quality of the late afternoon.

Quinn took a nervous sip of her drink, worried, now, that she would get emotional once she explained the situation. It was one thing to cry in front of Molly, whom she'd known for a few years now, but another in front of the guys. After all, they didn't even know about Nicole. She'd never talked about her around them before.

Dane, as if sensing some of this dilemma, put a hand over hers and patted it. "You look upset, Quinn. You don't have to tell us if you don't want to."

"Your business isn't necessarily our business," Rico said.

"No—I want to tell you both, but I'm probably overreacting. You'll think I'm being ridiculous."

They both frowned, and Dane shook his head.

"That would never happen. Anything that has you this shaken must be a big deal."

"Agreed," Rico said.

Quinn felt slightly better, and she relaxed somewhat, leaning back in her chair. She took a deep breath, let it out, and began her story.

"Okay. So, there was this girl back in high school. I had a terrible crush on her all through school, and one time I helped her get this scholarship by doing something kind of stupid. Her name is Nicole..."

❖

Eighteen Years Ago: April 2000

The party was in full swing by the time Quinn made it to the hotel. She'd gone back and forth with herself so many times about coming, that even now, actually and for real here inside the door, she was still tempted to leave. She hated crowds, and she still found it hard to be happy about all of this. Nicole won the big scholarship, and Quinn got nothing. But she couldn't blame Nicole for any of that. It was her own damn fault. But that didn't make it any easier to be happy for her.

Nicole had rented out one of the bigger event rooms for this party, but Quinn was still surprised to see so many people here. At most of the high school parties she'd attended, maybe ten or twenty people showed up, and this was clearly way more than that—a hundred, maybe more. It was kind of hard to tell for sure with all the flashing lights and the undulating movement of the people dancing in the middle of the room, but it looked like most of their graduating class was here. She even spotted some people that she and her friends despised on principle—the jocks and the cowboy ropers. It was bizarre that they'd be at Nicole's big celebration.

But Quinn also knew Nicole had gotten the art club involved last week in making the advertisements and decorations for this party. Quinn was in the club herself and had done one of the flyers, which was when she'd learned about the scholarship. All the flyers had ended up very cool, and as they'd been plastered all over school, they'd obviously caught people's eyes. Nicole had called this event the "Non-Prom," and apparently that idea appealed to a lot of different kinds of folks. Word had gotten out, and so some of the normies were here with them tonight. To Quinn, it seemed like she'd ended up going to prom after all, though with much better music. Still, she'd been hoping for something more intimate—a last chance to see all her friends in one place.

She counted Nicole among those friends now, despite the situation with the scholarship. Ever since that whole thing in the computer lab last December, they'd been seeing a lot of each other. Well, no, that wasn't quite true. They sat in in the closer spaces than they used to, and they talked a whole hell of a lot more than they had before, but they'd still never hung out, just the two of them. Their interactions were still mostly the usual bumping into each other at this party or that, one diner or another. Only now, instead of Nicole panicking and running away, she would come say hello, ask how she was doing, and they sometimes talked a little more. This was an improvement, but it wasn't what Quinn really wanted. She wanted Nicole to ask her out.

Not that Quinn could fault Nicole for that, either. After all, she was herself perfectly capable of asking the other girl on a date, for God's sake, and she'd almost worked herself up to it once or twice, but she'd chickened out, like she knew Nicole had done several times now. They were pathetic.

Finally breaking through the initial crush of people near the door, Quinn spotted a group of her friends hiding in one of the corners, all of them hunched around a high-top table like a flock of gargoyles in their heavy black clothes. She smiled wistfully, wondering, then, and not for the first time, if they would ever be together like this again after this summer, when everyone scattered into their adult lives. College-acceptance letters were rolling in now, and many of her friends were going off to far-off places for school. Why on earth would they ever come back here?

Her friend Josh spotted her and waved with somewhat uncharacteristic enthusiasm before obviously remembering where he was, and who he was supposed to be. He toned down his reaction a bit, sending her a salute with two fingers. She chuckled lightly, starting to find some parts of goth culture a bit harder to take seriously. As she approached, her friend Heidi turned around in her full-on goth-princess dress of black lace in a faux-Victorian style, complete with a corset and a half-veil.

"You look amazing!" Quinn shouted.

Heidi squealed before wrapping her in a tight hug. "You look great, too! That dress is amazing on you!"

Quinn was proud of her thrift-store find. She and another friend had restored a vintage forties shirt-dress with a Mandarin collar. The dress was maroon and fit her so well it was like it had been made for her.

"Thanks!"

"Did you wear that dress just for her?" Heidi asked, her eyebrows going up and down.

"What? Who?"

Heidi rolled her eyes. "Nicole, dummy! She's going to eat you alive when she sees you in this!"

Quinn couldn't help the heat rising in her cheeks, and she pushed at Heidi's arm. "Shut up!"

Heidi laughed. "Oh, come on. We all know the two of you want to hump each other's brains out. So go ahead and do it already! Put the rest of us out of our misery!"

Almost as if talking about her had conjured her, Nicole appeared some ten or fifteen feet away from behind a crowd of dancers. She was staring at Quinn with that familiar dazed, dopey expression. Quinn had seen that look on her face a thousand times before. She was always flattered in a way, but the look could also be unnerving. Quinn never had that kind of effect on anyone else, and she wasn't entirely comfortable accepting the power she had over Nicole. Until last December, and sometimes even since, she'd suspected that some kind of trick was involved—that Nicole was pulling her leg acting like this. But she was finally ready to accept it, and tonight might be her last chance to act on it.

When she glanced back at Heidi, she was grinning, slyly.

"Are you going to help that poor girl out or what?" Heidi asked. "I'm not sure she's actually breathing right now."

Quinn hesitated and then squared her shoulders. "Yes. I am. Wish me luck!"

Heidi rolled her eyes. "You don't need it!"

She pushed Quinn slightly in Nicole's direction, and Quinn, not expecting it, stumbled forward, almost going down. Suddenly Nicole was there, her strong hands grabbing Quinn's and pulling her upright to steady her. They always avoided touching each other, and Quinn was suddenly struck with the overwhelming warmth of Nicole's hands in hers. She finally met Nicole's eyes, and the desperate longing she read there was enough to reassure her that being bold tonight was the right choice,

Nicole, as if suddenly aware of what she was doing, who she was touching, let go as if burned and rubbed her palms lightly on her thighs. "You look great! Amazing, I mean!" Nicole shouted.

Nicole looked incredible, too. She was in a slim-fitted black suit à la Johnny Cash, with a red silk shirt and smart, shiny black flats. Her long, dark hair had been styled into some kind of complicated up-do, with little red flowers braided throughout. Her makeup, always on point, was smokier, darker than usual, and incredibly appealing, her brown eyes sparkling under thick, dark lashes. Quinn had never wanted to kiss her as much as at that moment.

She'd planned to wait, at least for an hour, for what came next—that is, if she managed to get herself to do it at all. Emboldened, finally, or maybe too afraid she would chicken out again, Quinn grabbed one of Nicole's hands and started dragging her toward the door.

"Where are we going?" Nicole shouted. "Do you want some punch?"

They burst through the doors of the event room into the hotel lobby, the music muffled once the doors swung closed behind them.

"Woo!" Nicole said, shaking her head and pulling on one earlobe. "That's better. You don't realize how loud it is in there until you step out for a minute."

Quinn could tell she was nervous and simply making small talk. Then Nicole stared down at their still-clasped hands as if she couldn't believe what she was seeing.

"Come with me," Quinn said, leading her over to the elevator.

"What? Where are we going? Don't you want to dance or something?"

Quinn pushed the button and then looked up at Nicole, waiting until she met her eyes.

"I got us a room," Quinn said.

Nicole blanched slightly but said, "Yes. Yes, that would be good. Great, I mean."

They stood there quietly as they waited for the elevator, and then again when they were inside, their hands still clutched and damp with heated sweat. They continued to hold hands until they reached the door to the room, when Quinn had to dig around in her purse for the key and open the door. Nicole walked in ahead of her, and Quinn followed, almost choking with nerves.

Nicole peered around, smiling slightly. "Nice."

"What?" Quinn asked.

"It's one of the suites," she said. Then, seeing Quinn's confused expression, she chuckled, embarrassed. "Sorry. My mom works here, and I've done some shifts here, too. It's one of the nicer rooms is all."

"I know. I paid for it."

Nicole tried to laugh and then shook her head, her eyes downcast. "I'm sorry. I'm not good at this kind of thing. I don't know what I'm doing or saying. Obviously."

Quinn took pity on her and stepped closer. "It's okay, Nicole. I don't know what I'm doing, either."

"Oh? You mean you haven't gotten a hotel room with someone before?"

Quinn laughed, knowing she was teasing. "No. Of course not." She swallowed. "I've never wanted to get a room with someone before."

Something about this remark seemed to trigger some of Nicole's hidden confidence. Her expression suddenly cleared, and she stepped into Quinn's space and pulled her into a kiss. To Quinn, the sensation was like falling. She was suddenly lighter, as if she were drifting backward, the heat of the kiss sweeping through her like fire. She clutched at Nicole, tugging her closer, and Nicole moved nearly flush with her, their bodies touching lightly through their clothes. The longer the kiss lasted, the more and more Quinn wanted it to go on and on— the two of them here, lips locked together, for the rest of their lives.

Nicole finally drew back with a somewhat pained expression.

"What is it?" Quinn asked.

"I'm just so…mad at myself, I guess," Nicole said. "I've wanted to do that for…God, I don't know how long. Years and years, anyway. I wasted so much time."

Quinn tried to look coy. "That means we have some catching up to do."

Nicole smiled, a sight that always caught Quinn off guard. She'd seen Nicole staring at her, dumbfounded and sometimes almost upset, since they were little kids. Smiling was much, much better.

Nicole moved away a bit. She was staring at the bed, clearly anxious again, and Quinn needed to help both of them relax more, whether they tried sleeping together tonight or not. Luckily, she'd prepared for this scenario. When she'd finally decided to get the room, on the almost-certain chance that Nicole would come up here with her after the party, she'd also done some reconnaissance. She'd been here at the hotel earlier this afternoon and brought some things to help them out.

"Let's play some music," Quinn said, pointing at a portable stereo she'd set up then.

Nicole grinned, clearly relieved as her shoulders dropped. She squeezed Quinn's hand before walking across the room. Quinn took the chance to take a deep breath, calling on her inner confidence. Nicole wanted to be here with her, and she needed to keep that fact in mind.

Nicole examined the stereo, bent over, and then hit play. Quinn had set the volume low, and Nicole, clearly understanding why she'd done that, turned back around, grinning.

"Depeche Mode," Nicole said, indicating the stereo. "Nice."

Quinn relaxed. She'd spent hours making the mix CD for tonight, but she'd still been more than a little worried about her music choices.

"Do you want a drink?" Quinn asked.

Nicole opened her mouth, clearly stunned. "Uh, yes. Hell yes. What do you have?"

"Some champagne I stole from my dad. He uses it for, what do you call it, the one with orange juice? Mamacita or something like that? Anyway, he has like a whole case of it. He won't miss a bottle."

"Sounds great. I've never had champagne before."

"Me either, actually."

Having seen it in a movie, Quinn had put the bottle in a bucket of ice a couple of hours ago, and it was nicely chilled when she picked it up. She'd watched her dad open bottles like this before, and the instructions were printed on the foil around the cap, but opening it was harder than it looked. She struggled for a while before the cork finally popped off, startling them. Quinn had to work quickly to pour the overflow into two glass tumblers as it spilled around the neck of the bottle. She handed one glass to Nicole and held hers aloft in a toast.

"To us," she said.

Nicole held her glass up. "To us," and they clinked glasses.

The drink was tarter than she'd expected, and Quinn had to fight the urge to spit it out. Nicole's expression—disgusted, surprised— likely matched her own, and they both grimaced at their glass.

"Needs sugar," Nicole said, her lips peeled back a bit.

"Right? Do you think we can add something to it?"

Nicole shrugged. "I don't see why not. Maybe Sprite or something?"

"Good idea. I think I saw one in the mini bar. Doctor them up a bit while I…slip into something more comfortable." She winced after saying this, realizing how corny it sounded, but Nicole's expression remained vague and almost pained.

Her voice was rough when she spoke. "That sounds good. You do that."

Quinn grabbed her overnight bag and closed the bathroom door behind her. Her heart was racing now, and though she suspected she was imagining it, that sip of champagne seemed to have made her skin even hotter than it had been before. She grinned at her reflection and then started taking her dress off, careful to fold it as she set it on top of the toilet.

Shopping for lingerie by herself two days ago had been a terrifying experience. She'd wanted to invite her friend Heidi but had thought better of it in the end. If she'd told Heidi her plan and then ended up chickening out, she'd never hear the end of it. Instead, the saleswoman had walked her through the first sexy purchase of her life and been incredibly kind about it, answering all Quinn's questions and pointing her toward something reasonably priced and a lot tamer than some of the more adventurous stuff at the front of the store. The piece she was wearing now was easy to put on by herself, and, while tight and silky and in her signature maroon, it still left a lot to the imagination.

It took her a couple of minutes to work herself up to opening the door, and when she did, Nicole's back was to her as she stood by the little table with their drinks. The music had switched to something harder, Nine Inch Nails, but Quinn had chosen the song on purpose since she knew how much Nicole liked that band.

"It's much better with Sprite," Nicole said, turning her way with two glasses. Nicole's face contorted with something like pain and then wonder when she saw her. She visibly paled, and the drinks dipped dangerously low, almost spilling. Just in time, she jerked them up, splashing herself, and then turned, woodenly, to set the glasses on a side table. She took a half step toward Quinn, and then, as if thinking better of it, backed away, sitting down rather quickly on one of the armchairs.

"Are you okay?" Quinn asked, rushing toward her.

Nicole stared up at her from her chair, still pale, and shook her head. "I felt dizzy for a second. I'll be okay. It's nerves, I think."

Quinn sat in the other chair and took Nicole's hands in hers. "I'm sorry. Was it something I did?"

Nicole shook her head even before she finished speaking. "No. It's not you at all. It's me. I've…dreamt of something like this with you for so long, I don't know how to accept it. I feel like I'm dreaming. And then you came out of there looking like that and…I about passed out."

A lock of her dark hair had fallen loose from her elaborate style, and Quinn leant forward and tucked it behind her ear.

"We don't have to do anything, Nicole. We could just talk to each other a little first. I mean, I've known you my whole life, in a way, but I don't really know you, either, you know?"

Nicole shook her head. "I mean, I get what you mean, but Quinn— but I want this. I want you. You're all I've ever wanted."

Quinn flushed with pleasure.

"You're all I've ever wanted, too, Nicole. So why don't we take it easy for a while? There's no rush. We have this room all night." She glanced down at her exposed legs. "Do you want me to put something over this?"

Nicole glanced down at Quinn's legs, and she paled again. She closed her eyes and nodded. "I don't *want* you to, but that might be better. At least for now."

"Good. I was getting cold anyway."

Nicole gave her a grateful smile, and Quinn went back to the bathroom to grab one of the thick, luxurious robes hanging from the door. Quinn had almost no experience with hotels herself, but this must be a nice one with all these fancy extras.

Nicole's color had returned by the time Quinn returned, and she looked calmer, her posture more natural than that strange wooden rigidity before. She'd unbuttoned a bit of her shirt, too, and her neck and collarbone peeked out at Quinn, appealing and kissable. Later, she told herself.

Nicole patted the seat of the second armchair, and Quinn sat down again, taking the drink Nicole offered her. Mazzy Star was playing on the stereo now, and despite the low volume, the singer's fragile, broken voice and light, strumming guitar filled the room. The melody was calming and sweet, the perfect song to help them relax.

"This *is* better with Sprite," Quinn said, nearly draining her glass.

"Good thing to know before college, I guess," Nicole said.

A sinking sensation struck her then, and Quinn tried to dismiss it. College meant whatever came next. It meant moving on, leaving Glenwood, at least for a while. And it almost certainly meant never seeing Nicole again. She'd wanted to ask her, since her own acceptance letter arrived two weeks ago, where she'd decided to go with her fancy full-ride scholarship, but she'd also dreaded learning the truth. Some part of her hoped, no prayed, that Nicole would be going to Rocky, in Denver, like she was.

Nicole, clearly thinking along the same lines, suddenly said, "But hey, speaking of college, maybe you can come visit me? In Chicago?"

"Chicago?"

Nicole seemed puzzled, her brow creased. "Yeah—at the Art Institute? Didn't I tell you?"

"No."

"Oh. I guess I hadn't gotten around to it. I got all my acceptance letters a couple of weeks ago. I couldn't decide between SCAD or Chicago, but Chicago won out in the end. We have some family there, so I've been before, and Savannah seemed too far away from my folks. So like I said I'd love to see you there. Where are you going to school?"

Quinn didn't respond, the idea of Chicago clanging around in her mind with a thunderclap of jealous horror. Nicole had gotten into one of the most prestigious art schools in the world, and she could afford to go there because of that scholarship. Quinn hadn't even applied, knowing the tuition was beyond her dad's means and her own paltry savings.

Nicole set her drink down and took Quinn's hand. "What is it? What's the matter? You seem upset."

Quinn regarded her evenly. "Did you ever...?" She shook her head. "You know what, never mind."

"What were you going to say?"

Quinn paused again, that jealous dread fluttering her heart. Stop now, you idiot, she told herself, but didn't listen.

"Did you ever wonder why *I* didn't apply for that scholarship, Nicole?"

Nicole frowned. "You didn't? Why not?"

Quinn's heart dropped again, that awful feeling rising full force. She could still stop this, change the topic, but almost as if compelled, she kept talking.

"Do you think it would have mattered? I mean, if the two of us were competing for the scholarship, do you think I would have even had a shot at getting it?"

Nicole's frown deepened. "Are you kidding me right now?"

Quinn's temper flared. "Do I sound like I'm kidding?"

Nicole leaned forward, waiting until Quinn met her eyes. "Of course you could have won. Your work is really good, Quinn."

"But not *as* good as yours, right?"

"I didn't say that."

"But you must have thought it. Didn't you?"

Nicole looked completely dumbfounded, frowning deeply. "I seriously don't know what you mean, Quinn. You're incredibly talented." Her eyes narrowed. "Do you mean to say you didn't apply because you didn't think you could compete with me?"

Quinn stared at her for another long beat, a jealous fit of temper rising and falling again. She was beyond foolish for bringing this up, but she couldn't help herself.

"No, Nicole," she said, almost whispering. "Not at first anyway. But then you needed my Zip drive—"

Nicole waved her hands in front of her. "Whoa, whoa, whoa. Hold on a second here. Do you mean you were afraid to compete with me, so you let me use the Zip drive you needed yourself? Is that what you're saying?"

"And you didn't even seem to notice. I mean, even if you didn't know about the Zip drive, didn't it occur to you that I might want to apply to the scholarship, too?"

Nicole shrugged. "I mean, I guess, but then why didn't you say anything about it last December?"

Quinn stared at her again, a sullen rage now seeping into her heart. "I don't know." She stood up. "Nicole—I think I have to go."

Nicole leapt to her feet. "What? No way! You can't do this, Quinn! What about," she gestured wildly at the room, "what about all this? We were just talking! It's all some big misunderstanding—"

Quinn laughed bitterly, slipping her shoes on. "No. It isn't. You're self-centered. And I'm a fucking pushover. That's what's happening. And you're leaving for Chicago, and I'll never see you again, and after college, I'll spend the rest of my goddamn life here in this town. So what are we even doing here?"

Nicole reached for her arm, and Quinn flung her hand off, storming away as quickly as she could. Nicole called to her, but Quinn was already at the door, grabbing her coat and purse, and trying her damnedest to ignore Nicole's pleas.

The voice, the one that had protested this entire conversation, was trying to speak up over the rushing blood in her ears, trying to tell her to turn around, but when the hotel room door closed behind her, Quinn kept going, running down the stairs and outside into the chilly nighttime air.

CHAPTER THREE: NICOLE

Present Day

Nicole studied herself in the mirror critically. She would never admit to anyone that she was dressing up for her first encounter with Quinn, but that was, in fact, exactly what she was doing. She'd kept her dark hair as long as it'd been in high school, but she'd styled it in a Bettie Page since her freshman year in college. It draped past the middle of her back. She'd started seeing a few stray grays here and there, but overall, her hair was dark and luscious, in better shape now than ever before. Her clothes were better now, too. Then, she'd worn a kind of half-goth, half-punk, or as near to it as she could with her limited income. Now, she favored vintage-style or actual vintage dresses and suits. Today's outfit was a navy 40s-style A-line skirt dress with short sleeves and a white Peter Pan collar. She was wearing heavy stockings underneath to help with the chill, and she had a nice, complementary blazer—not quite of the period of her dress, but still nice. Her makeup was impeccable and tasteful, as always. Yes, on the whole, Nicole looked better now than then.

After telling her mom about the Quinn situation with this job yesterday, the two of them had decided to try to forget about it with some Christmas margaritas—a red and green frozen cocktail that was a Steele family classic. They'd both gotten a little sloppy and silly at first, dancing around and singing along to Christmas music as they decorated the tree. On her third drink, Nicole had gotten a bit maudlin about Quinn again. She and her mom spent some time reminiscing about that awful morning in high school after the Non-Prom. Nicole had come home the next morning weeping and screaming about Quinn, and both of her parents had spent most of the day calming her. Annette recalled the situation well and remembered different details because of her slightly more objective perspective. Both parents had been afraid she was going to hurt herself. Her dad had finally given her a shot of whiskey with some honey to knock her out late that afternoon. That had been the same day Nicole had come out to them, somewhat by accident, since she'd told them all about Quinn. Both had been stunned, they later admitted, but Nicole was too upset at the time to notice.

Another margarita later, and she and her mom were cyberstalking Quinn on Facebook and Instagram, trying to find a recent photo. Not that Nicole didn't know what she looked like now. She'd seen Quinn here and there on visits home, but always from a distance, and always in secret. From what she'd noticed over the years, and what they saw online, Quinn hadn't changed much. Fewer pieces of black and maroon clothing and fewer piercings, but she was basically the same person except for some fine lines around her eyes.

"She's still cute, though," Annette said, slurring slightly.

Nicole sighed. "She is."

Now, the next morning, and nursing a hangover, Nicole stared at her slightly bloodshot eyes in the mirror and winked impishly at her reflection.

"She might be cute, but you're gorgeous, baby," she told herself.

"What was that, dear?" her mom called from the living room.

"Nothing!"

"Well, come on out here and let me see you, honey. You're going to have to leave soon if you don't want to be late."

"Coming!" Nicole called. How many times had she yelled something like this at her mom through the same door from the same place in front of this same mirror?

Annette was sitting in front of the TV, half-watching *White Christmas* and knitting one of the dogs a sweater. Though this was their third Christmas without her dad, Nicole was struck, once again, by the empty armchair next to her mom's. In years past, her dad would have been singing along.

As if reading her mind, her mom gestured at the TV and said, "This was his favorite, you know."

"I know. I'm sorry, Mom, for not bringing him up more. I miss him, too."

Annette shrugged. "We had other things to talk about last night. You look great, by the way—very chic! How's your head?"

"Like shit."

Annette laughed. "If it's anything like mine, you've got your work cut out for you at that meeting. Wouldn't want to be you today."

"It shouldn't be long, or at least I hope not."

"Will you be back for lunch?"

"I don't know. I'll try to call, but don't wait for me if you get hungry."

She kissed her mom's cheek and walked outside into a bright but very chilly morning. The neighborhood had improved quite a lot over the years as Glenwood gentrified. The little house next door, which had always been something of a pigsty, was now trim and clean, and decorated to the nines for the holidays. Lots of expensive cars were parked in nearby driveways, and Nicole thanked the powers-that-be that her dad had the foresight to buy when he did. At least her mom was safe here, now, and she would make a small fortune if she ever decided to sell and move.

After a quick drive to city hall, Nicole went inside as quickly as possible, glad to be out of the chill despite the short distance from her car. A friendly person at the front desk pointed her in the right direction, and when she pushed through a set of double doors, she saw Quinn waiting at the end of the hall on a bench. Quinn hadn't seen her yet. She was looking at her phone, and Nicole was glad for the chance to train her expression into neutral before she looked up at her. Quinn's lips twisted, briefly, with something like distaste, but she gave a polite smile.

"Nicole. Nice to see you again."

"Quinn—same."

They remained silent, and after a while, Nicole's heart slowed from a gallop to a light trot. Quinn had gone back to her phone, and Nicole stared straight ahead at the door to the boardroom they'd been sent to, trying her damnedest not to look at her.

So this is how we're going to play it then, I guess. Nicole didn't know what she'd expected. Of course Quinn wasn't going to greet her with open arms—that would have been weird. They hadn't even been like that as teenagers. She also hadn't expected her to be rude or mean. And it wasn't as if Nicole expected an apology either, certainly not here and now. After that night in the hotel, they'd avoided each other entirely. Quinn's words as she stormed out of the room had been their last spoken encounter. If there had been a time for an apology, it would have been back then, or that summer. Once or twice before she left for college, Nicole had driven past the Old West studio, thinking she might go inside and confront Quinn, but she'd chickened out. No, here and now, polite disinterest was best. They might have to collaborate, after all, and bringing up any of that crap from when they were kids wouldn't make their work any easier.

Nicole's gaze, however, almost of its own accord, flickered down Quinn's way several times as she stood there. She remembered then that Quinn didn't photograph well. In pictures of parties when they were teenagers, and in yearbook photos, she hadn't seemed like herself. Some people were like that—their essence, or something, couldn't be captured on film—ironic, considering Quinn's profession, but a fact, nonetheless. Nicole had run into this issue several times during her career, and she had learned techniques to deal with it, but it took some extra work during a shoot and in post-production. Apparently, whoever had taken the photos of Quinn on social media didn't know how to correct for this trait, as Quinn looked about a thousand times better in person.

Like Nicole, she'd dressed up for this meeting. She wore a gray pantsuit and a light blue shirt, the colors flattering with her pale complexion and eyes. Her hair was arranged in a style similar to the one when they'd been in school together—shaved on one side with a chin-length comb-over, the blond waves much more defined and clearly cared for. She'd removed her facial piercings at some point but still had several running up the length of the visible ear. Nicole could also see some tattoos peeking out from under her sleeves on both wrists. She was, in a word, gorgeous, and with this, Nicole recognized the depths of how difficult the next few weeks were going to be. She would have to avoid her as much as possible.

The double doors at the end of the hall swung open again, and a man and a woman appeared. The woman was carrying a stack of paperwork, and the man held a cardboard carrier with four takeaway coffees.

"Nicole, Quinn?" he asked.

"I'm Nicole," she said, moving toward him. "Do you need me to take that from you?"

"Would you? I have to get my keys and unlock the door. Here. I'm sorry we made you wait. It took me and Linda a bit to find the right paperwork."

Nicole and Quinn followed Linda and the man inside the little boardroom, and he held out his hand after Nicole set the drinks down.

"Hello, hello! I'm sure you know from our emails, but I'm John

Rivers, commissioner for the city's tourism board, and this is Linda Tuck, from HR."

Everyone shook hands, Nicole and Quinn introducing themselves.

"Okay. Let's sit down and talk a bit," John said, indicating the chairs. "And please help yourself to a coffee. I brought them for all of us."

As an outcome of the seat John chose, Nicole was forced to sit next to Quinn. Selecting a chair farther away would have been awkward in this small space. She saw Quinn wheel her own chair almost imperceptibly farther away when Nicole sat down and couldn't help a strange stab of something like resentment. Everyone spent a minute doctoring their coffee, John chatting about the weather, and Nicole took the opportunity to calm down. This is a job, she told herself. Just ignore Quinn.

"All righty then," John said. "I take it you both had a chance to review your folders?"

"Yes," they said at the same time.

"Great! In that case, you know what we're looking for. I had to have you guys in to do this paperwork for HR, but I also wanted to have at least one meeting in person so I could see the two of you face-to-face, answer any questions you have, and give you some insight into my vision for the project, as it were." He winced when he finished. "Sorry, That sounded kind of corporate."

Nicole waited for Quinn to speak first, and when she didn't, she shot her a quick look. Quinn was staring down at her folder, flipping through it as if searching for something, so Nicole turned to John again.

"I was wondering first about that list of photos you gave us."

"Yes," Quinn said, her voice somewhat subdued and her forehead creased. "Me, too."

John nodded. "I bet you were. I imagine you saw that and thought, 'This guy's out of his gourd!' Am I right?"

She saw Quinn nodding in her peripheral vision.

"Well, yes," Nicole said. "Frankly, I was a bit..."

"Overwhelmed," Quinn said.

"Exactly," Nicole added.

John laughed. "I can imagine! Look—let me put it to you this way. The list is—what's the word?—aspirational. I might be a city employee, and a businessman beyond that, which means I don't know an aperture from an F-stop, but I *do* know there's no fricking way the two of you could take all of those photographs on the list. So let me ease your mind. The staged wedding and the New Year's Eve ball are musts. Beyond that, I want to know what you *think* you could do, and what you absolutely *could* do. Does that sound fair?"

Once again, Nicole and Quinn made eye contact. Quinn looked as relieved as Nicole, that tension in her forehead much slighter.

"I don't want to speak for Quinn," Nicole said, "but with what, a little over five weeks until the deadline? It's all due the eleventh, right?"

"Yes."

"With about twenty-five weekdays, and some work on the weekends, I could do about twenty-five shots beyond the wedding and the ball."

Quinn was nodding. "That's exactly what I would say for me. Twenty-five and the wedding and the ball is completely doable. That allows extra days for reshoots, time off for the holidays, and maybe a weekend day or two off beyond that."

"And if you pushed a bit?" John asked, grinning again.

Nicole grinned back. "Thirty and the wedding and ball."

"Exactly," Quinn said. "That would be the very upper limit."

"Great!" John clapped once. "In that case, I'm going back to my office while the two of you do some paperwork with Linda here. I'll come back in in a while with a list of the top fifty, if you will, and a second list with the top sixty in case you can get to any of the others. We'll talk some more details, and then you'll be on your way. Sound like a plan?"

"Perfect," Quinn said.

They spent the rest of the hour completing the paperwork, finishing as John returned. Linda excused herself, and John closed the door behind her. He handed them two new lists—the top fifty on one sheet of paper, the top sixty on the next. He then explained his vision at very boring length, illustrating the differences he pictured by pointing out some of the flaws in the current photos on the tourist brochures and on the website. While he wanted Glenwood to continue to attract families, he also wanted to attract single people, young people, and he wanted more diversity represented in the tourism materials. Most of the current pictures showed young, white families, and that wasn't good for anyone but that kind of family. All of this was a smart marketing move, Nicole thought, already considering at least one subtly LGBTQ shoot with some local models, as they were allowed a small budget to use models when they needed them.

"I can already see the wheels spinning in your heads," John said, "and I want you to know that I have absolute confidence in you. You make the shots every time." He chuckled at his pun and then checked his watch. "Jeez! Wow. I'm sorry. I've been talking for over an hour already. Do either of you have any questions before I let you get out of here?"

"I'm wondering about oversight, that kind of thing," Quinn said.

"Exactly. How often do you want to see progress?" Nicole asked.

John shrugged. "Let's do this. Send everything you have right before Christmas, and we'll talk after the holiday. You can send me stuff more often if you want me to review anything, but let's set Thursday, the twenty-seventh, as our next official meeting here at city hall. And you can call me any time you have questions."

He stood, and she and Quinn exchanged a confused glance.

"Um. I guess we also need to know how to divide the work," Nicole said.

John held up a finger and dug around for a minute in his pockets before pulling out a gift card. He handed it to Nicole. "I forgot to mention that lunch is on me today, ladies. Why don't you go together right now and work that out yourselves? I'm sure you have a much better sense of how to divide the photos than I do." He glanced at his watch, muttering a curse. "Now, if you don't mind, I'll follow you out. I have a meeting with the mayor soon."

Nicole pocketed the gift card, careful not to look Quinn's way as they gathered their folders and other belongings. Her heart was started hammering again, and she was afraid now that she'd managed to completely fool herself earlier when she'd pretended that all of this was no big deal. The last thing she was ready for right now was a quiet tête-à-tête with Quinn. She'd never make it through a meal without cracking from the pressure.

CHAPTER FOUR: QUINN

Quinn trained her eyes on the menu, too terrified to look anywhere else. Any time she met Nicole's gaze, her heart seemed to quite literally stop. This whole morning had been absolute torture, and now here they were, at the best date restaurant in town, alone together. The menu was trembling in her hands.

When Nicole had showed up this morning at city hall, traipsing through the door like she owned the place, Quinn had barely managed to keep her cool, and only because she'd prepared for that moment. She'd gotten to city hall ridiculously early and sat down on that bench waiting, pretending to look at her phone the whole time. Every time those double doors opened, her stomach had dropped to the point that when Nicole finally did waltz through, Quinn was almost sick with nerves. Still, she'd gotten through the first exchange well, though it had taken every ounce of Quinn's willpower not to look up from her phone a single time as they waited for John. That one exchange, however, had been enough for Quinn to see her in her full glory. Nicole looked incredible.

It didn't help that she'd barely aged. She was older, sure, but her face was unlined, and those high cheekbones and her patrician facial structure were still strikingly pretty—not a sag in sight. It also didn't help that she'd apparently learned how to dress for her figure in a way that highlighted her height and all her deadly curves. Like Quinn herself, she'd had some colorful tattoos done—a gorgeous upper sleeve was revealed when she removed her blazer in that overheated boardroom. Her makeup was flawless, her haircut was flattering, and her hair was still that luxuriant, almost black brown—hardly a strand of gray in sight. Quinn would never be able to act normally around her.

Then she'd had to sit next to her for over two hours, so shaken she could hardly drink her coffee or choke out a single word. And now here they were, in an intimate, dimly lit booth in a nearly empty gourmet restaurant, playacting as if they had nothing whatsoever between them. Quinn, on her side, was so overwhelmed she could think of nothing whatsoever to say.

"Is it too early for a cocktail?" Nicole asked, breaking the silence.

"Um," Quinn said, almost murmuring. It was the first thing she'd said since they'd awkwardly greeted each other outside the restaurant.

Nicole chuckled falsely, clearly uneasy. "I mean, what the hell, right? He gave us a hundred bucks. Might as well enjoy ourselves."

Quinn could think of a thousand reasons why drinking with Nicole was a bad idea, but when the waitress appeared, she ordered one of the Christmas cocktails—the First Noel, it was called—a watermelon mojito, of all things. Hardly fit for the birth of Christ. The waitress excused herself, and Quinn tried to focus on the menu again.

"See something interesting?" Nicole asked.

Quinn jerked her head up. Nicole watched her, one eyebrow raised. Her lips were twisted in a knowing grin.

"Um," Quinn said, desperately trying to remember what Nicole had asked. Nicole's features fell, and she squinted at Quinn.

"Are you okay? You look…like you felt sick for a second, maybe."

"Just nervous," Quinn admitted, and could have slapped herself. "About the job, I mean."

Nicole's eyebrow stayed up, her lips pursed skeptically. Finally, her face relaxed into a lazy grin. "Yeah—it's kind of a big deal, right? Not the money, but the work, of course."

For Quinn, the money was a big deal. It represented a huge boost to her usual income. The idea that Nicole thought so little of it was telling.

"It does seem like a lot of work," she said instead.

Nicole's brows lowered a bit, but she shrugged it off a moment later. "So anyway—how do you want to do this thing? Should we draw straws for the best shots?"

Quinn took a careful sip of her water, trying to hide her trembling hands.

"Well, some of them make more sense for one or the other of us to do."

Nicole frowned. "Oh?"

"I mean, you're obviously better with candid and action shots with people, hands down."

Nicole's smile was open and warm. "You've seen my work? I mean since high school?"

Quinn realized her mistake. Damn it, she thought. She's going to think you're some kind of stalker. However, being familiar with her work would be natural to some extent. Almost anyone in the business that paid attention to noteworthy photographers would know who Nicole Steele was. Her photographs were in museums, for God's sake.

"Yes," she said. "Of course I have. I even went to your last exhibit in Denver." Again, realizing her mistake, she added, "I mean when I was there. For something else. I happened to catch it."

If Nicole sensed this lie, she hid it well. "Well, that's flattering. Thank you. But you're no slouch yourself, Quinn. I'll admit right now you're better with the nature and animal shots than I am."

Quinn was shocked. "You've seen *my* work?"

Nicole snorted. "Of course! That hummingbird in *Nature* was amazing. They should have given you a full page instead of a quarter. How did you get that shot?"

If possible, Quinn's face was even hotter than before. The idea that Nicole of all people would have kept up with her photography was more than flattering. Nicole was world-renowned, for Christ's sake, and Quinn was nobody. Nicole would have had to go out of her way to see anything Quinn had produced. Sure, the hummingbird had been in a major magazine, but that didn't mean everyone read it. Nicole couldn't have seen it by chance.

Remembering that Nicole had asked her a question some time ago now, Quinn shook herself back into the moment.

"Uh...very carefully."

Nicole laughed. "No shit. Seriously, though, I'd like to learn how you take pictures like that. Maybe we could do one of the animal shoots together, and you could show me the ropes?"

Quinn swallowed and managed to nod. "Of course."

The return of the waitress saved her, and as Nicole ordered her food, Quinn took a moment to reassess the situation. Maybe this wouldn't be the disaster she'd predicted. Nicole was a professional, after all. Maybe getting to know her would be a good thing. It might mean getting some more connections to the broader photography world, and, perhaps, if things went well, they could put the past to rest, become colleagues of a sort. That would be nice. She needed to ignore this ridiculous crush.

"And for you, miss?" the waitress asked her.

Quinn still hadn't had a chance to read the menu. "What? Oh. Um, I'll have what she's having."

If the waitress was surprised, she didn't say, simply taking note and excusing herself. Nicole was watching her as she took another sip of her drink. Quinn's cheeks were hot again, but she tried to keep her expression as neutral as possible.

"What?"

Nicole shook her head. "Nothing. It's just, well, funny. After all this time. Being here together, of all places." She paused, frowned a little. "When we were kids, I was going to ask you—"

Quinn's heart rate spiked in true panic. "Nicole can we, maybe, forget about all that stuff in the past? While we're working together, I mean. I don't want to…"

Nicole waved her hands dismissively. "Of course. I'm sorry I brought it up." She fiddled with her napkin and silverware before she picked up her cocktail again, that cocky smirk back full force. She held out her glass. "Here's to us and this project."

Quinn's heart was still racing, but she picked up her own cocktail and clinked glasses with Nicole, using the momentary pause as she took a sip to try to calm herself. Part of her, of course, desperately wanted to talk about it—the past, that incredible kiss, that stupid, terrible thing she'd done to Nicole at the hotel. But a much larger part of her knew that bringing it up would make all the work they had to do much harder.

"So shall we start choosing the photos as we wait?" Nicole asked.

"Yes. Good idea."

They both opened their folders and pulled out the lists. Quinn hadn't read the new version yet, but even the longer, top-sixty list was less than half the length of the original. If she didn't have to put in so many hours at her Old West studio, she might have been able to do closer to thirty or forty of these on her own.

She glanced up to see Nicole stowing away her phone.

"Sorry," Nicole said. "Had to tell my mom to eat without me. If I didn't, she'd make a spread of food so impressive you'd think the Denver Broncos were coming to lunch."

Quinn smiled. "Is that where you're staying? At your folks' place?"

"My mom's, yes. Dad died a couple of years ago."

"I'm sorry. I didn't mean to—"

Nicole waved dismissively. "It's okay. You couldn't have known."

Quinn had known. She'd seen the obituary but had forgotten all about it. She felt terrible for the slip.

"How about your...it's only your dad, right?" Nicole asked. "Is he still here in town?"

Quinn shook her head. "No. He retired a few years ago and lives in Arizona. He comes back for a couple of weeks in the summer, and he'll be here soon for Christmas through New Year, to see me and go skiing."

"Ah, skiing," Nicole said. "I can't wait to hit the slopes myself. That's part of the reason I was so excited to take this gig—all the skiing I can sneak in between shoots. Getting to a resort where I live is a major hassle."

"You ski, huh?" Quinn asked. "That makes that part of this list easy, then. Why don't you do the two ski resorts?"

"Really? You don't mind?"

"Not at all."

They both wrote Nicole's name next to the resorts.

"Two down, fifty-eight to go," Nicole said, laughing and downing the rest of her cocktail.

"I can do the animals here," Quinn said.

"Which one should we do together?"

"The elk would probably be easiest—easiest to find and easiest to shoot." Then, seeing Nicole's expression, she backpedaled. "Not that you need something easy—"

Nicole grinned. "I was screwing with you. Easy would be good. Just let me know when you want to go."

They both put Quinn's name down next to the animals. The rest of the list was just as easy to divide. The food was delivered about halfway through the process, and they continued eating as they worked. By the time they made it through the longer list, they had only three points of contention—the Pioneer Cemetery, the brewery, and the hot springs.

"Let me have the cemetery," Nicole said. "That was like my main hang when I was a teenager. And it's the place—"

"Doc Holliday is buried. I know. I live here, Nicole. And it was also one of my hangouts, and I also love Doc Holliday."

"Are we talking about the same—?"

"I've seen *Wynonna Earp*, Nicole. And yes, it's one of my favorites. We get queer tourists all the time because of that show now."

"Oh?"

"Yes—lots. There's like a pipeline of them between here and Calgary, where the show is filmed. My friend Molly works at the brewery, and she's met a lot of the actors."

"That's really cool. I was kind of thinking that maybe I could, I mean, maybe *we* could do an LGBTQ photo spread. It's not specifically on this list, but we could make any one of these places work for it. The brewery might be a good spot."

"That's a good idea," Quinn said.

Nicole had some pink in her cheeks now, whether because of her drink or the conversation, but either way, she seemed happy, excited even. Quinn's defenses were down a bit herself. So far, working with Nicole was easy. Maybe they could have some fun together. Innocent fun, anyway.

"All right," Nicole said, eyes on the list again. "And you also said your friend works at the brewery, right?"

"Yes. We could do the shoot any time."

"I've been meaning to get over there," Nicole said. "Usually, I'm here in town and gone again, and all of that time is with my mom. I'll be glad to have a chance to visit."

"We can go anytime. Even without the photos, I mean," Quinn said, blurting out the idea before she could think better of it. Nicole looked surprised, so she kept talking, rambling really. "I get a discount. If Molly's there, I mean, and they have good beer and food—"

"That sounds nice. Whenever you want to go, I'm down."

"Deal."

"Okay—if we're both doing the brewery, then let's do the hot springs and the cemetery together, too. That way, we both get to do exactly what we want. How's that sound?"

Quinn had a momentary pang of unease. Already, with the brewery, the phony wedding, the elk, and the New Year's Eve ball, they'd be seeing each other far more than she'd originally hoped. On the other hand, despite the initial awkwardness, it had been a pleasant lunch. The cocktails helped, of course, but maybe they'd simply gotten over the initial hump, as it were.

"Perfect," she said.

Nicole glanced at her watch. "Not that I *have* to be anywhere, but I did want to start planning today. I need to check my equipment, decide what order to do things in, that kind of thing. I think I'll start tomorrow morning."

"Same."

"Let me find the waitress, and we can get out of here. Call me when you want to do those shots together. Maybe we could do one together once a week or so?"

"Sure. I need your number, though."

Nicole reached into the inside pocket of her blazer, pulled out a slim metal case, and opened it to give Quinn a business card. The card was beautifully done in a peacock pattern, with embossed gold and black ink. Quinn put it carefully in her wallet and then grabbed a cocktail napkin, writing her name and number on it and sliding it over to Nicole. Nicole chuckled and folded it, slipping it into her pocket.

"Should we do one of the shoots together this week?" Nicole asked. "Like the day after tomorrow? What is that, Friday?"

"Sure. That sounds good. I'll talk to Molly, and if we can do the brewery then, let's plan for the afternoon. It's usually quieter before dinner, and…"

"The light will be best." Nicole smiled slightly. "I agree. Are you heading out?" She stood up and pulled on her blazer and overcoat.

"I'm going to stay here and get another cocktail, I think, start writing down some plans myself."

"On another cocktail napkin?"

Quinn smiled. "Something like that."

Nicole hesitated and glanced at her watch again. Then she reached into her pocket and gave Quinn the gift card and some cash for her part of the tip.

"See you Friday, then," Nicole said. Even though Quinn was still seated, Nicole took a few steps toward her, her arms rising slightly, and then, as if remembering, she furrowed her brow and stepped back, a strange half-smile twisting her lips. She saluted briefly before she turned and walked away.

Quinn waited until she'd left through the front door before calling Molly.

"Sooooo…" Molly said. "You saw her. Are you having another freak-out?"

"Yes."

"I'll have your beer waiting for you."

"Thanks," Quinn said, hanging up and closing her eyes. She took a couple of deep breaths, trying to calm her racing heart. Right before Nicole left, it looked as if she'd wanted to hug her, or maybe something else—something more.

"Shit," Quinn said. That wasn't good.

CHAPTER FIVE: NICOLE

Nicole was about halfway back to Glenwood when she saw the small car parked crookedly on the shoulder of the highway. On this stretch between Aspen and Glenwood, pulling over was dangerous. The road had blind curves and very little room to get out of the way of traffic. Two men crouched in the mud by the car's rear tire, which was clearly flat. One was gesturing widely, the other watching him. She switched on her directional and pulled over past their car onto a slightly widened stretch of shoulder. She waited for a car to pass, then jumped outside, jogging back toward them. As she approached, she could hear the men arguing.

"It's not working!" one of them said.

"Well, try harder!" the other said.

They hadn't noticed her yet, and she was briefly tempted to go back to her car and turn around to return to the slopes. She'd had one of the nicest mornings skiing that she could remember.

Early this morning, she'd driven up to Aspen and set up her equipment before the ski resort officially opened. She'd taken photographs of Aspen village, as well as the beautiful ski slopes that rose behind it. Then, as more and more people arrived or came out of their hotels, she took pictures of the crowds. Her last shot was from the top of one of the tallest peaks, and, wanting to put her equipment away, she'd skied back down. She'd spent the rest of the morning and early afternoon on some of the best snow she'd ever experienced.

Altogether, the day so far had been absolute bliss, and the last thing she wanted now was to get in the middle of some dude fight. Unfortunately, the man closest to her noticed before she could escape.

"Oh! Hello! Who are you?"

He stood up from a crouch, and Nicole was struck by his

looming height—well over six feet, maybe even beyond six and a half. Impeccably dressed in upscale skiwear, he had sun-kissed golden skin and strikingly white-blond hair. Normally she might have been a little afraid to be on the side of a road in the relative middle of nowhere with a man this large, but his open, friendly expression put her immediately at ease.

"Uh, hi! I'm Nicole. I, uh, saw you here and wanted to see if I could help."

"A Good Samaritan?" the man asked, putting a hand to his chest, pretending to be aghast. "In Aspen?"

She laughed. "Something like that."

The other man had also joined them. He was also handsome and much shorter, with dark skin and a thick, black beard and wavy hair. He, too, wore expensive skiwear. This was surprising, given the jalopy they were driving. Maybe it was a rental.

"Hi, Nicole," the second man said, holding out his hand. "I'm Rico, and this is Dane."

Everyone shook.

"Could we use your phone to call Triple A?" Dane asked. "I left mine at the lodge, and Rico's is dead."

Rico rolled his eyes. "Which wouldn't matter if you remembered your phone, like, ever!"

Dane barked a laugh. "Which wouldn't matter if you remembered to charge *yours*, like, ever!"

"Sure," Nicole said, reaching into her pocket. She held the phone out. "Though, if you have a spare, I can change the tire for you. Then you won't have to wait."

Both men looked surprised.

"Really?" Dane asked.

Nicole nodded. "Of course. Is it a doughnut or a real spare?"

"Doughnut," Rico said, frowning.

Nicole lifted a shoulder. "It should still be okay—at least into town. Are you driving to Glenwood?"

They nodded.

"A doughnut's totally fine for that. Just go slowly, and make sure to get a new tire before driving anywhere else."

"You're a lifesaver," Rico said.

"Yes," Dane said. "A real hero. Thank you."

"No problem. Let's take a look," Nicole said.

After a careful check of the road, she hustled over to the back of their car and crouched next to the flat tire. Dane and Rico squatted on either side of her, evidently to watch. She was about to start when she realized it might be better to teach them how to do this, so she talked as she worked, explaining. Having grown up with inexpensive cars with cheap tires, she was quite practiced, and it took her very little time to get the tire sorted.

All three moved back to the front of the car, safely away from the road.

"I seriously don't know how to thank you," Dane said, shaking her hand again.

"For real," Rico added.

"You're like a real American hero."

Nicole rolled her eyes. "Don't exaggerate. My dad was a truck driver. He taught me lots of stuff like this."

Dane and Rico shared a look and grinned at each other.

"Neither one of our dads taught us stuff like that. Probably 'cause, you know," Rico said, and shrugged one shoulder.

It struck Nicole then that that the two men were holding hands.

"Ah," she said. "Well, now you know how to do it yourself!"

"I'd still like to thank you," Dane said. "Are you coming from Aspen?"

"Yes. I was skiing all morning. The snow was awesome."

"That's where we work!" Rico said.

"Oh, yeah? How cool! That must be a blast."

Dane snapped his fingers and pointed at her. "Aha! Now I know what to give you."

Nicole held up her hands. "You don't have to give me anything, guys. Really. Maybe we'll run into each other in Glenwood, or something, and you can buy me a beer."

"No, no," Dane said, moving to the driver's door. "This is better."

He climbed inside, leaned over, and started digging around in the glovebox. A moment later, he got out of the car again and handed her a season's ski pass to Aspen.

"What?" Nicole said. "Are you serious?"

Dane laughed. "I am. My hero deserves the best."

The pass was the premier level, which gave her a free meal and hot beverage every time she visited.

"This is…wow," Nicole said. She hesitated, not sure if she should accept. Her lift ticket this morning had been so expensive, she could hardly afford to go to Aspen again the whole time she was here. She couldn't even imagine how much a season pass cost. Still, considering how easily Dane had given it to her, it might be a job perk. She slipped it into her coat pocket.

"Wow," she said. "I don't know how to thank you."

"You earned it, hero," Dane said.

All three shook hands and went back to their cars, and as she drove away, Nicole wished she'd thought to get their phone numbers. It was rare to meet local queer people up here in the mountains, and she'd immediately connected to them, somehow. That was unusual anywhere.

The rest of the drive down from Aspen was picturesque and lovely, and the roads were still relatively clear of other cars. Over the next few weeks, in the lead-up to Christmas, she'd run into a lot of traffic on this road, but it was relatively pleasant now.

Back into Glenwood, she decided to park by the brewery. She'd been planning to drop off some of her equipment at her mom's and then drive and walk back—a lovely twenty-minute stroll—so she could drink a little more, but she was already a few minutes late.

Only a few guests sat at two tables, so she spotted Quinn right away. She was seated at the bar chatting with the bartender—Molly, if Nicole remembered right. From here, they seemed very friendly, hunched close together across the bar, Quinn laughing at something the other woman had said. Molly was quite pretty, in that all-American, strawberry-blond way. Were they together? Quinn had called her a friend at lunch the other day, but that could mean anything.

As if sensing her gaze, Quinn suddenly looked her way, her smile lifting into something broader, more excited than before. She waved, and for a moment, Nicole was taken back to those few months in high school when they'd been more like friends. After all that photo scanning, Nicole had seen her at a few parties and the like, and Quinn had always greeted her just like that—a bright smile and a wave. After spending most of her childhood trying to ignore her, it had been like a gift to see that expression all the time.

Nicole's hands were taken up with her camera equipment, so she lifted her chin before walking as quickly as possible to set the bags down next to Quinn's, relieved to put the heavy things down.

"Hi, Nicole. This is Molly," Quinn said.

Molly held out her hand, her eyes narrowed slightly with appraisal and suspicion. "Nice to meet you."

"Same here."

"What can I get you?"

Nicole dragged the beer list closer and reviewed the choices. "I'll have the Winter Stout, please."

Molly looked strangely pleased and walked away to the taps.

"Don't mind her," Quinn said, indicating the stool next to hers. "She likes it when women order what she calls 'real beer.'"

"What are you having?" Nicole said, sitting down. "Is that a real beer, too?"

Quinn grinned. "Yes, actually. It's an Irish Red." She slid the glass closer. "Feel free to try it, if you want."

Quinn's cheeks colored slightly after she said this, which made Nicole's stomach swoop around in delight. Nicole took a careful mouthful, rolling it around her palate briefly before swallowing.

"That's wonderful. I'll have to get a glass of that next."

Quinn grinned. "Sounds like you have the whole afternoon planned."

Nicole tried to cover her slip. "I mean, the next time I'm here, or whatever."

Quinn laughed. "I was joking, Nicole. The shoot will probably take long enough that we'll need some refreshment later, anyway."

"Right. Of course," Nicole said, still feeling hot. She was flustered, but she also hadn't had a chance to change out of her ski clothes, and she was overheating now in this warm, dark room. Thinking it would give her a chance to cool off in more than one way, she asked, "Where's the restroom?"

Quinn pointed at a large sign on a nearby hallway that said *Restroom*, and Nicole used the excuse of grabbing some lighter clothes from a bag as cover and rushed away to change.

Back in regular clothes, she splashed some cold water on her face and neck and stared at herself evenly in the mirror for a long moment.

"Get it together, Nicole," she told herself. "You're making a fool of yourself."

As she left the restroom, she heard loud, boisterous, excited voices and came out of the hall only to stop immediately. The two men she'd helped earlier—Dane, the tall blond, and Rico, the shorter, bearded brunet—stood at the bar, near Quinn's chair. Dane spotted her first, and his eyebrows lifted at once into his perfect, wavy, golden bangs.

"What are *you* doing here?" he asked as she approached.

"What are *you* doing here?" Nicole replied, and she and the men laughed.

"You three know each other?" Quinn asked, clearly confused.

"This is the woman I was telling you about!" Dane said. "The one who saved us! The hero of the hour!"

Nicole waved at them dismissively. "It was nothing—really."

Quinn looked surprised, too. "Wow! That is strange. Well, uh, Dane, Rico—this is Nicole Steele."

The two men reacted as if slapped, both of them jerking back.

"What on earth?" Rico said.

"What are the ever-loving odds?" Dane asked. "I mean, you told us your name, Nicole, but I didn't know you were *that* Nicole—"

Quinn laughed, the sound fake and forced, and she waved her hands to cut him off. Everyone turned her way, and her face went a dark shade of red. "Uh, N-Nicole," she sputtered. "Um, I asked the guys here today to help with the shoot. You know, uh, since we wanted to do an LGBTQ thing? I wasn't sure if we could find a couple of men, uh, willing to pretend to be gay. Or another gay couple, come to that."

Nicole smiled. "That's a great idea. Hi, guys. Nice to meet you again, properly this time." She held out her hand, and they shook it, Dane grinning widely.

"Oh, wow, Quinn. When you told us about her the other day—"

"So anyway," Quinn said, her tone high and panicky again. "Um, do you guys want to wear that ski stuff for this, or did you bring other outfits?"

Nicole had caught both not-so-subtle interruptions. Clearly Quinn had told these men about their past together at some point, which meant Molly probably knew, too, which would explain Molly's earlier suspicious appraisal. Nicole didn't exactly want to know what Quinn had told them, but on the other hand, she could barely stop herself from asking.

Molly finally appeared, this time coming out from behind the bar to join them. All five of them moved the various bags of equipment over to one of the more isolated tables and sat down to finish their beers.

"Do you think we could get Toni in any of the pictures?" Quinn asked, nudging Molly with her elbow.

"Fuck you," Molly said, pushing her back.

The others laughed, and Dane leaned close to Nicole, fake-whispering as if they were sharing a secret, but loud enough that everyone could hear. "Molly is head over heels for her boss, Toni, but she's too chicken to ask her out."

"The hell I am!" Molly said, slamming her beer onto the table. She frowned and looked at Nicole. "It's just, you shouldn't, you know, at work. It's about being professional is all."

"No—the fact is you're a damn coward," Rico said, and bocked a few times like a chicken, his arms bent and flapping like wings.

"Screw you guys," Molly said, and everyone laughed.

"Is that her?" Nicole asked Dane, subtly pointing at the handsome butch woman behind the counter.

Dane touched his nose. "Bingo."

"She's pretty hot."

"Screw you too, Nicole," Molly said, making everyone laugh again.

"I was serious, though, Molly," Quinn said, a hint of mischief pulling at her lips.

"About what?"

"About getting Toni in a shot. It would be great to have her in a few, or at least one. She's probably the most, well, obvious of any of us."

All five of them stared at Toni, who, apparently sensing their gaze, turned their way and waved, seeming confused the longer they stared back at her. She had very short, dark hair and was muscular and fit, the sleeves of her uniform shirt stretching over bulging biceps underneath.

"Again, screw all of you," Molly said again.

As they all continued to rib Molly, Nicole realized that she was enjoying herself, feeling, strangely, like she was among friends. She hung around with a group like this back in the Loveland-Fort Collins area—a very similar group in many ways, made up of mixed queer couples. It seemed, for the first time since she'd gotten here, almost like she was home.

She caught Quinn smiling at her, specifically, and that dropping sensation caught her up once again. How long would it be before that smile struck her as normal? Part of her never wanted it to seem normal. She liked the unmoored feelings she always had around her.

And, of course, Nicole couldn't help but feel a little relieved. Molly and Quinn weren't together, after all. It shouldn't matter, but it did.

CHAPTER SIX: QUINN

Quinn and her friends waved as Nicole left, Dane and Rico shouting their good-byes across the busy room. All of them had been here at the brewery for hours now taking photos, and the dinner rush was well underway. Nicole had excused herself by saying she needed to be home.

They'd had a perfectly lovely afternoon. This was surprising on the one hand, as Quinn had been dreading so much contact with her, but on the other, she should have expected that her friends would like her, and with the three of them here, she and Nicole hadn't had time to be awkward. She and Nicole worked well together.

The door closed after Nicole, and Dane looked at her, grinning.

"That woman is seriously hot, Quinn."

Rico and Molly agreed.

"And she obviously still likes you," Dane added.

"Pshaw." Quinn waved a dismissive hand. "Come on. That was almost..." She grimaced. "God. Almost twenty years ago, now. She couldn't possibly *still* like me."

"Whatever. Then she likes you now, if that's more accurate."

"You think?"

"Oh, for sure," Molly said. "She was watching you anytime she knew she wouldn't be caught."

Rico nodded enthusiastically. "Her eyes were like magnets on your," he gestured at her broadly, "everything."

Quinn shrugged, trying to keep her expression neutral. "I mean, yeah, I think we're attracted to each other—"

"I knew it!" Dane said, slapping the table.

Quinn laughed. "I have eyes, don't I? Even so, it doesn't mean anything. She lives like four hours away. What could possibly come of it?"

Dane and Rico shared a look.

"What?"

"Well, that's the thing," Rico said. "When you and Molly were doing that shot with Toni, we had a chance to chat with her. She told us she wants to move back here."

Quinn was floored. No one ever came back. Even her dad, who was born and lived here his whole life, had left the city the day after he retired. All her high school friends had scattered, and most of the time, when she made new friends, they eventually left, too. People always left Glenwood. But return? Never.

"I think you broke her," Molly said, chuckling.

Dane put a hand on hers briefly. "Is that something you'd want? For her to move here, I mean?"

Quinn peered up at him, frowning. Truthfully, she'd never given it a thought. After that disaster at the hotel when they were kids, she'd avoided Nicole all summer. Then Nicole left for Chicago, and while she visited a couple of times a year, they hadn't spoken once. Never, in all that time, had Quinn ever believed Nicole might return and had no way of absorbing what that could mean for them.

"I'm not sure," she said, frowning. "I don't know what to think."

Dane patted her hand again. "It's okay, Quinn. You don't need to make up your mind overnight or anything. But you know, you *could* see if something's there, right? While she's here, I mean?"

"And if it doesn't work out, a Christmas romance never hurt anyone," Rico said, winking.

"Ain't that the truth?" Molly asked. "I could use a Christmas romance myself."

"Then have one, you ninny!" Dane said, pushing her shoulder. "Just ask her out. I'm sure Toni's into you."

Molly rolled her eyes. "No, she isn't. I'm just another peon to her."

Rico laughed. "Yeah, right. You're just chicken."

Molly pushed him back. Then, glancing around, she said, "Shit. It's getting late, guys, and I'm supposed to work the dinner shift. If Toni catches me sitting here while we're slammed, she's going to have kittens."

Dane checked his watch and grimaced. "Damn. Me and Rico need to get home soon, too."

"Let's talk soon," Molly said, giving Quinn a quick hug. "Try not to overthink it. You and Nicole seem to get along, and you don't have to see her all the time, or anything. Feel free to stop by if you flip out again, okay? And call soon so we can do some Christmas shopping."

"I will. And thanks, Molls."

They hugged again, and Molly disappeared into the staff area.

After they paid, she followed Dane and Rico outside with her equipment. The night was brisk, but still strangely warm for this time of year. From here, the scent of the hot springs was sharp with that sulfuric bite some visitors complained about. She rarely thought about it, living here, but sometimes the scent was too strong to ignore, even for her. The three of them peered in the direction of the springs, lit up at night and festooned with special, colorful lights for the holidays.

She and the guys hugged and parted, and she walked as quickly as she could back to her apartment, stopping twice to put down her cameras and lights to rest her arms.

She spent the evening reviewing her shots, organizing them by theme and by the people in them—groups and couples—and then noted the best two or three from each set. She'd taken several shots of individual people, too, in case they'd work better for the brewery's advertising campaign, but most of these individuals were, she now saw, of Nicole. Nicole, laughing at something Molly had said and leaning on the bar casually, happy, like a hipster beer model. After seeing several more like this, Quinn couldn't help a sharp pang of embarrassment. All the pictures of Nicole seemed a little too intimate, and she and Nicole were anything but. She quickly dragged these photos into another folder on her laptop, hoping Nicole would never find out how creepy she'd been.

Finished, she noted the time with alarm and got ready for bed. She wanted to get up as early as possible to see if she could catch some of the animals on her list. John had simply listed "birds" as one of the animals he wanted, and she knew a great spot to catch a lot of them that wintered here.

Sleep didn't come easily. She was still worked up from her afternoon with Nicole. And after a night of tossing and turning, she finally got up and left her apartment well before sunrise. She had to be at the studio by ten to help her assistant with the weekend rush. Anyway, she usually took most of her best wildlife shots either early in the morning or right before sunset. Despite the frigid chill, she decided to ride her bike to the spot she'd been thinking of for the shoot this morning. Some years ago, the city and county had put in a walk-bike path along the Colorado River for more than thirty miles east from town, and the trail was entirely deserted as she coasted, the river roaring nearby the whole ride.

The day was waking as she parked her bike. She hiked down a steep slope to a rock shelf that gave her a good view of the brush and the water in a stream pool. It took her about twenty minutes to set up all her equipment. Finally ready, she sat back on her camp chair, trying to remain as still as possible. The birds and animals would have seen her arrival, but they had short memories.

She was soon rewarded with a number of song and marsh birds. While birdwatching wasn't as thrilling here as in the mid-summer, when she might see twenty or thirty different kinds of birds in a single visit, she caught several ducks, some geese, a solo American coot, and several different jays. Right as she began to get cold, and the very moment she was about to get up and move around to warm up, she spotted a belted kingfisher—a female with her huge, gray-blue crested head and bright white and chestnut chest feathers. Quinn managed to get several shots of her, still and in flight, and captured the very moment the bird caught a fish before flying away. She was thrilled. These birds were rare enough that she'd never managed to get a female before.

"Was that a kingfisher?" someone called to her.

Quinn peered up the hill to the trail, where an older woman stood with a pair of binoculars.

"Sorry," the woman said, slightly shy of shouting. "Didn't mean to startle you."

"No problem," Quinn hollered back before standing and stretching. She hiked up to the woman, not wanting to yell their entire conversation over the distance and rumble of the rushing river.

"It *was* a kingfisher," Quinn said, smiling as they met. "A female."

"Oh, dang," the woman said, snapping her fingers. "I've never seen a female. I've been looking for years now."

The woman seemed familiar, but Quinn couldn't place her. In a small town like this, they'd likely run into each other a few times, but the recognition seemed stronger somehow.

"I've never seen a female, either," Quinn said. "Not until today, anyway. Want to see the shots I took?"

The woman smiled. "Yes, actually, I'd love to. Though it wouldn't count. For my app, I mean. But I'd still like to see them."

"App?"

The woman pulled out her phone and showed Quinn her birding app. It apparently kept a tally of her sightings for her.

"That's handy," Quinn said.

"I'm aiming for a hundred by the New Year," the woman explained, crossing her fingers. "But I'm ten short."

"You'll get them if you hang out here, I bet."

"That's what I'm hoping."

Quinn pointed down at her spot. "Let me grab my cameras real quick, and I'll show you what I got."

"Oh, gosh—I don't want to be a bother."

"It's no problem. I was about to wrap up for the day, anyway. Getting cold sitting here. Just give me a few minutes to get my things."

She always found it easier to pack up than to set up, and soon Quinn had her gear and chair zipped up tight again, ready to make the steep climb once more. As she labored up the hill, she heard voices, and by the time she made it to the top, the older woman had company.

It was Nicole.

"What are you—" they both said, then burst out laughing. The older woman seemed confused, and Nicole gestured between them.

"Mom, this is Quinn Zelinski. Quinn, this is my mom, Annette."

"Oh!" Annette said, her eyebrows shooting up with surprise. "My goodness! What are the odds?"

Quinn guessed, then, that like herself with her friends, Nicole had probably told her mom about her. Actually, considering that disastrous night eighteen years ago, Annette probably knew the whole damn story almost as well as the two of them did. Now, seeing them side by side, she realized that earlier she'd recognized the resemblance without knowing it. Annette's face had a similar pretty sharpness to Nicole's. They also had the same eyes, and Annette's hair, though a solid silvery gray, was thick like her daughter's.

Quinn held out a hand. "So nice to meet you."

"You too, dear," Annette said, her tone warmer than Quinn might have expected, considering.

The three of them stood there awkwardly before Quinn said, "Oh! The photos."

She unzipped one of her bags and pulled out a camera, turning it on and scrolling until she found the first shot of the kingfisher. Nicole took it from her and held up the viewfinder to her mom, the two of them hunched up to look at it together. Nicole scrolled through, Annette making sounds of excited joy the entire time. Finished, Nicole gave her the camera again.

"They're beautiful," Annette said. "You're really talented, dear. Like my girl, here."

"They are gorgeous shots," Nicole said, nodding and smiling.

Quinn was hot, likely blushing furiously, and could only stammer her thanks.

"I'm going to head down to that little spot of yours, Quinn, see if I can spot that bird for myself. You have a nice day, now, and I hope we see you again, soon."

Quinn could tell Annette was giving them a minute alone, and while she was still somewhat terrified, she was thankful for it, too.

"Be careful, Mom!" Nicole called.

"So…you're birding, now?" Quinn asked her, grinning slightly.

Nicole sighed. "I know, I know. But Mom loves it, and I like being with her. And it's nice to get outside."

Quinn could only agree. Now that the sun was starting to warm the day, it was incredibly pleasant out here. The air was clear and sweet with melting frost.

"I should probably get down there," Nicole said. "Make sure she doesn't fall in."

Quinn laughed. "No problem. Go ahead."

She turned toward her bike to leave, but Nicole touched her shoulder.

"Uh, wait a sec. Are you busy? I mean after this? My mom and I were going to get breakfast at the Daily Bread. If you wanted to join us, I mean."

Quinn's heart skipped. She didn't need to be at the studio for another two hours, but the idea of having another meal with Nicole so soon, especially when they didn't have work to distract them, was too much.

"Sorry," she said instead. "I have to get going."

"Ah. No problem. Some other time. See you soon."

Nicole turned to join her mom, and Quinn watched her descent until she was safely down there with her. Hands trembling, she took longer than normal to get her camera equipment into the saddlebags on her bike, but her anxiety gradually turned into something like happy excitement as she rode.

Nicole wanted to spend time with her outside of their job together. Quinn didn't know what that meant yet, but she was starting to like the idea.

CHAPTER SEVEN: NICOLE

Nicole peered out the living-room window of her mom's house before letting the curtain slip closed again. She managed not to pace, but it was a near thing, her foot tapping impatiently. Quinn was five minutes late now, and Nicole didn't know if this was usual for her. She'd been ready herself for over an hour, always an early bird.

When Quinn had called her last night to set up their shared photo shoot at the hot springs today, Nicole had agreed to basically everything she'd said, including the idea of driving together. Now, as she waited, she realized that had been incredibly stupid. Not only would Quinn see her mom's modest home, but they'd also be stuck all day together. She wouldn't have a chance to make a quick exit if things became awkward.

That is, if Quinn even showed.

That earlier teen trauma flashed through Nicole's mind. How ridiculous. After almost nineteen years, she still felt the searing pain of residual abandonment from that terrible night at the hotel. In all the years since, she'd avoided thinking about that night and about Quinn as much as possible, yet sometimes the memory would float to the top. She no longer felt resentful or even overly hurt—nothing like she had at the time, anyway. In fact, when she'd thought of that night or Quinn at all during the last two decades, she'd regretted her own lack of follow-through. She'd been an absolute coward. She should have chased her out of the hotel room or talked to her the next day or later that week—anything would have been better than leaving things like that. She should have asked her out when she'd had the chance much earlier that semester, too. Instead, she'd avoided her all summer, and they never spoke again. Until last week.

So her current feelings—the attraction, anyway—held an echo of that earlier pain, but even more of that nervous excitement, that can't-wait-to-see-you pinch in the pit of her stomach any time she planned to be around her again. Yet that fear of abandonment was still there, and this waiting wasn't helping.

Today was Thursday, and it had been almost a week since that lucky happenstance with Quinn by the river. Her mom had teased her about the two of them at least once a day since. It had been obvious, at least to her mom, that Nicole was still attracted to her, and Nicole hadn't said differently. Her mom seemed to like the idea of them together, for some reason. Nicole blamed the Hallmark Channel, which, besides *White Christmas*, was playing nonstop on the TV this month.

She checked her phone again and sighed. No messages. Apparently, Quinn was one of those people who, when running late, didn't think to text ahead.

Her mom emerged from her bedroom then, her red-and-green Christmas-themed bathrobe garish and bright. The dogs were at her heels, both of them blinking stupidly. Her mom rubbed her eyes and startled slightly at the sight of Nicole.

"Jesus! You're up early."

"I told you last night. Quinn and I are doing the hot springs today. We thought we'd get there before the crowds congregate and set up together."

"Hmm," her mom said, grinning slightly.

"What?"

"Oh, nothing!" She headed toward the kitchen, dogs at her heels, and Nicole was compelled to follow them all.

"No, what?"

Her mom ignored her, opening the door for the dogs, both of whom dashed out into the backyard. She poured a cup of coffee and finally turned toward her. "Are you going to spend the whole day with her?"

"Well, yes, I guess so. We need night and day pictures, but the sun sets pretty early, so it shouldn't be too late."

"That's good. You should invite her over to dinner if she doesn't have plans. Tell her I'm making enchiladas."

"Why would I do that?"

"Because you want to," her mom said simply.

"No, I don't. What makes you think I would—"

"Nicole. I know you better than anyone, and I can tell when you like someone. Give me some credit, for goodness' sake."

Nicole almost protested, but she sighed. "She *is* cute."

"She sure is. Much cuter than her pictures."

"I barely know her."

"You've known her for over thirty years."

Nicole shook her head. "No. That's just it. I don't know her now, and I didn't know her then. We barely talked to each other in school. I was too dang flustered all the time to say anything to her."

"Well, then, now's your chance! I imagine you're much smoother than when you were eighteen."

"Mom!"

"It's true! Or I hope it is, anyway. Invite her to dinner."

"And you'll, what, watch us eat?" Nicole asked.

Her mom rolled her eyes. "I'll eat with you. I want to see the two of you being idiots around each other some more. You were both darling at the river the other day, flustered and stammering. It was cute."

"Gee, thanks."

Hearing a knock at the door, she and her mom jumped lightly Nicole's heart began to race, and her mom squeezed her hand.

"You'll be great. Relax. She seems like a lovely girl."

"You make it sound like a date."

"Isn't it?"

Nicole rolled her eyes and went for the door, pausing long enough to take a deep, long breath before opening it. Quinn's hand was raised, ready to knock again, and Quinn startled at the sight of her.

"I didn't think you were up. I thought you'd slept in," Quinn said.

"I got tired of waiting."

Quinn winced. "I'm sorry. Stupid car wouldn't start. Had to borrow Molly's. I'd have let you know, but I forgot my phone, as usual."

"Would you like some coffee, dear?" Nicole's mom asked from behind her.

"No thanks, Mrs. Steele. I already had one too many this morning."

"Okay, but call me Annette."

"This is a cute place, Mrs., I mean Annette. Great neighborhood, great location. You're lucky to have it."

Her mom and Quinn started discussing the changes to the area in the last ten years or so, and Nicole used their distraction to start gathering her equipment and to hide her own surprise. While she'd always been proud of her parents for buying their home and keeping it, she couldn't deny that she'd always avoided having friends over because of its size. Now here was Quinn, genuinely interested and pleased with her folks' house. Nicole should have expected Quinn's response, now that she knew Quinn wasn't a snob, but she was still more than a little taken aback by her enthusiasm. It made her like Quinn even more, and she wasn't sure what that meant.

"You two have fun today, even if it is work," her mom said.

"Will do. Thanks, Mom."

"Thanks, Annette."

Nicole gave her a quick hug and kiss and followed Quinn toward a purple Subaru Outback in the driveway, grinning a bit at its hideousness. Her hands were full of equipment, another camera case strapped to her back.

"Got everything?" Quinn asked, taking two of her heavy bags.

"Yep."

"Did you bring your suit?"

"My what?"

"Your swimsuit?"

Nicole was surprised. She'd brought it with her from Fort Collins. Every year she and her mom went to the springs the day after Christmas, like she had with both of her parents growing up. But bringing it today, when they were going to a professional shoot together? It hadn't even occurred to her.

"Uh, well..."

Quinn's gaze darted to the side. "I'm sorry. I don't know what I'm thinking. I'm sure we'll be too busy. We have so much work to do, and—"

"No, no! You're right! We should take advantage of being there. We can get a soak in when we're done."

Quinn smiled brightly, and Nicole dashed back inside. Her mom looked up from her armchair, clearly surprised to see her so soon, and laughed when she saw what Nicole was holding when she came out of her bedroom.

"That woman wants to see you in a swimsuit?" Annette asked. "She's even worse than you are."

"Quiet, you," Nicole said, trying not to smile.

The Subaru smelled like hops and yeast, and despite the hour, Nicole suddenly craved a beer. Of course, uneasiness caused part of that urge. She tried hard not to stare at Quinn. She was even cuter than usual today in her heavier winterwear—a faux-fur-lined gray parka and matching maroon hat-and-glove set. Her cheeks were colored from the chill, and her blue eyes seemed somehow even lighter in the morning sunlight.

"Cold today," Quinn said, startling her.

"What? Oh, yes. It is. Very." She made herself look out at the road again. Quinn must have sensed her gaze.

"I sure hope we get some snow before Christmas," Quinn said.

"Yeah. Me, too. I'd love to take the snowshoes out."

That was the extent of their conversation all the way to the springs. At one point, Quinn turned the radio on, and they caught the middle of one of Nicole's favorite songs—"Fade Into You," by Mazzy Star. Nicole was about to start singing along, but Quinn quickly turned the radio off without explanation, and the rest of the drive passed in silence.

Jesus! Nicole thought. Ask about anything! Pets, hobbies, anything! But it was too late. They were turning into the parking lot, which, despite the early hour, was surprisingly full.

"Locals are here in force," Quinn said as she searched for a spot. "Pretty soon it'll be totally packed with tourists. Everyone in town likes to take advantage while they can."

"Oh? I guess it's true for me, too. I almost always go a couple of times when I visit."

Quinn's face soured slightly, her brow lowering, lips thinning.

"Is that so?"

"Yep."

Nicole wasn't sure what she'd said wrong, but a palpable tension pervaded the car now. Perhaps it was just the reminder that Nicole didn't live here like she did, but she wasn't sure why that would bother Quinn. Luckily, she didn't need to worry about it much longer as they finally found a spot and parked. Quinn got out of the car without a word.

"Oh boy," Nicole said, rolling her eyes. Today was going to be a joy.

Luckily, Quinn's mood had already shifted by the time she met her at the trunk, and they started chatting and making plans for the first shots right there in the parking lot.

"Someone should get a shot from up on the bridge," Quinn said, pointing at the stairs that led to a pedestrian bridge that overlooked the springs and the spa.

"Good idea. We should get a night shot from up there, too."

"And we should include the front of the entrance. Maybe from an angle? To avoid some of the cars and stuff?"

Both were good ideas—the perfect first shots. Quinn seemed to have a real knack for this type of shoot. Strange that she hadn't gone pro after all these years. Having seen at least some of her work now and then, Nicole was certain she had the talent. But Nicole also knew that she spent most of her time running that Old West studio downtown. Her talent and her day job were hard to reconcile.

Rather than bringing up the subject, Nicole agreed. "Sounds good! Do you want me to do the bridge?"

Quinn grinned. "I was hoping you'd volunteer. The last thing I need is to lug all my stuff up there." She mimicked back pain. "I'm getting too old for acrobatics."

Nicole waved at her dismissively. "Sure, sure. You want to get out of the hard stuff."

"Of course!"

Nicole spent the next fifteen minutes huffing her way up the stairs to the pedestrian bridge, the cameras and the tripod weighing her down. She didn't mind the exercise, and she hadn't been on the bridge in a long time, either. While she went to the springs with her mom every year, they always drove. And her visits in general were almost always rooted to her mom's place—she barely knew the town now.

With brisk winds, it was bracingly cold up here, and Nicole was forced to put on her gloves almost as soon as she had set up the cameras and light reflectors. They hampered her movements quite a lot and made every shot that much harder, as she couldn't always depress the button when she hit it the first time. She had to wait a few times for a passing high cloud, reminded, once again, why she hated photographing water.

The mountains behind the pool were nicely lit this morning, and despite the crowded parking lot, only a handful of people were in the water. She wanted to show the full extent of the great pool, the striking brick spa and athletic club, with the majestic red hills rising behind everything. If she could just get the right lighting, she'd have it.

By the time she'd captured a few images she was happy with, she was chilled through and fumbled her way through repacking her gear, shivering hard. She'd need the hot pool sooner at this rate.

Thankfully Quinn seemed genuinely grateful and a little contrite when they met at the front door.

"Jeez, Nicole. You look frozen solid. Now I'm sorry for asking you to do that." She pointed to a far part of the parking lot. "I was crouched down over there in that bush for my shots, so if it makes you feel any better, I have some pine needles where they don't belong."

Nicole chuckled and shrugged, that flicker of earlier resentment completely forgiven. "No problem. You can do the nighttime version of that shot up on the bridge, though, okay?"

Quinn saluted and smiled that heartbreaking grin. "Sure thing, boss," she said. She started walking toward the door and then turned back to Nicole, her brow furrowed. "You coming?"

Nicole had to force her shocked legs to move and her lips to smile back. For a moment, she'd been eighteen again, struck completely stupid by one of Quinn's gorgeous smiles.

CHAPTER EIGHT: QUINN

Quinn's tension melted away with the hammering jets of hot water. She'd been in here for ten minutes now, letting them work their magic, and she did, in fact, feel a lot better than before.

She and Nicole spent most of their day outside in the bitter cold. They'd been so busy, they'd barely spoken, and had even eaten lunch separately. Quinn was worn out and grateful to be done.

Nicole was still inside changing. She had wrapped up her last photo for the day after Quinn and still needed to store her equipment and get her suit on, so she'd be a while yet. Still, Quinn couldn't help but watch for her, her hopes rising anytime she saw a brunette coming outside. Nervous again, she closed her eyes and leaned her head back, the hot water bubbling up behind her neck and on her shoulders.

"Sleeping on the job, Zelinski?" Nicole asked a few minutes later, startling her.

Quinn bolted forward, spinning toward her voice.

This had been a terrible idea. A wonderful idea, too, maybe, but also terrible. For the rest of her life, she could picture Nicole like this. Her modest swimsuit—a simple black one-piece—still left a lot of skin on display. Quinn's heart raced. She should have expected that a tall, curvy woman like her should look incredible in a swimsuit, yet Quinn was struck dumb. Nicole waited for a reply, grinning ever wider the longer Quinn gawked, but Quinn couldn't stop herself in any way. She stared, openly and likely obviously, as well as unashamedly.

Finally, Nicole slid into the water next to her, wincing slightly at the heat.

"I almost never come in here," Nicole said. "I usually stick to the cooler pool."

"Really?" Quinn asked. "I'm the opposite. I could sit in here in the heat all day."

The springs had two larger pools and a kiddie pond. One pool was more like a warmer swimming pool, set at about 90°F. This therapy pool, on the other hand, was set at about 100°F. It had massaging jets, like a hot tub.

Nicole settled herself into one of the areas with jets next to her, closing her eyes. "It is nice," she finally said, speaking up over the noise of bubbling water.

Quinn was still staring at her, but with Nicole's eyes closed like that, she could get away with it. Nicole's long hair was up in a messy bun, but tendrils of it hung down, bobbing in the water. She'd removed her makeup, too, and Quinn wasn't sure she'd ever seen her face completely bare like this, at least since middle school.

Nicole cracked one eye open, her face splitting into a wide grin the moment she caught Quinn's eye.

"What are you looking at?" she asked.

"I, uh…" Quinn desperately tried to think of some excuse. "Oh, I just wondered about your hair. It's so…great." Quinn could have kicked herself. She sounded like a straight-up idiot.

Nicole opened her eyes fully and raised one eyebrow. "Yeah? Well, thanks. I've always liked yours, too."

Despite the heat, Quinn was blushing, so she was grateful that the hot water masked her reaction. She touched her hair lightly. "What? This? It's basically the cut I've always had. Same old, same old."

"It suits you."

Quinn had no response, and she finally made herself pull her eyes away and attempt to relax back into the roiling jets. That was, of course, easier said than done, and she was tense now, anxious lest she say or do anything stupid. She was entirely aware that she was being ridiculous, that reacting this way would only lead to disappointment, but she also knew that she couldn't help it. She couldn't control the way she responded. Take today, for example. She'd stolen some more snapshots of Nicole, knowing, without question, that she was being creepy. But she hadn't been able to help herself—it was like a compulsion.

All week, she'd look at her phone, her fingers hovering over Nicole's number, desperate to call her and knowing she shouldn't. Molly had teased her at first. Then, as if recognizing how worked up she was about Nicole, she'd stopped teasing and started to encourage her. And still, Quinn couldn't make herself even send a quick text. She'd managed to call her last night only after several beers with Molly, Dane, and Rico. She was, in a word, a mess.

She'd been busy—very busy—with the other photo shoots she had done and her business, which was now well into the holiday rush. The store wasn't as busy as it would be a week or especially two weeks from now, but plenty of walk-ins and appointments kept her and her assistant on their toes most days.

Her dad was coming tomorrow, and she hadn't had a chance to buy a gift for him or any of her friends—something she normally finished by now. Actually, when she considered shopping at all, she more or less shut down. Part of her wanted to buy something for Nicole. She probably shouldn't, but she also couldn't let the idea go. Not that she planned anything grand or over-the-top. No, she wanted to give her something small—a gesture, of sorts. But she couldn't think of anything that fit the idea she had in her head.

"Hey," Nicole said, startling her.

"Hmm?"

Nicole's face twisted, uncertain. "Uh, my mom asked me to invite you to dinner. Tonight, I mean, if you don't have plans. We're having enchiladas."

This was, Quinn realized, the second time Nicole had asked her to a meal. When they'd run into each other by the river, she'd panicked and made up an excuse. This time, however, she had a real one.

"I'd love to, Nicole, but I can't."

Nicole's face fell. "Oh, okay. No problem."

Quinn touched her arm, removing her hand almost as quickly when she realized what she'd done. The two of them avoided touching each other—they always had.

"No, I'd *really* like to. But I can't. My dad is coming to town, and my place is a disaster. He's staying at a hotel, but we always spend time together at my apartment. And I'm working the closing shift at the store tomorrow, so I won't have a chance to clean before he gets here."

Nicole's expression cleared. "Oh, yeah? Any way I could help?"

Quinn couldn't help but laugh. "Help clean? Gee. What fun."

"No. I mean it! I'd love to see it. And help."

Quinn bit her lip. The idea of having Nicole in her apartment was both appealing and horrifying. Her apartment was a pit right now, and having Nicole clean up after her was more than she could bear. Still, some parts of her apartment wouldn't be too embarrassing—the kitchen and the living room, namely. They needed dusting, wiping down, and the dishes put away.

"What about your mom? Won't she be sitting there with too many enchiladas?"

"She won't put them in the oven until I head home. We can have them tomorrow."

"Are you sure? It won't put her out in any way?"

Nicole shook her head. "Not at all. If I know my mom, she's been sitting around nibbling on Christmas cookies all day. I'm sure she'll be fine waiting."

"Okay, well, thanks. If you're sure you want to, and she won't mind."

Nicole grinned and sank back into the jets again, closing her eyes. Quinn was struck with a strong sense of déjà vu. She remembered that Nicole was like this—accommodating, helpful. In high school, she always seemed so remote, almost too cool to talk to, and then, when you did talk to her, you realized she was actually lovely. Nice, sweet even. But helping clean her apartment? Quinn wouldn't even ask Molly to do that, and Nicole had volunteered. Maybe she was motivated by more than simple helpfulness. Was this Nicole's way of flirting? If so, it wasn't particularly obvious, nor did Quinn know what to think about the possibility.

"Woo! I'm getting hot now," Nicole said, standing up and moving away from the jets.

"Isn't that the point?"

Nicole laughed. "Well, maybe, but like I said, I'm more of a cool-water kinda gal. Wanna take a quick dip in the other pool together?"

Quinn didn't, but she also didn't want to be a spoilsport. Nicole had been nice enough to hang out with her here, so she could at least return the favor.

"Sure. As long as we get back in here before we leave."

Nicole made her way over to the stairs, waiting for Quinn to join her before climbing out into the night air. It was so cold, carpets had been set up between the hot thermal pool and the cooler swimming pool so no one would slip on the ice, but Quinn's feet and the rest of her were instantly chilled. Suddenly Nicole grabbed her hand and, laughing, dragged Quinn forward toward the bigger pool. They paused at the edge before jumping in, Quinn coming up shrieking from the blast of cooler water. The water was still warmer than the average pool, but after soaking in the thermal-therapy water for the last half hour, she found it bracingly cold.

"Yikes!" Nicole said, standing and rubbing her arms. "It's like ice water!"

"I told you!"

"Yeah, well, normally it feels totally fine—hot even. You ruined it for me."

"*I* ruined it?"

Nicole smirked. "Well, no, but getting in the hot pool first ruined this water for me. Let's swim around before we go back in there."

She dove and swam away, and Quinn was forced to hurry to catch up. By the time they reached the far end, she did, in fact, feel warmer. They floated there together, panting slightly, grinning at each other stupidly.

"This is fun," Quinn said.

"It is. All work and no play and all that. I'm glad we got a chance to…well, hang out, I guess."

"Me, too."

The dopey grin on her face matched Nicole's, and she didn't bother trying to hide it. She liked being here. She liked being around her. Why fight it?

She glanced up at the huge pool clock, surprised to see the time. They'd been here taking photos and swimming for almost ten hours now. No wonder she was so worn down.

"We better head out," Quinn said.

"I guess so. But I wish we didn't have to."

Quinn grinned. "Same."

They did another quick dip in the hotter, thermal pool before going into the changing room together. Luckily there were privacy stalls, as Quinn wouldn't even think of getting dressed in front of her. They soon emerged, Quinn smiling at the sight of her. It had been only a few minutes, yet she was glad to see her again. How ridiculous was that? Luckily, to judge by Nicole's excited smile, she felt the same.

"Ready?" Quinn asked.

"Yes. Let's go. I hope you have something to drink at your place. I could use something after that day."

"I do. Molly keeps me in beer at all times."

"Useful friend to have around."

"For sure."

By the time they were at her apartment, several bags of equipment in tow, Quinn was drooping with fatigue. Nicole looked similarly tired, but after she put the bags of cameras and lights down, she glanced around the one-room apartment before focusing on the framed photos covering many of the walls. Quinn tried not to watch her reactions, turning her attention to getting them both a glass of beer. She had several crowlers in the fridge from the Glenwood Brewery. She opened and poured one evenly into two pint glasses.

"I love your place!" Nicole called. "It's cool in here. I didn't know Glenwood had apartments like this. It's very industrial chic. I like this exposed brick and the wood floors. And the location is amazing. It's nice being downtown. Everything's right outside."

As Quinn turned around with the pints, she found Nicole studying one of her photographs on the apartment wall. A family of otters played in the river near an abandoned homestead, the snow-capped Rocky Mountains rising dramatically behind them. She'd waited weeks to get that photo, going to that spot once a week in the spring, knowing that if she did, she could get more than the single male otter she usually saw there. Finally, the female and her four pups emerged from their den, and she'd taken hundreds of all six playing and eating together.

"I love this," Nicole said, pointing at the photo and turning her way.

"Thanks," Quinn said, handing her the pint glass.

Nicole took a long swallow, closing her eyes briefly before holding up the glass. "And I love this, too."

Quinn chuckled. "Thanks, though it's really Molly's work."

Nicole pointed at the picture of the otters again. "That's amazing, Quinn. All the photos in here are great. It's better than the stuff *National Geographic* has been putting out lately."

Quinn rolled her eyes and indicated the loveseat and armchair. Nicole, surprisingly, joined her on the loveseat, and Quinn had to force herself to sit next to her, immediately fighting a distinct urge to fidget.

"So why don't you?" Nicole asked.

Quinn had lost track of the conversation. "Why don't I what?"

"Work for *National Geographic*?"

Quinn laughed. "Oh, please. Give me a break."

"I'm serious!"

Quinn couldn't help a slight stab of resentment. Easy enough for Nicole to think something like that.

Some of this reaction must have shown on her face, and Nicole winced and touched her hand. They both stared down at the fingers on Quinn's hands at the same time before Nicole moved hers away.

"I'm sorry, Quinn. I shouldn't have asked."

They sat quietly drinking, Quinn waiting for her jealousy and heart rate to subside a little. Finally, she set her beer down and turned toward Nicole, and waited for her to do the same.

"You don't have to apologize, Nicole. You just don't know what it's like. For people like me."

Nicole's brows lowered. "Like you?"

"People without fancy art degrees and a million contacts. You think I wouldn't give my, well, anything, to work for *National Geographic*? Of course I would! But they won't even look at photographs from someone like me. They'd go in the slush pile, with the other amateurs."

Nicole's brows lowered more, and her mouth twisted into a frown. "I didn't get where I am with my 'fancy degree' and a million contacts, Quinn. I worked for it."

Quinn couldn't hold back a puff of exasperated air, and Nicole's frown deepened. This time Quinn touched her hand and left her fingers there. Eventually Nicole relaxed a little, smiling sheepishly.

"I'm sorry," Nicole finally said, "Like I said earlier, I shouldn't have brought it up. I'm sure you know your...circumstances better than I do. But if you do ever want to use my 'millions of contacts' to help you out, let me know."

Quinn swallowed nervously. The idea that Nicole meant what she'd said—that she was willing to help Quinn get some work, or at least meet some of the right people—was more than she could ever have hoped for. Quinn would never have asked her, yet Nicole was offering without a second thought.

"You'd do that for me?" Quinn asked.

Nicole's eyebrows lifted in surprise. "Of course! Anything I can do to help, you've got it."

They spent the next couple of hours chatting about the various shoots Nicole had done over the years, about their families, about college. They finished their first beer, and Nicole had a second, both making only the vaguest of gestures at cleaning as they hung out, though they did some of the dishes together. Finally, she had to drive Nicole home.

She helped Nicole drag all her equipment inside her mom's place, greeting Annette and petting the dogs, who were very excited to meet her. They ran in circles around her several times, barking at her until she knelt to pet them, both devolving into fits of joy, wriggling their stout little bodies as she tried to pet them at the same time. When she looked up at Nicole and her mom from the floor, both dogs crazily licking her face and hands, they were watching her, clearly confused.

"What?"

"Those dogs ignore every person on earth but my mom," Nicole explained, helping her stand.

"They know good people, Nicole," Annette said, patting Quinn's arm.

Quinn's face was hot at the compliment, and after promising to come over for lunch on Sunday, Quinn excused herself. Nicole followed her outside, walking her back to the Subaru.

"Sorry my mom badgered you into a meal after all," Nicole said.

Quinn made a dismissive gesture. "It's no problem. I mean, my dad might think it's strange for me to disappear the whole weekend he arrives, but he'll deal."

"Bring him along!" Nicole said.

"Really?"

"For sure. If he wants to, I mean."

"Okay. I'll ask."

She opened the door to the car and paused. "So we'll see each other on Saturday, I guess. For the wedding?"

Nicole groaned. "Oh my God. I almost forgot. I was looking forward to a few days off. But yeah. I'll see you there. What time will you show up?"

"Around ten."

"Okay. I'll aim for that."

They stood there awkwardly for a long moment, Quinn desperate to do something—hug her, at the very least. Instead, Nicole finally squeezed her arm.

"Have a good night, Quinn."

"You too, Nicole."

Quinn watched as Nicole went back to the house, and waved once again at Annette, who'd apparently watched their entire exchange. Finally, she got in the car and started driving. The arm Nicole had squeezed was somehow warmer, and Quinn couldn't help smiling the entire drive home.

CHAPTER NINE: NICOLE

When Nicole had taken this job for the city, she'd envisioned something entirely different. She'd pictured skiing a couple of days a week, taking photos most mornings, spending time with her mom in the afternoons, and then editing a couple of hours in the evening. But as she closed her laptop Saturday morning, she realized she hadn't had more than an hour or two to herself the entire week. She'd barely seen her mom except in passing, and she'd gone skiing only that single time last week.

She'd finished edits on the hot springs, which brought the grand total of finished shoots to four for the week, which meant six total since she started. With the wedding today, she would have to edit all day tomorrow, which meant no break at all this weekend. Altogether, she hadn't anticipated the work being this time-consuming.

She glanced at her watch and sighed, rubbing her face. She would have to shower right now if she was going to be on time to meet Quinn.

Coming out of her bedroom, she was surprised to see her mom all gussied up. Now in retirement, her mom was always the definition of Colorado casual—khakis or jeans and T-shirts or sweatshirts, basically. Her mom went birding most mornings, but either she'd skipped it today or had finished early to come back to change. She had on a midcalf red and gold floral dress with a nice white shawl and low heels, and she was wearing mascara, lipstick, and her pearl necklace and earrings, all of which was unheard of, even when she used to work. She looked nice enough for a date, and Nicole couldn't think of any other explanation.

"Why are you dressed like that?"

Her mom scowled slightly. "That's a fine greeting, Nicole. Good morning to you, too."

"Sorry, Mom. I mean, wow! You look great! Going somewhere special?"

Her mom laughed. "Yes, actually. Same place you're going—to this sham wedding today. Do you remember my friend Susan? From work? She left the hotel when I did and started working at the ski resort last summer. Apparently, they forgot to hire the mother of the bride for some of the photos, so she asked if I would step in to play the role."

"That sounds like fun," Nicole said. "Let me get ready, and we can drive together."

Nicole had brought one nice, plain black suit to wear for the wedding today and the New Year's Eve ball. She wasn't going to be in any of her own photographs, of course, but it was weird showing up to a big event dressed down, even if, like today, the event was a fake one. She had another reason to dress up and look a bit nicer than usual. The city's tourism commissioner John would be there today, too. She would have to tell him she was falling behind, barely over a week on the job. Looking like a professional could only help her break that news.

When Nicole came out of her bedroom, her mom stood up from her armchair and held out her arms for a hug.

"You look fantastic, honey."

"Thanks, Mom. You do, too. I mean it."

"It's kind of fun getting dolled up, isn't it? I haven't done anything like this since your father died."

Her mom hadn't dated since he passed, and while she claimed not to be interested in moving on, Nicole nevertheless felt an overwhelming sorrow at the idea that, as relatively young as she was, her mom didn't have any reason to dress up anymore.

As if seeing this regret in her expression, her mom patted her shoulder. "Hey—don't you worry about me. You never know. Maybe I'll have another chance to get fancy for *your* wedding one of these days."

Nicole rolled her eyes. "Oh, Mom. Come on. I'm not even dating anyone right now. That's a long way off, if ever."

"I wouldn't be too sure of that, honey."

Ever since Quinn had come over to the house two days ago, her mom had been teasing her like this. According to her mom, despite everything in their past, Quinn was apparently the perfect woman for her. Nicole ignored the comments as best as she could, but part of her was secretly pleased. She liked to be around Quinn. She liked the idea of the two of them starting over together, now that they were adults and could be around each other without a full-on meltdown. The tension was still there, but they might get past that with time.

So yes, altogether, she didn't resent her mom's teasing, but she also didn't want to talk about it yet. It seemed premature, when the farthest she and Quinn had gone so far was a couple of brief, careful touches—the kind she normally gave her friends. She decided to change the subject.

"We better get going if we don't want to be late."

Her mom sighed but followed Nicole outside, helping her with the equipment before they started the drive. By the time they parked at the Sunlight Mountain Resort near the service entrance to the lodge, as instructed, it seemed as if a full-scale wedding was about to happen. Several people were carrying flowers and other decorations through the big industrial doors here in the back of the hotel. A large crowd milled around nearby under some heat lamps. Nicole was surprised by the scale of it all. Normally, in a fake shoot like this, the client did whatever they could to cut corners—reusing props in multiple shoots, for example. This, on the other hand, was like the real deal, as if the pretty woman in the white dress over there was actually marrying that handsome guy next to her, not two models getting paid to look cute together.

Her mom spotted her friend Susan in the crowd of extras and models and excused herself. Nicole peered around, searching for John, and spotted him and Quinn near a heat lamp away from the larger crowd. He saw her first and waved her over, and when Quinn looked her way, a slight smile lifted the corners of her mouth. She was wearing a long coat, but she'd styled her makeup and hair more elaborately than usual. She'd done smoky eyes, wore striking lipstick, and her carefully braided hair was beaded with sparkling rhinestones.

"Hi," Quinn said.

"Hi."

"I was just telling Quinn," John said, "the shoot here today can serve two functions, at least in part, to cut back on your work a bit. After the wedding and reception, you can also shoot the slopes and the rest of the lodge while you're here together. Quinn was telling me that she's having a hard time keeping up with the number of shoots she agreed to do, so this will save some time."

Nicole was surprised. She'd been wondering how to admit this same thing to him, but apparently Quinn had come right out and told him.

"Me, too," Nicole said.

John smiled, clearly unsurprised. "And I'll tell you what I told her. Basically, don't worry about it. Like we agreed already, get what you can get done through Christmas. We'll meet after the holiday and reevaluate. I'll review what you give me, and the two of you can focus on the shots we still *have* to have after Christmas."

"Gosh, John, thanks. I was starting to worry."

He made a dismissive gesture. "Don't. Like I said, I know how hard you're working, and I trust that you're doing all you can. We'll figure it out as we go, okay?"

Quinn seemed equally relieved, and Nicole had to stop herself from touching her reassuringly. She clenched that hand into a fist.

"Okay, then," John said, waving at someone gesturing behind them. "That's the wedding planner here at the resort. He just let me know that the ceremony space on the deck is ready. I'm going to go corral our models, and we'll meet you there."

He moved off to the crowd of people, which had ballooned even more. About fifty people were here to act as guests, as well as several very attractive stand-ins for the wedding party. She saw her mom waiting next to a tall, handsome older man. He was impeccably dressed in a smart gray suit and wore a flower boutonniere that matched a corsage on her mother's wrist. They were chatting, her mom peering up at him somewhat shyly, her hands crossed in front of her and her lids lowered. Nicole couldn't be certain in the chilly air out here, but she appeared to be blushing. The man was most likely a model. He had striking dark gray hair and chiseled, almost rugged features.

"Oh—how funny!" Quinn said, pointing. "Your mom and my dad are talking."

"What? Why is he here?"

"They needed a father of the bride. I guess someone forgot to hire older models. John called me, totally desperate last night, asking if I knew anyone in town. My dad got in right before he called and was game to do this when I asked him."

The sight of their parents together gave Nicole a strange twinge in the pit of her stomach. It wasn't as if the two of them were dating, but the idea of them pretending to be a couple all morning and afternoon was still disquieting on some deep, fundamental level. She and Quinn would be what, like sisters? Nicole shuddered.

She followed Quinn to the deck, where the ceremony portion would be shot—one of the outdoor options at this resort. It was certainly cold out here, but the staff of the resort had done a lot of work to set up a series of heat lamps to keep the models and the guests warm—just like they would if this were a real wedding. While an indoor space was available, it was clear why they'd chosen to feature this space today. The backdrop was stunning—the mountains and ski slopes rising behind the seats in breathtaking, snowy splendor.

She and Quinn decided to split up, agreeing that it was best to focus on different kinds of photos as much as possible. Quinn would get most of the setting and large group shots, while Nicole would do individuals and couples. Unlike a real wedding, they were trying to suggest that anyone could be married here at the hotel. They wouldn't take many wedding-party specific photos, for example, like they would at a real wedding, instead focusing on near-candid photos.

Eventually, the fake guests and party appeared, each directed by John and the wedding planner to sit or stand in specific places. Some hair and makeup people rushed around once Quinn pointed out some shiny foreheads and messy hair, and they were finally able to get their large group shot of expectant guests as they waited for the bride. They took some shots of the bride with her "parents" walking from the back, then of the party up front with a fake officiant. It went on like this for about an hour. Once they'd wrapped the ceremony portion, her mom sought them out before going inside.

"This is fun!"

Nicole laughed. "I'm glad you think so."

"It's also interesting to see you in action. Both of you, I mean. You two knew exactly what you wanted with us models and where to put us and things. I can't wait to see the results."

"You look great today, Annette," Quinn said. "I'm sure you'll be the center of attention in any photo you're in."

Her mom swatted her arm, playfully. "Oh, you. That's only because I'm next to your dad in all of them. He's a real silver fox."

"Mom!" Nicole said, covering her face with one hand.

She shrugged. "Well, it's true."

Annette excused herself, and Nicole and Quinn took a moment alone to compare photos. Nicole realized now that doing a shoot like this together meant that they would likely have to get together later to coordinate. Unlike their days at the hot springs and at the brewery, where they'd planned different individual shots so they wouldn't repeat things, there was a lot of overlap today, and they'd want to choose the best versions to submit to John.

Quinn, anticipating this possibility, said, "It's useless trying to do this here and now. We should get together and sort through everything as we edit."

Nicole smiled. "You totally read my mind. Let's keep doing what we're doing for today and not worry about overlap."

John and the wedding planner led everyone inside the reception room. As Nicole made her way in, following everyone else, she was struck, once again, by how realistic everything looked. She saw a table with name tags for the seating arrangements, and flowers festooned everything. The wedding was, of course, in a Christmas theme, which meant a lot of poinsettias, holly, red roses, snowberries, and white anemones, matching the bride's bouquet. Every inch of the place was decorated in creamy whites and reds with splashes of green. Having done several staged sessions like this over the years—weddings and otherwise—Nicole had never seen anything like this. Altogether, with the heavy silk linens and real silverware and crystal, this was possibly the classiest wedding Nicole had ever been to, fake or not.

Without speaking about it, she and Quinn immediately started snapping shots of people streaming into the room, grabbing their fake seating arrangements, sitting down wherever they were told. They spent the next stretch of time getting shots of the bride and groom doing the usual wedding activities—the cake, the first dance, and then pictures of other people offering toasts nearby, dancing, and lots and lots of fake laughter. On the whole, Nicole found these sorts of staged but almost candid photos much easier to take than at a real wedding, as she could reshoot whatever she wanted. She also managed to get a nice one of her mom laughing at something Quinn's dad had said—a genuine laugh, which made it her favorite picture of the day. Everything went so smoothly, she and Quinn shot what they needed from the reception in less than two hours.

Once they let him know they were finished, John took a microphone from the wedding planner and thanked the whole crowd. Then he gestured for Quinn and Nicole to step closer.

"And I wanted to give a very special thanks to the two people who are going to bring this vision together and no doubt make all of you and our little city and its fabulous resorts and businesses look their very best. The reason we're all here—our photographers."

During a burst of wild applause, she and Quinn shared a warm smile. It was nice to be acknowledged—also a very different experience than a real wedding, where she tried to stay as invisible as possible.

The crowd dispersed very quickly, and Nicole watched, somewhat dumbstruck, as her mom left with Quinn's dad without even glancing her way to explain. Well, Nicole thought, maybe her place was on the way to his hotel.

"So," Quinn said. "You saw that too, I take it?"

"What? Oh, yes. They left together."

Quinn's expression was sly, almost mischievous, but when she met Nicole's eye, she laughed. "Sorry. I think it's funny that they're hitting it off."

"Funny ha-ha, or funny gross?"

"Ha-ha, I guess, but kind of gross, too. Not that I have any problem with him dating. I think it would be great if he did."

"Me, too. My mom, I mean."

"It's just that the two of them together is a little bit…yuck."

Nicole agreed. She knew exactly what Quinn meant. Though why it might also be unsettling for Quinn was pretty telling. Without a touch of vanity, she could sense these unsettled feelings weren't one-sided. She'd seen the way Quinn froze up around her sometimes, and she'd caught her staring even more often than that. But did that mean anything beyond attraction?

"So I guess we need to shoot the rest of the resort now," Quinn said, sighing.

Nicole had almost forgotten that detail. She sighed too. "I guess we better. I don't know about you, but I'm pretty beat."

"Should we come back another day?"

Nicole hesitated, remembering how hard it had been to complete the four sessions earlier this week. It wasn't a small thing to get her equipment loaded and ready for a shoot, and if she put off the rest of the resort now, she would be losing all that time driving up here and loading and unloading again. Still, she wouldn't do much justice to this place if she worked more today, tired as she was now.

"Okay. Let's do it later."

"Maybe on the same day we look at the wedding shots together?"

"Totally. We can plan it out when you come to lunch tomorrow."

"Will do."

"Is your dad coming?"

Quinn shrugged. "I didn't ask him yet. But now that he's met your mom, he might be more likely to be there."

They laughed, and Nicole trailed Quinn outside to the parking lot, helping each other load their equipment in their separate cars, which, by chance, were parked right next to each other.

Before they left, they paused, each by her driver's side door gazing at the other across Nicole's roof. They were grinning, and Nicole was very tempted to ask her out for drinks. It was still early—only after three now, and a cocktail or two would be a nice end-of-day.

"See you tomorrow?" Quinn asked.

Nicole tried to force the question out of her lips, desperate, as she had been many times in the past, to ask her out.

"See you then," Nicole said instead.

She cursed her cowardice all the way home, which, she wasn't exactly surprised to see, was completely empty—her mom nowhere in sight.

CHAPTER TEN: QUINN

The next morning, as they drove the short distance together, Quinn was tempted to ask her dad where he'd been all evening. After the fake wedding, she'd gone home, taken a nap, and then waited for him to show for dinner. When he hadn't responded to her calls or messages early that evening, she started calling around town at some of his favorite haunts, and, right as she was about to devolve into a full-on panic, she managed to find a trace of him. His friend Ronnie was running the bar at his favorite restaurant, and she'd spoken with him briefly about two hours earlier. Ronnie told her that he'd been with an older, pretty woman who matched the description of Nicole's mom. Quinn spent the rest of the evening trying to not think about what that meant.

Now they were here in his rental car, driving together to Nicole's mom's place. Her dad was humming along to his favorite show tunes on the radio, spruced up and far more dapper than a simple lunch with relative strangers dictated. In fact, next to him, she was distinctly underdressed.

Quinn had never really known her birth mother. When she was about eight years old, her mom left them and never came back, and Quinn had no idea where she'd gone then or where she was now. Her dad hadn't exactly forbidden talk of her, but he hadn't invited questions, either. Eventually Quinn didn't want to ask. Except for the divorce papers that appeared in the mail a couple of years after her mother left, her parents never had contact again, as far as she knew.

Her dad had dated quite a lot when he was younger, but never seriously. Back then, he'd see women off and on for a couple of months, sometimes longer, but Quinn rarely met any of them. Then, sometime in her late twenties, he'd either stopped dating altogether or stopped telling her about it. She'd suspected, once, that he was involved with someone in Flagstaff, where he lived now, but when she finally outright asked him about her, he'd claimed they were just friends.

So all of this—disappearing for an evening, getting dressed up for lunch, his obvious enthusiasm to see Annette again—was entirely out of character.

"Uh, Dad?"

"Yes?"

Quinn glanced his way and then stared out the windshield again, mouth dry. She wanted to know, but she also didn't want to know—the two feelings equal in strength.

"Never mind."

He grabbed her hand, squeezing it. "You okay? You seem a little nervous."

"I'm okay. Tired, I guess."

"I bet. You're working two jobs this month. That's rough on anyone. I'm glad you have such a great assistant this year at the studio."

Normally, even with an assistant, Quinn worked every weekend. The studio was always busy during the holidays. But her assistant Kim was entirely competent and levelheaded. She was a master's student doing fieldwork for her thesis in geology in the nearby caves, but she needed real cash. It was now Kim's school break, so she was able to work fulltime through mid-January, which had essentially made this job for the city possible.

"Yeah. She's great. I don't know what I'd do without her."

He was quiet for a long beat before he glanced her way. He hesitated a moment longer before asking, "Are you worried about seeing Nicole again?"

Eighteen years ago, she'd come home from the Non-Prom at the hotel dressed in lingerie and a coat and nothing else, face streaked with tears and makeup. He'd been so startled when she came in, he hadn't even tried to stop her as she stormed up to her room. He'd given her an hour and then insisted on coming in. He'd gotten the whole story out of her, being remarkably decent about everything, including the fact that she was gay and had stolen some of his champagne. They'd spent the next day on the couch together, eating ice cream and pizza, watching and laughing at bad 70s science-fiction films together—their comfort viewing to this day.

Quinn sighed. "I mean, I sort of am, but I'm starting to get used to seeing her, too."

He nodded, focused on the road. They were close to Annette's place now, and a trill of nerves fluttered her stomach. She was fooling herself and basically lying to her dad. She was never going to "get used" to Nicole. She would always feel this giddy and stupid and panicky just thinking about her.

As they pulled into the driveway, Quinn saw new decorations throughout the front yard and lights strung up around the eaves, windows, and several trees. Knowing how busy the last few days had been for Nicole, Annette must have decided to go all out on her own.

As she and her dad got out of the car, the front door opened, and Nicole came out to greet them, Annette standing inside the doorway.

"Hello!" Nicole said, holding out a hand to her dad. "I'm sorry I didn't get a chance to properly meet you yesterday. It's Jack, right?"

He shook her hand. "That's right. Nice to meet you, too, Nicole."

Nicole turned her way, gesturing to the side a bit. "Can I talk to you about a work thing real quick?"

Quinn frowned, confused, but when she saw Nicole's head tilt briefly toward her dad, she realized what this was about.

"Sure. We'll be right there, Dad."

Her dad looked confused, but Annette called to him, and he joined her, the two of them hugging in the doorway before disappearing inside.

"Did you see your dad last night?" Nicole asked.

Quinn shook her head. "Nope. Not once. And he didn't explain anything this morning, either. Didn't even mention all the texts I sent him or anything. It's like he was pretending nothing happened."

"Same here. My mom wasn't home when I went to sleep. I don't even know if she came home last night at all. I was really tired and slept until about nine this morning, so I don't know when she made it back."

Quinn couldn't help a giggle, and Nicole joined her a moment later, each of them covering her mouth with one hand.

"So are they—" Quinn began.

Nicole shook her head. "I don't know, and I'm not sure I want to. Not until they tell us, anyway. They can keep their secrets, for now."

"I never thought of my dad as a Lothario before."

"Well, he better be a nice one."

Quinn squeezed her arm, briefly. "He's a very nice man. I can't imagine he'd do anything to hurt your mom."

Nicole grinned at her and winked. "Let's hope so, or I'll have to give him a stern talking-to."

They went inside, and Quinn was not at all surprised to see their parents standing somewhat close together, the heads bent near each other. Her dad was grinning, broadly, and Annette was laughing at something. It took a long time for the two of them to notice her and Nicole, and neither seemed even remotely embarrassed or aware of how they appeared, standing so close.

"Are you okay?" Annette finally asked. "You look…" She glanced at her dad. "What's the expression on their faces, Jack?"

"Suspicious," her dad said, squinting.

"We were just wondering—" Nicole said, but Quinn elbowed her, hard, to stop her. Nicole winced, her mouth pinched against laughter.

"Never mind!" Quinn said, taking her hand. "Let's eat. I'm starving."

Quinn wasn't sure why she didn't want to hear the response to Nicole's question. Actually, if their parents came right out and told them they were dating, or whatever they were doing, she'd be happy for them. But interrogating them about it was another thing entirely. She'd rather they spoke up when they were ready to do so. Already, they looked cozy and comfortable together, like old friends, if nothing else.

Annette had set up a kind of buffet lunch in the kitchen. Quinn had forgotten that she was holding Nicole's hand until the four of them were crowded around the food. Nicole didn't seem to notice their hands either, but both of their parents had, her dad's eyes bugging slightly at the sight, Annette's eyebrows so high they were hidden in her bangs. Quinn dropped her hand naturally, reaching for a plate, keeping her eyes averted from their curious gaze.

Quinn's hands were shaking slightly as she loaded up with food, and she cursed her nerves. She was going to give something away if she kept acting like this. Nicole, as if sensing some of this anxiety, met her gaze and winked. Nicole was wearing her glasses today—square and black and bold, and more attractive than they had any right to be. She, like her mom and Quinn's dad, had dressed up a bit for what was supposed to be a casual lunch. Nicole was in a cute, retro-style knee-length red-and-white dress with a green ascot, looking very much like a punk Christmas queen. More than the food was making Quinn's mouth water.

"You okay?" Nicole asked, almost whispering.

Quinn, realizing she'd been staring at her, managed to turn her daze into a wide smile. They stood on the other side of the kitchen from their parents, but she kept her voice low nonetheless.

"I'm great." She glanced around, trying to distract from the blush warming her cheeks. "Uh, where are the dogs?"

"They're at doggy daycare today. Mom thought it was best. They're not great with strange men."

Quinn laughed. "Well, my dad's not great with dogs, either. We'll have to make sure that's not a problem."

"Drinks, everyone?" Annette called, indicating an enormous punch bowl next to her.

They all grabbed a glass of what Annette called Holly Jolly—a red concoction that smelled sweet and boozy. Then, loaded with food and drink, they went back into the tiny living room, where a card table had been set up near the little Christmas tree. The room had been thoroughly decorated—red and green and white streamers, cardboard cutouts that reminded her of elementary school, oversized plastic candy canes, decorative Christmas pillows, a Christmas blanket on each of the armchairs, and crocheted candles on nearly every surface. The card table had a vinyl Santa-themed tablecloth, and the centerpiece was a tiny, battery-powered lighted tree with miniature ornaments.

As the four of them sat down, Quinn glanced over at her dad, wondering how he was taking all of this. When she was growing up, he'd essentially banned holiday decor. She'd always assumed it had something to do with her mom but had never gotten up the courage to ask for an explanation. Theirs had been the only house on the block without a wreath or any outside lights, and while he'd allowed a Christmas tree, they put only lights on it—none of the glittery tinsel, garland, or baubles and ornaments hanging on the tree here. To this day, she didn't even decorate the studio, some part of her knowing her dad wouldn't like it, even if he stopped in only once or twice while he visited for the holidays.

If he objected to the overwhelming decor, he didn't let on, his gaze rooted on Annette, Annette's on his. Quinn shared an amused exchange with Nicole, both trying very hard not to laugh.

Her dad, as if suddenly coming back to reality, shook himself a bit and held up his glass of punch. "Well, then. Thanks for welcoming us to your home. Here's to old and new friends."

"Hear, hear!" Quinn and the others said, and then everyone clinked glasses.

Quinn took a long swallow and almost choked at the burn of

booze that hit her throat. Her dad started coughing and laughing, and Annette pounded him on the back, laughing with him. As she watched the two of them continue to interact, she couldn't help a rising sense of something like hope. Her dad was a calm, subdued kind of guy. A woman like Annette, who was clearly a bit livelier, frankly, would be a good influence. Regardless of what kind of relationship might develop, she liked them together. Nicole was smiling at them too, clearly thinking something similar.

"Jack," Annette said. "Now that we've eaten, can I ask you and Quinn for some help today?"

"Mom..." Nicole said, shaking her head.

"Oh, pooh-pooh, Nicole," Annette said, swatting a hand at her. "We need help, and you know it. I have some more lights to hang, and the cookies need doing. Would you be willing to stay a bit after lunch?"

"Of course," her dad said, gaze rooted on Annette. "Anything we can do to help."

Quinn sat quietly with Nicole as their parents bustled into their outdoor wear, chatting and heading outside. She and Nicole were still seated at the table when they closed the door behind them, their focus entirely on each other.

"Well, well," Nicole said. "I guess things are moving along faster than I thought."

Quinn almost reached out to take her hand again, but stopped herself at the last moment, clenching it in her lap.

"We've been left to our own devices, I guess," she said.

"Yes," Nicole said. "But we do have like a million cookies to do."

"So early?" Christmas was still over a week away.

"Uh-huh," Nicole said. "My mom makes them for all her friends and their families. They stay pretty fresh in the freezer, believe it or not. Well, if we remember to save some of them for ourselves."

"So what do we need to do?"

"Decorate," Nicole said, standing up. She started gathering plates. "We can work in here or in the kitchen, whatever you like."

"If it's easier in the kitchen, let's do it in there."

Quinn grabbed the rest of the glasses and cutlery and followed Nicole. They worked together to put the lunch things away and clean up before Nicole started getting the decorating materials out. This took some time. There were several different kinds of frosting applicators, big and small, as well as a number of different kinds of jimmies and sprinkles and other candy toppers. Nicole continued to put things onto the island for a couple of minutes—so much that Quinn could almost believe this was a joke, the materials were so over-the-top.

"Uh, wow," Quinn said when Nicole finally stopped.

Nicole's expression was slightly grim. "Yeah. I know. It's kind of crazy. Listen—you don't have to do any of this if you don't want to. You could watch a movie or something instead. It's a lot to ask."

Quinn shook her head. "No. It's fine. I'm just surprised. And I'll need you to show me how, okay?"

Nicole's returning smile was breathtaking. "Of course! Let me get some of the cookies from the freezer. We'll do a couple together, and then we can work on our own."

She came back a couple of minutes later from the basement carrying four plastic trays with frozen sugar cookies.

Seeing her expression, Nicole laughed. "You should see the freezer down there. My mom does chocolate chip, ginger snaps, oatmeal raisin, shortbread, peanut-butter blossoms, raspberry Linzer, and spritzes. It's insane. Lucky for us, she does all the simpler decorating on the others last-minute—you know, dusting with sugar, that kind of thing. We only have to decorate the sugar cookies ahead of time."

"Wow. Pretty different than what I'm used to."

"No Christmas cookies at your house?"

She shrugged. "No, never like this. I mean, sometimes we'll get something from the store—"

Nicole covered her ears dramatically. "Don't tell me that! I can't hear about it, or you'll be literally drowning in cookies when my mom finds out." She paused, standing on her tiptoes to look outside in the backyard. "It might be too late already. She has a sixth sense about this kind of thing."

Quinn's face was warm and hot, like the rest of her. She liked being here in this tiny kitchen, joking around like this. She and her dad always had such a quiet holiday together, it was hard to remember that other people went all out like this. Plus, both Nicole and her mom were nice—approachable, friendly, easy to be with. Now that some of the awkwardness had worn off between the two of them, Quinn could honestly say she liked being around Nicole, even if she was tempted, sometimes, to say or do something she'd regret. She wasn't sure she'd ever get over that.

"So," she said, turning to her tray of cookies. "What do you want me to do?"

"How about I decorate one first to show you what we're going for. Or, if you prefer, I could just show you one without demonstrating first?"

"Do one first, please, and tell me what you're doing as you go along."

Nicole picked up a tree-shape cookie and then grabbed a very narrow-tipped tube of white frosting.

"With the tree, I like to outline first. That helps the rest of the frosting stay inside the lines." She traced around the entire tree and picked up some green frosting with a slightly broader tip. "Then I color it in," which took a bit longer, "and then I decorate it." She took some pieces of the red, bead-like candy and placed them strategically in the field of green. Then, using the narrow white again, she drew some branches. Finished, she reviewed it before turning it Quinn's way. "That's about it."

The resulting cookie looked as if it had come from an upscale bakery. Nicole obviously didn't recognize what an incredibly expert job she'd done, nor that she'd made it look very easy with her practiced technique.

"Oh, that's all?" Quinn asked.

Nicole's brows lowered "What?"

Quinn shook her head and took the white frosting from her, their fingers touching briefly. She attempted the smooth, one-line edging Nicole had used all the way around one of her tree-shaped cookies and made an immediate mess.

"You can't squeeze that hard," Nicole said, frowning and peering down at the cookie.

Quinn laughed. "I was barely touching it."

Nicole's frown deepened. "Let's try another. I'll do the outline for you, and then you can fill in the green. Okay?"

"Sure."

Nicole passed her the outlined tree a few seconds later, and when Quinn tried to squeeze out the green, very gently, a big glob of it gushed out, immediately ruining the cookie.

"Huh," Nicole said, clearly puzzled.

"I told you I'd never done this before," Quinn said, her face heating with mortification.

Nicole shrugged. "I'm sorry, Quinn. Don't worry about it. We'll figure it out together, okay? I'm sure it'll take some practice, and maybe a new technique."

She came around the edge of the island to Quinn's side and stood close enough that her body was flush with Quinn's on one side. Quinn was at once joyous and horrified, wanting her there yet wanting, very much, to move away.

"Let's try one of the snowmen next, okay?" Nicole asked, smiling down at her. "They're all white, so there's no need to outline."

"Okay," Quinn managed to say.

Again, Nicole demonstrated, creating a perfect, café-quality snowman with a jaunty hat and scarf and a happy smile in less than a minute. Quinn took a deep breath and tried to recreate what she'd seen Nicole do, immediately shooting white frosting all over her hand.

"Oh, shit!" Quinn said, jerking back.

Nicole took her other hand, leading her to the sink. "Hey—don't worry about it. It's just sugar. Comes right off."

They were standing by the sink together, still holding hands. Quinn forgot all about the frosting and the embarrassment of the last few minutes, staring up into Nicole's eyes. Nicole was smiling at her, the expression behind her glasses somewhat glazed and unfocused—a replica of the one she'd had most of the time they were growing up together. Nicole took a slight step toward her, leaning down, and Quinn moved forward, suddenly very hungry for what came next.

At the sound of the door opening, they sprang apart, Nicole walking quickly away to the far counter to pick up a frosting applicator as if nothing had happened. Nothing *had* happened, of course, but Quinn stood there, dazed, as if it had.

"How's it going in there, girls?" Annette called from the living room.

"Fine!" Nicole called back.

"Good. Could you bring me and Jack some more punch? Hanging lights is thirsty work."

"Sure thing!" Quinn called, moving to the punch bowl.

She used the opportunity to calm down, getting the drinks and carrying them to Annette and her dad. By the time she was back in the kitchen, Nicole was intently decorating the cookies and spared her only a quick glance, her lips lifting a bit in greeting before she went back to work.

Whatever had almost happened had come to nothing after all, and Nicole didn't seem inclined to talk about it. The situation was too depressing to ignore. Quinn made her excuses soon after, wondering, all the while, at Nicole's behavior. Why had Nicole almost kissed her if, minutes later, she wanted to pretend she hadn't tried?

CHAPTER ELEVEN: NICOLE

Nicole tightened the scarf around her neck and reviewed her appearance one more time. Her dark hair was nicely styled but in a way that looked casual. She'd also kept her makeup lighter than usual, and she was wearing her glasses. In her nearly solid-black outfit, she was aware that she was very much the grown-up goth with some money in her pocket. Her clothes were the kind she'd dreamed about as a kid—nicer, smarter, more stylish than they ever could have been then. It was crisp and chilly today—she'd been out earlier birding with her mom—so she should be wearing her heavier winter parka, but she looked better in this knee-length wool, and as she was meeting Quinn and her friends, that's all that mattered.

She was being ridiculous. In every interaction with Quinn they moved closer to something disastrous—a kiss or something else—but she still couldn't help herself. The other day in the kitchen, it had seemed like Quinn wanted that, too. She'd almost kissed her, after all. But then they'd been interrupted, and afterward Quinn had seemed upset, jumping away, not bringing it up, and then going home. Nicole hadn't behaved much better. Still, even knowing with absolute certainty that Quinn was reluctant to pursue whatever was between them, Nicole couldn't help but dress up for her today, even if she'd be cold the entire time they were outside.

The drive to the trailhead to Linwood Pioneer Cemetery was very short, and when she parked on the street, she saw Quinn and her friends waiting. Dane and Rico sat at the foot of the trail, perched on the side of a boulder. Molly stood next to Quinn and Quinn's car. Everyone waved, and Quinn walked over to meet her. Quinn was apparently smarter than her, wearing a heavy winter coat, unflattering thick wool pants, and hiking boots. Yet even wearing these bulky clothes, Nicole found it hard not to stare at her.

"Doomed," she whispered to herself, opening her trunk.

"Hi!" Quinn said, coming closer. "What cameras did you bring?"

"Just a couple of smaller ones. I can't stomach the thought of carrying my heavier stuff up there."

"The guys don't mind," Quinn said, gesturing toward them. "They carry all sorts of stuff up mountains all the time at work."

"No. It's okay. These two should be fine." She slung one of her camera bags around her neck and another around her shoulder.

"Molly brought snacks," Quinn said as they walked toward her friends, "And whiskey."

Nicole laughed. "For us or Doc Holliday?"

"Both."

"Hey, hey! Here's the hero again!" Dane said, coming closer. He held out his hands. "Let me carry those bags for you."

"No, no," Nicole said. "It's fine."

"I insist!"

She shrugged and slid both straps off her shoulders, giving him the camera bags. They weren't particularly heavy, and the trail up to the cemetery wasn't long, but it was steep in a couple of spots.

"Haven't seen you on the slopes," he said.

Nicole sighed. "I know. And it's killing me. I guess I didn't realize how busy I'd be."

"That's what Quinn said. We've barely seen her since you two started this thing."

"Sorry, guys," Quinn said. "I've missed you, too."

Molly made a dismissive gesture. "It's all good. It's work. We all know how it goes. But we're going to make up for it today." She grinned at Nicole. "Maybe you want to join us after this?"

Nicole glanced at Quinn, who was glaring at her friend.

"Uh, maybe? What are you guys doing?"

"First lunch, then ice-skating."

"The city always sets up a rink for the holidays," Rico explained.

"Okay," Nicole said. "Lunch, ice-skating—that sounds great."

"And then we're going Christmas shopping," Molly added.

This time Quinn elbowed her, hard, and Molly winced.

Nicole, recognizing what that meant, held up her hands. "Well. I'm not sure about shopping, but I'd love to come to lunch and skating with you guys. Thanks for inviting me."

"We like you, hero," Dane said, hugging her with one arm. "We like you for Quinn, too."

"What do you mean?"

Quinn, bright red, nearly shouted. "I think we should get going. Those clouds look a bit menacing."

Everyone looked up at the sky, which was the usual bright, blinding, cloudless blue of most Colorado days, but Quinn began heading up the trail before anyone could call her on this strange statement. The four of them had to jog to catch up, and then Molly grabbed Quinn's arm and scuttled ahead with her a bit, out of earshot. Dane and Rico, apparently in on the conspiracy, hemmed Nicole in on either side, walking slower to keep her behind.

"You know, I've been in the area for a while, almost three years, but I've never been up here," Dane said.

"Oh?"

"Me neither," Rico said.

"Quinn was saying it was a hangout when she was a kid," Dane said.

"A lot of us hung out up there," Nicole explained. "Drinking, smoking, that kind of thing. Small towns aren't great for teenagers. We didn't have a lot to do, otherwise."

"Both of you were up there at the same time?" Dane asked, raising and lowering his eyebrows.

Nicole shook her head. "It wasn't like that between us."

"But you wanted it to be?" Rico asked. His eyes were focused on the trail, so she couldn't see his expression well, but she could tell he was grilling her. They both were.

She stopped walking, and the two of them stopped with her. Quinn and Molly were already too far ahead to notice.

"What is this, guys? Twenty questions?"

The men shared a guilty glance, and Rico frowned and shrugged. "Yeah. I guess you're right. We're sorry."

"We...we both wanted to know if you..." Dane turned to his boyfriend as if for help.

Rico laughed. "Fine—I'll just say it. The answer is kind of obvious, seeing you two together, but we want to ask anyway. We were wondering if you liked her, too."

"Liked her, *too*?" Nicole's heart started pounding, and not from the hike.

Dane sighed. "Oh, come on. You have to know."

"No one could be that oblivious," Rico added.

Nicole almost denied her feelings, but their expressions suggested that they wouldn't buy it. She peered up the trail, checking to make sure that Quinn was nowhere in sight before responding.

"I mean, okay, yes. Of course I like her."

"Then what's the problem?" Rico asked. "She likes you, and you like her."

"And you have some history. Who doesn't?" Dane asked.

Nicole sighed. "It's not that simple, guys. And anytime I try anything, she pushes me away."

"That sounds like our Quinn," Dane said, sighing.

"Doesn't know a good thing when it's right there in front of her," Rico added.

"Or undermines it on purpose," Dane said.

"She does this a lot?" Nicole asked.

They both nodded.

"She drove the last one away," Dane explained.

"And the one before that, and the one before that..." Rico said, rolling his hands.

Nicole was starting to feel guilty about hearing all this. Quinn should be the one to tell her about her feelings and about her ex-girlfriends, or not tell her anything. Dane, as if sensing her train of thought, held up his hands.

"Hey—I'm sorry. We're being nosy and intrusive."

"He's right," Rico said. "We won't say anything more."

"We just want her to be happy."

Nicole relaxed. "I want that, too. But I don't know how to get her to open up. She keeps running away from me. She has since we were kids."

"Run harder," Dane said, grinning.

"And faster," Rico added.

They started hiking up the trail again, all three of them soon huffing and focused on breathing and walking. Nicole meditated on what they'd said. She'd sensed all month that Quinn liked her, or was, at least, attracted to her. But when they almost kissed the other day, she'd run away, just as she'd done almost twenty years ago. How could Nicole convince her to try? Thinking back on the last few times she'd seen her—at lunch, and the fake wedding, at the hot springs, the brewery—all those encounters had been nice, fun even. She liked being around her, even when they had to work. Maybe she needed to be more obvious. Braver, in fact, than she'd ever been with her. She'd been such a coward as a teenager and wasted all that time they might have had together. She believed she'd grown out of that shy awkwardness since then. She'd never had problems asking women out before—at least not since high school. She didn't even particularly mind being rejected, as she always bounced right back. Yet here she was, acting as if she were eighteen again. Something about Quinn brought it out in her.

That had to be the solution: something bold, something brave. The next chance she got, she'd flirt with her, compliment her, say something so obvious Quinn couldn't mistake her intentions or meaning. And the next time she had a chance to kiss her, she would take it the second Quinn wanted it too, even if it meant kissing her in front of her own mother.

She chuckled, knowing how her mom would react. The other day, after Quinn and her dad had left, her mom had spent twenty minutes grilling her about them holding hands. What would she do if she saw them kissing?

Nicole paused at the last and highest curve of the trail. Here, the entire City of Glenwood Springs spread out beneath them. A bench had been placed here, and she called Dane over for her cameras, spending a couple of minutes setting up and taking a few shots of the city and the freshly snow-dusted mountains rising behind it.

By the time she made it up to the cemetery with Dane, the others were already spread out. Quinn was shooting some of the graves for establishing shots, so Nicole and Dane immediately walked over to the main attraction—Doc Holliday's grave. Like at other celebrity graves she'd seen over the years, tourists left souvenirs—cards, cigarettes, and booze in his case. The maintenance people discouraged it, but leaving little gifts was tradition. She pulled out the pack of unfiltered cigarettes she'd bought for the occasion and placed them on his grave, giving a quick, two-fingered salute before moving to set up her tripods and cameras.

Quinn and the others soon joined her, and she and Quinn spent some time adjusting their positions and light boxes before taking several different shots of the grave.

"Did you want to get our friends in a couple of them?" Quinn asked.

Nicole was secretly pleased with the easy use of "our" in her question.

"Absolutely. In fact, we should get all four of you, a little like at the brewery. This is, after all, a queer attraction now, too."

"But not too obvious for the straights, right?" Dane asked before kissing Rico, deeply.

Everyone laughed.

"Exactly," Nicole said. "The idea is to suggest it, not necessarily show it."

They took a few shots with the real couple, then Molly and Quinn, Nicole and Quinn, Molly and Nicole, everyone, four people, and then different combinations of the women with the men.

"I think we've got what we need," Quinn finally said, scrolling through her photos.

"Agreed," Nicole said.

The others relaxed their poses, and Molly, Rico, and Dane wandered away as she and Quinn started to review and compare shots. They were standing shoulder to shoulder, close enough that she could smell Quinn's lightly floral shampoo. Nicole had, in fact, warmed up as they were hiking up here, but Doc's grave lay in shadow, and while it was nearly noon now, the sun hadn't warmed the thin air. She shivered and moved closer to Quinn's warmth, their arms flush now. Quinn tensed next to her, and Nicole stared at her face until she looked up at her. Their lips were very close. Quinn's eyes were dark and troubled, her lips thin and narrow.

Nicole licked her own lips, took a deep breath, and said, "Quinn, I want to kiss—"

Quinn kissed her then, surging forward and nearly dropping her camera. They both giggled, taking a moment to set their cameras down before continuing. Nicole made herself hold back a little, exploring Quinn's lips gently for now. They were a bit chapped and cold, but the sensation of them pressed against hers warmed her to her very core. She kept her hands innocently pressed to Quinn's sides, fighting the urge to run them up her back and pull her closer. When Quinn drew back, finally, Nicole didn't chase her lips, letting the kiss end naturally. They simply stood there, smiling at each other and still close.

"Well," Quinn said.

"Well," Nicole echoed, making them both laugh.

Quinn immediately seemed worried again, stepping back and chewing her lip.

Nicole grabbed her hand and squeezed it. "Hey. Stop that. I wanted to kiss you, you wanted to kiss me. So we kissed."

"Yeah, but is that all it was? A kiss? What does it mean?" Quinn asked.

Nicole pretended to think hard, squinting up at the sky, before giving her a broad smile. "It means I like you. I've always liked you."

Quinn's cheeks colored, and Nicole wanted, very much, to pull her into another kiss. But she still looked worried and upset, her gaze darting around, not meeting hers. Nicole was going to have to take this very slowly—far more so than she had possibly ever done. But, now that they'd cleared the first hurdle, she couldn't think of anything she'd like to do more.

"Here come Molly and the others," Quinn said, stepping even farther away. She seemed momentarily guilty. "I'm not trying to hide anything between us from them, or whatever, but is it okay, I mean, can we wait until—?"

"Of course. We don't have to tell anyone unless you want to."

"Do you need any reshoots?" Molly asked as she came closer.

Nicole and Quinn shared a look. They'd barely reviewed any of their photos.

Still, as if by telepathy, they said, at the same time, "Nope."

"Great!" Molly said. "We should head to lunch then. Oh, wait!" She reached into her parka and pulled out a small bottle of cheap whiskey. "Should I put this on the grave or something?"

"No, no, no!" Dane said, taking it from her. "We have to toast to him, and *then* we leave the rest of it for his ghost."

"I thought you'd never been here before," Quinn said, frowning at him.

He shrugged. "It's obvious."

"Okay, then," Molly said, unscrewing the bottle cap. "Here's to you, Doc! The fastest gun in the West."

They all took a brief sip of the liquor, wincing from the taste. Nicole liked whiskey and scotch, but this was rotgut. Molly put the cap back on and left the rest of the bottle near the headstone.

The five of them made short time of the trail on the way down. Nicole wanted, very much, to hold Quinn's hand as they descended, but she settled for walking near her. Molly peered back at them a few times, clearly suspicious, and she and Quinn shot each other knowing glances every time she turned away. Something about the sneaking around made this whole thing between her and Quinn a little more exciting. Yes, Nicole thought. She could do this. Taking things slow could be fun.

CHAPTER TWELVE: QUINN

The ice rink was blissfully empty when Quinn and her friends arrived after lunch. The local school holiday break didn't start until this weekend, so it wasn't packed yet. Still, Glenwood was between several ski resorts, and this time of year everything could be busy, even on a weekday. The chilly, almost bitter weather was the likely culprit today, and Quinn certainly didn't mind having the place to themselves, and not only because they wouldn't have to dodge around kids and newbies. They could also all be more open, and Rico and Dane could be as affectionate as they wanted. But not her. Holding hands or something with Nicole would be a little too much, too obvious, and not just for her friends, but for anyone who saw them. The rink was empty now, but that didn't mean it would stay that way. She wasn't ready to be out with Nicole in public, yet.

That kiss had been everything she'd wanted since she'd seen Nicole again almost two weeks ago. Still, she couldn't help the strong sense of misgiving that kept trying to ruin her enjoyment of it. She couldn't even blame Nicole. Nicole had asked for consent, or tried to, and she'd leapt at the chance to kiss her. And the kiss had stayed mostly sweet, almost chaste. Had that been her choice or Nicole's? Either way, she'd taken her chance, and that was risky. She needed to play this situation cool—far cooler than her instincts urged. She didn't want Nicole to think she was desperate.

Nicole had insisted on driving herself today, and Quinn watched the parking lot anxiously for her car as Molly, Rico, and Dane sorted their rental gear. Quinn had her own skates, but she waited to put them on until everyone else was ready, and, honestly, she was also waiting for Nicole to show. They'd all left the restaurant at the same time, so it was strange that she wasn't here already.

"Looking for someone?" Molly said behind her, so close to her ear that she jumped slightly.

"Jesus, Molly! You scared the hell out of me!"

Molly grinned and peered out at the parking lot with her. "Not here yet?"

"No."

"Maybe she stopped for gas or something. Come on. Let's lace up and get out there before we all freeze to death."

Quinn followed, a little reluctantly, but moving at all made her realize how cold she was. She shivered and pulled her hat down over her ears, wishing now that she'd worn her long underwear today. Soon, however, as the four of them took to the ice, she'd forgotten the chill and was loosening her scarf. Rico and Dane were racing around the rink, both occasionally trying to drag the other man down, and she and Molly were doing their best to stay out of their way, laughing at their antics.

Her friends skated away from her, racing now, and she glanced nervously again at the nearly empty parking lot. Nicole's car had pulled up at some point when she'd been distracted. Quinn looked around, confused, and finally spotted Nicole standing by the side of the rink, taking pictures of them.

"Hey!" she shouted and skated over to her.

The rink had a waist-high barrier at the edge, and Nicole had crouched behind the farther side, her camera resting on the ledge.

"Hey, yourself," Nicole said, standing up and smiling.

"I was waiting for you earlier. Everything okay?"

Nicole gestured at her outfit—a more seasonally appropriate parka and heavy pants. "Sorry—I went home to change. I should have texted."

She was also wearing those glasses Quinn loved so much, but she didn't mention them. "How long have you been here?"

Nicole shrugged. "Twenty minutes? Basically since Rico and Dane started screwing around."

"And you thought you could take pictures without asking?"

Nicole's face fell a bit, a hint of worry pinching her lips. "What? Oh, you mean you mind?"

Quinn pretended to be put out a while longer and then grinned. "Sorry. I'm just messing with you. No one cares."

Nicole pretended to wipe the sweat from her brow. "Whew! You had me worried."

"And it's a good idea, too. John didn't even think to ask us to get photos of the ice rink, but it's so pretty here, right on the water like this."

The rink was in Two Rivers Park, in an area that had been an empty lot when they were younger. The city put the ice rink here every holiday season near the skateboard ramps. Today, the river roiled loudly below them. Across the water, the mountains rose in striking red majesty, capped with bright, new snow.

"Gorgeous," Nicole said. Then she shivered.

"Get your skates on," Quinn said, gesturing toward the ice. "You'll warm up in no time."

Nicole winced. "Actually...I don't skate."

"What? Then why did you agree to come with us?"

Nicole held up her camera. "You guys look great out there. And it's very seasonally appropriate for the website and brochures."

"Uh-huh. No way. Go rent some skates. I'll teach you. You can't be entirely bad if you know how to ski. It's mostly about balance, anyway."

Nicole hesitated and then grinned, her eyes sparkling merrily. "Actually, I've kind of always wanted to learn. You don't mind baby-sitting me?"

"No. Not at all."

Not even a little. Quinn watched her head toward the rentals. After all, if she was helping Nicole learn how to skate, she'd have an excuse to hold her hands again. No one would think anything of it.

Soon, Nicole sat down at the edge of the rink to lace up. Quinn skated toward her, stepped onto the rubber mat, slipped on her blade guards, and awkwardly clumped over to her before kneeling to help.

"You want these as tight as possible," she told Nicole, and yanked at the laces. Nicole winced and she laughed. "Baby."

"Hey!"

She helped Nicole stand, grabbing her waist when she wobbled, and the two of them shared a smile.

"Maybe this isn't a good idea," Nicole said.

"You'll probably be a natural once we get out there."

Nicole looked determined, and they lumbered their way to the edge of the rink. Quinn slipped off the blade guards before stepping onto the ice and turning around. She held out her hands.

"Okay, then. Take it easy on the first step."

Nicole was biting her lip, her eyes wide and frightened, but she took her first step a moment later, almost slapping her blade onto the ice.

"Easy," Quinn said, backing up a bit. "Now the other foot."

Nicole did the same thing, almost driving her foot into the ice with a strong step. She wobbled, briefly, and then stood fully upright, clenching Quinn's hands.

"Not bad," Quinn said, trying not to laugh. "Your blades are probably so far in, you couldn't fall if you tried."

"Ha, ha," Nicole said. "So now what?"

"Did you ever roller-skate or roller-blade?"

Nicole shook her head. She opened her mouth as if to comment further and then shook her head again.

"Here," Quinn said, drawing Nicole's hand to the barrier around the rink. "Watch me skate first so you can see the basic moves."

She moved across the rink as slowly as possible, exaggerating her gait to show the movement of her feet and legs. Then she turned around and came back just as slowly.

"It's like cross-country skiing," Nicole said

"Okay, sure," Quinn said. "I've never been, so I don't know."

Nicole rolled her eyes. "And you call yourself a Coloradoan?"

Quinn shrugged and held out her hands, preparing to skate backward. "Work on your footwork for a lap or so. You can use me as balance for a bit."

Nicole's grip was panicky, almost painful, but Quinn didn't say anything. Instead, as Nicole let go of the barrier, she moved back a bit, letting her glide and find her balance again. Nicole was staring down at her feet, and when she lifted one, they both wobbled. Nicole yanked her arm, hard, but Quinn managed to keep the two of them upright. They repeated the whole process several times, and on the fourth, longer straightaway, Nicole managed to move her feet correctly, propelling herself evenly.

"Can we rest a second?" Nicole asked. "It's killing my neck to look down like this."

"Sure." Quinn moved them closer to the barrier.

Nicole grabbed it in a kind of death grip, but unsurprisingly she was relatively balanced already, hardly wobbling now.

Quinn had noticed but not commented on the fact that the others had been giving them some distance and privacy, but when she glanced their way across the rink, Molly lifted her chin and skated closer.

"Looking good out here, Nicole!" she said. "The guys and I are going inside for a warm-up drink. See ya in there?"

"In a little while," Quinn said.

Nicole watched their friends leave, her expression a little wistful.

"Hey," Quinn said, touching her arm. "I'm sorry if I forced you to skate. We don't have to do this if you don't want to."

Nicole shook her head. "No. I'm being a wimp. I want to learn."

"Okay. How about this? We skate for ten more minutes and take a break. Sound like a deal?"

Nicole nodded, appearing entirely serious and determined. They started skating again, Quinn still going backward, still holding Nicole's hands, and by the fifth lap around after that pause, Nicole started to look as if she knew what she was doing. She'd already stopped watching her feet as much, mostly smiling at Quinn, and she wasn't as hunched up on herself. The minutes ticked away, and as their break approached, Nicole was almost standing up, her hands holding Quinn's somewhat casually.

"I think I'm getting the hang of it," Nicole said, seconds before going down entirely. The sound of her body hitting the ice—that solid, clunking pop of it—was very loud, and she spun away from Quinn with her momentum. She ended up entirely on her back, spread-eagle.

"Shit, Nicole!" Quinn said, skating over and kneeling next to her. "Are you okay?"

Nicole's eyes were closed, and she slitted one open.

"Maybe?"

"I'm so sorry," Quinn said. "You were so steady that I wasn't being as cautious as I should have been."

Nicole groaned and sat upright, rubbing her shoulder. "It's okay. I got cocky."

"Let me help you up."

Nicole kept sliding, dragging Quinn with her, her skates slipping in all directions. Then, when she finally climbed to her feet, either from fatigue or simple lack of skill, she slipped forward again, and Quinn was forced to bear-hug her to keep her from going down again. Nicole's face ended up in Quinn's chest, one of her hands on her ass, and both of them, as if realizing what had happened at the same time, froze in place.

Quinn laughed nervously and drew back, letting Nicole use her forearms to pull herself completely upright.

"I need a drink," Nicole said. Her cheeks were red, whether from the chilly air or from the brush with her chest, and neither of them could seem to make eye contact.

"Let's go inside," Quinn said, clearing her throat. "And maybe that's enough of a lesson for the day?"

Nicole eagerly agreed, and they managed to get to the edge of the rink without another incident.

Skates off and Nicole's rentals returned, they went inside the cozy warming shack. A gas fireplace kept it warm. Molly and the others were sitting near the fire, well into their second drink, and Molly insisted on buying everyone a round of hot toddies.

She and Nicole had to sit in the only two-person loveseat by the fire, though Quinn guessed their friends had arranged for the two of them to end up there together. Nicole, however, didn't seem to mind or notice, and their legs pressed together on one side. Molly returned with their drinks, and Nicole regaled them with a story of her epic fall on the ice, leaving out the whole face-in-boobs-thing at the end. Their friends laughed uproariously when she was finished, and though Quinn suspected their response had more to do with the booze than the humor, Nicole did have a way with words. She was a good storyteller, making a simple fall sound like a major disaster.

All five of them were quiet for a long beat, watching the flames dance around in the fireplace. Suddenly, Dane leaned forward, resting his forearms on his lap.

"Soooo," he said, squinting at all of them. "What are you getting me for Christmas?"

Quinn barked a laugh, more at his serious expression than anything else.

"Wouldn't *you* like to know?" Nicole said.

All four of them looked at her.

"You got me a present?" Dane said, his voice rising in surprise and sounding overly pleased.

"Of course! We're friends, aren't we? And anyway, it's just a little something. No big deal." She flapped a hand dismissively.

Molly groaned. "Don't tell me I have to shop for *another* person today."

Nicole chuckled. "No, no. Don't worry about it. I wanted to get you all something small. No biggie."

"How small?" Molly asked, frowning.

Nicole waved a hand again. "It's barely anything. You don't need to buy me a thing."

Molly was frowning, clearly still put out by the idea. Quinn's heart was racing. She'd planned several times to get Nicole a present but had decided, finally, not to, worried how it would look. But now that Nicole had gotten her something, she was horrified by the idea. What on earth would she give her?

"Let me get you the next drink, Molly," Nicole said. "Will that make you feel better?"

Molly considered, frowning, and then smiled. "Of course. And sorry. It was very nice of you to think of me. I just hate shopping. That's not your fault."

"We're going to Grand Junction this afternoon," Quinn explained. "Mostly so we can do all our shopping at once."

"Ah," Nicole said. "Gotcha."

Nicole went to get the drinks, and Quinn's stomach dropped. This morning, when Molly had asked Nicole to join them shopping this afternoon, she'd hated the very idea. Now, as the time approached to part with her, she cursed herself for being such a coward. She wanted Nicole to come with them for the same reason she'd wanted to kiss her up at the cemetery. She liked Nicole, and every moment without her was starting to feel as if it was missing something.

Eyes trained on Nicole's very appealing backside, she didn't notice that the others had fallen silent until she wrenched her gaze away. They were all grinning, somewhat mischievously, and Rico shook his head when she met his eyes.

"You got it bad, girlfriend."

Quinn could only agree.

CHAPTER THIRTEEN: NICOLE

It had snowed a bit overnight, so when Nicole was leaving, her car was crusted with ice. Her mom helped load her cameras into the trunk as Nicole cursed and scraped at the ice, letting the engine warm as she worked. When she finally climbed inside, she was freezing. The idea of being out in this all morning was entirely unappealing. But calling Quinn and canceling barely crossed her mind. This would be the first meeting since they'd kissed a couple of days ago, and they'd be alone together all day. So no—a little cold weather wouldn't keep her from that.

Two tourists were waiting outside the Old West studio chatting about their photos this morning, their excitement clear. For an early Thursday morning, it was bustling here downtown, with shoppers and tourists loping along, peeking in windows and packing the restaurants for breakfast and brunch. Nicole peered inside the studio and could see Quinn talking to her assistant. Both women waved at them, the assistant holding up a finger in a "wait a moment" sign. The studio was set to open now, strikingly early in the morning. Quinn and her assistant spoke a moment longer, the assistant nodding and smiling. Nicole saw the moment Quinn relaxed, her shoulders dropping and her expression clearing as they finished talking. Finally, Quinn unlocked and opened the door. She welcomed the tourists inside, holding the door for them before she stepped outside to join Nicole.

"Wow!" Nicole said, lifting her chin at the door. "So eager!"

"It's been like this all week. Every appointment is booked through New Year's, even with all the extra hours. We have some walk-in hours in the afternoons, but they've been really crazy, too. We'll be working like mad all weekend. But I'm closing the store Christmas

Eve, Christmas, and the day after. My assistant and I need a break, even if I lose some money."

"It sounds hard, but it's great that you're so busy, Quinn."

Nicole was, in fact, very glad for Quinn's success. It was difficult to keep a small business running anywhere, let alone in a small town. True, the establishment was ideally located in the very heart of downtown, but Glenwood was neither Estes Park nor Aspen, not yet anyway, and still she'd made a success of it.

"Thanks," Quinn said, grinning. "I know you think it's cheesy—"

"What? I don't think that."

Quinn's expression faltered, and then she smiled. "Sorry. I remember you using that term when we were kids."

Nicole frowned, trying to recall. "Hmm. I don't remember that. Anyway, I'm sorry. I was clearly being an asshole. And I don't think that now. It's really cool, actually. I love all the costumes and things in there—they're much nicer than most places like that. And it's neat that you get to take photographs all day. And the fact that it's stayed open all this time and is clearly thriving is impressive. You should be proud of it."

Quinn's cheeks were red, and she beamed up at Nicole before glancing around them. No one was nearby, and Quinn stood on her tiptoes and kissed her, lightly and very briefly, letting fingers rest on Nicole's chest. The kiss was cute, innocent even, but Nicole almost floated right off the sidewalk.

"Thanks," Quinn said. "I needed to hear that. Sometimes I feel like…" She hesitated, her gaze shifting before she lifted one shoulder. "Like it's silly, I guess. A waste of time."

Stunned, Nicole grabbed Quinn's hands and waited until she met her eyes.

"I can't tell you how to feel, Quinn, but I hope you change your mind. Running a small, successful business is nothing to be ashamed of, and it's certainly not silly. It's admirable. I mean that."

Quinn's lips quirked nervously. "Okay. Thanks, Nicole. I appreciate it."

Nicole wasn't sure Quinn believed her, but she let go of Quinn's hands anyway, letting the slight tension of the moment fade.

"So which car should we take?" Quinn asked.

"Mine? I don't want to get a ticket."

Quinn slapped her forehead. "Oh, crap—I'm sorry. I should have brought my street permit down. But that's fine—let's take yours. Can you help me move my stuff over?"

They walked over together, Nicole almost itching to grab Quinn's hand, but she fought the urge. Take it slow, lady, she told herself. Like everything else, she'd let Quinn take the lead on PDA.

As they drove, Nicole let Quinn direct her outside of town, south and into the mountains. The road, as predicted, was quite busy, the ski and holiday traffic up to Sunlight and Aspen significant this close to the holiday weekend. Still, they hadn't been on the highway long before Quinn told her to turn onto a snow-packed dirt road that wound up and then over some low-lying foothills. This was all state forest, and they passed several trailheads before pulling into an empty parking lot.

Both stretched once they were out of the car, and then Quinn frowned up at the sky, holding a hand over her eyes and squinting at the light.

"Damn," she said.

"What?"

"We should have been here sooner. The elk are much livelier and easier to find early in the morning. Right after dawn is best." She shook her head. "Sorry—it's on me, I should have planned better."

Nicole bit her lip. Giving up might mean losing the rest of this day with Quinn, and that was the last thing she wanted. Time together was more important to her than the photos.

"Why don't we check? Just in case we see some," Nicole suggested. "And then maybe, if we don't find anything in, I don't know, an hour, we go do something else?"

Quinn shrugged. "Sure—why not? It's not like we need some giant herd or anything. We might find a couple elk no matter what time of day it is."

It took some time to choose their gear. While the snow was only a few inches deep in most places, even here in the lower foothills it would be treacherous and slippery to walk in. It wasn't deep enough for snowshoes or skis in most places, but snow of any kind was still wet and slick. And, because of the terrain, everything they carried needed to be in a backpack for safety, which limited the scope of their equipment. Nicole had brought almost all her cameras in the car, not entirely sure what to leave behind, and Quinn gave her some advice on which camera and lenses to choose for the shoot today.

Finally, they headed out on the trail, walking toward a lake where

Quinn had found elk in the past, both silent and focused on staying balanced on the trail. Quinn led, and Nicole had to school herself to watch Quinn's feet, not her butt, to avoid distracting herself from the real task of staying upright. Today was uncharacteristically cloudy, and the lack of sunshine was making this hike far colder than she'd predicted. Normally, with any kind of physical activity, even in the snow, she was sweating in minutes, but while she was perspiring under all her layers, she was still chilled. Twenty minutes later, mincing precariously on the slippery trail, she longed for the coffee she'd left in her car.

"Phew!" Quinn said, stopping suddenly at the top of a rise. "Here we are, That's the lake there."

It looked like a picture postcard. Down below them in the gorgeous, tree-lined valley, she could see a partially frozen mountain lake. The mountains rose in stark relief of grays and reds behind the crystalline beauty of the icy water, everything kissed with fresh, sugar-like snow and frost.

"Incredible," Nicole said.

Quinn smiled. "Right? Hardly anyone comes here, but it's so pretty." She shivered and rubbed her arms. "Man, I'm cold!"

"No kidding—me, too. Frozen to the bone."

"Let's see if we can save some time, then. I'll check things out from up here before we hike down. If I can't see any elk, we might want to come back another day."

"Sounds good."

Quinn set her backpack down and pulled out some binoculars, lifting her sunglasses before peering into them. She'd been sweeping around for a few seconds before she paused and held out the binoculars to Nicole. It took a moment for Nicole to find what she'd spotted, but she soon saw a sizable group of elk, all lying huddled underneath a grove of pine trees at the edge of a meadow next to the lake.

"Wow! There's a lot of them."

Quinn nodded. "There will be others nearby, too. They act like lookouts, kind of, for the rest of the herd. But we won't see them until we get down there. They're good at staying out of sight."

"Okay, but how do we do this? I imagine we can't march down there."

Quinn shook her head. "No. You're right. It's more complicated than that. In fact, we have to sort of go around, slowly." She pointed far to the right of where the elk were huddled. "And we stay as far away as possible, ideally hidden somewhere. That zoom lens I told you to bring does some good stuff at a decent distance. I do birds with something similar, and you usually have to shoot those pretty far away."

They started heading down into the valley, this direction far more dangerous than the path upward had been. Nicole was soon sliding and stumbling, and Quinn wasn't doing much better. Luckily, the hill was short, and soon they were at the bottom and inside a pine forest. The branches almost entirely insulated the ground here, which was blissfully dry, and the lack of snow made the air much warmer.

"Let's get the cameras ready here," Quinn suggested, setting her backpack down.

"Really? Why?"

"You don't want to open a zipper near an animal. I don't know what they think it is, but they definitely recognize it as something unnatural. It's almost like setting off a bomb. It should be flat here, and safe to carry the cameras now."

"Okay," Nicole said, though still uncertain. She'd done so very little nature photography, and all what she had done was happenstance—in a park, for example, or at the beach on vacation. Essentially, she never went out of her way to do it on purpose. Her inexperience made her very nervous about carrying something so valuable as a camera through the woods. She had a strap, of course, and her equipment was insured, to a point, but it would still be a major inconvenience to hurt either her camera or her lenses. But Quinn was the expert here, so she did as suggested.

Quinn affixed an incredibly long prime lens to her camera before zipping two zoom lenses into her pockets. Nicole was impressed. Everything she was bringing was not only incredibly expensive, but state-of-the-art. Nicole rarely did long-distance work herself. She had only the one specific type of long-distance zoom lens for the work today, and that realization made her feel amateurish. Quinn was clearly in her element, and Nicole enjoyed seeing her like this—fired up and excited, and evidently very sure of what she was doing. She was sexy anyway, but incredibly so when confident like this.

After walking the main trail for another minute or two, Quinn held a finger up to her lips and indicated a small game trail that meandered off the established one. Nicole mimicked Quinn's crouched state, and the two of them wandered through the trees for a minute or two before the woods began to open again. Almost as if they'd planned it, a pile of boulders was clustered at the edge of the trees, near the meadow where they'd seen the elk. Quinn led them to the boulders, and they sat down, leaning back on the stone and breathing heavily. Quinn eventually made eye contact with her and signaled silently, "Okay?"

Nicole nodded, and Quinn moved into a crouch, still hidden behind the stones. Nicole kept her head low, and then, like Quinn, slowly raised her gaze over the boulders to peer out across the snowy meadow. She heard herself gasp and bit off the sound, almost slapping her hand over her mouth. There, some fifty yards away, stood an enormous bull elk. His antlers had multiple points, and his giant body was heavy with his winter coat, the ruff of fur around his neck and rump so thick and downy he looked like he was wearing a jacket. He was staring in their direction, as if he'd detected them, and she heard the quiet, almost silent sound of Quinn taking photographs. Then, as if losing interest, he looked outward toward the lake, and Nicole finally remembered to start taking her own pictures. Eventually, the bull started grazing again, kicking at the frosty snow over the grass to expose the roots. She took a couple of shots of him like this, but his stance was certainly less interesting than when he'd been looking their way.

Nicole eventually realized that Quinn was already focused on something else. She followed the direction of her lens before she saw the huddled herd. Three females were standing now, still near the herd, but slightly away from the others, many of whom appeared to be dozing. Nicole was frustrated with the limitations of her lens from this distance, but she took some shots anyway, hoping to clear things up a bit in post-production.

A loud series of bugles sounded off to their left, and Nicole turned that way in time to watch two bull elk emerge from the deeper woods. The big one nearest them seemed to lift his head, as if acknowledging the newcomers, and then he turned and lumbered back to the rest of the herd, collapsing near the others as if ready for a nap. The two new elk stationed themselves where the big bull had been, as if relieving his watch. Nicole had never been as riveted watching animals like this.

She and Quinn stayed there, crouched behind the rocks, for what seemed like hours. At one point, they were simply watching the elk, and Quinn's mittened hand slipped into hers. They beamed at each other, equally pleased and happy. For Nicole, being here with Quinn in this magical place and seeing these incredible animals up close like this was almost too good to be true.

Eventually the elk shifted around a bit, revealing different elk behind them, and she and Quinn went back to the task at hand. After a long time of shooting whatever she could, Nicole finally recognized that her legs were starting to cramp. She sat back down as quietly as she could, leaning her back on the boulders while Quinn continued to shoot, utterly absorbed and completely in her element. Nicole would be surprised if Quinn even noticed she'd taken another break. She seemed entirely focused on what she was doing.

Finally, when Nicole was certain she would have to interrupt her or start taking photos again to pass the time, Quinn seemed to come back to herself. She pulled her eyes away from her camera, looked down at Nicole, beamed at her, and sat next to her, squeezing her gloved hand again before leaving it there. The color was high in Quinn's cheeks, her expression the very definition of happiness with bright eyes and a gloriously open smile. Nicole was enchanted and leaned toward her, pausing, as she had before, one eyebrow up. Quinn scooted closer, closing the distance and kissing her, one mittened hand coming up to caress the side of Nicole's chilly face. When she drew back, Quinn's hand remained there, warming her further. Nicole shivered, exaggerating her reaction a bit, and Quinn pointed at the trail that led back to the car. They both soon snuck that way and moved safely back into the woods.

They paused when the game trail met the main trail.

"Wow," Nicole said. "That was amazing, Quinn. I've never been that close to them before."

"We lucked out. Normally, they'd be traveling south by now. This mild weather lately must have delayed them. You might get a bull or two this time of year here, but rarely a herd like that."

"Thank you for taking me with you. It was one of the coolest things I've ever done."

Quinn grinned at her and squeezed her hand again. "You're welcome. My pleasure. I can't wait to compare photos. Did you get the group of hares? Or the fox?"

"What? No! I didn't even see them."

"Oh," Quinn said, grimacing slightly. "Sorry. I should have pointed them out."

Nicole laughed. "No—that's fine. You're the expert here. I'm sure John will want to choose all your photos over mine."

Quinn waved a hand at her dismissively. "Oh, please. I'm sure you have some great stuff, too." She paused. "Maybe we can go back to my place and compare? We still need to edit the wedding photos together, too."

Nicole sighed. She'd been hoping to take the afternoon off.

Quinn, apparently misreading her pause, held up her hands. "I'm sorry. You're probably busy today. I didn't mean—"

Nicole shook her head and took Quinn's hand again. "Not at all. I'm just tired of working all the time. I wish we could, I don't know, take the afternoon off together or something."

Quinn tilted her head in confusion. "And do what?"

Nicole could think of a hundred things she'd like to do with and to Quinn, but it seemed premature to even suggest most of them. Instead, she focused on the immediate.

"Nothing. You're right. It's almost Christmas, and I want all of this wrapped up as much as possible, pun intended. It'd be nice to take the weekend through the holiday off, but I won't be able to relax with all this work hanging over my head."

"What do you still need to do?"

"Well, we both need to finish the rest of the ski resort. Except for that, for me it's mostly editing. I got some of that done yesterday, but I still have a few more hours of it, at least, especially with these new shots here and if we get some more at the resort."

"Let's compromise, then," Quinn said. "Let's do the rest of the ski resort together now, whatever edits we can do at my place after, and then we can have dinner. I have to work the opening shift at the studio tomorrow, but we can edit everything else together after that and send what we have to John tomorrow night before the holiday weekend."

Nicole had barely heard a word after "have dinner together," but she agreed eagerly anyway. At this point, Quinn apparently wanted to spend the rest of today and most of tomorrow with her. Nicole would be happy to do anything she wanted to make that happen.

CHAPTER FOURTEEN: QUINN

Their photo shoot at the resort that afternoon had taken far longer than Quinn expected. They'd driven more or less directly to Sunlight Mountain Resort from the trail with the elk, but even with the cameras already in the car, the trip, loading and unloading, and the work itself had eaten up the rest of the day.

Nicole was the consummate professional all afternoon, as always. She was nice, too, not bossing Quinn around like she'd expected earlier in the month, but once again asking for and often deferring to her suggestions. Before this project together, she'd never have expected Nicole to be like this—an expert, but not conceited or vain. Now that they'd worked together several times, Quinn realized that she needed to accept that her preconceived notions had been entirely wrong.

What was worse, and what she'd known for a long time, was that Nicole had never been vain or full of herself. Even when they were teenagers, and Nicole was winning award after award for her work, she'd been humble. And the whole situation with the scholarship had been Quinn's fault, not hers. She'd known that even then. She'd been afraid to compete with Nicole, and that was her problem, not Nicole's. The imaginary tyrannical, stuck-up Nicole that Quinn had envisioned all these years was simply a projection, a way to cope with and justify what she'd done when they were kids. Over the years, she found it easier to imagine leaving Nicole alone in a hotel room if she pretended Nicole was a terrible person, but this fantasy was much harder to maintain now that she knew her.

During their photo shoot at the resort, they took pictures of the outside of the lodge and the ski slopes from several angles. The holiday decorations had been up for a few weeks now, but today, dusted with new snow, they looked sharp, renewed, and appropriately seasonable.

With the approaching holiday, a great bustle of people streamed in and out of the resort, checking in or on their way to the slopes. They also took photos inside, which was similarly decked out in Christmas splendor.

When they finally walked back to Nicole's car, the sun was starting to set. Quinn could hardly believe it was almost five.

"Man, I'm beat," Nicole said, opening the trunk of her car. She put her cameras and lights inside and helped Quinn do the same. They paused there, Nicole's droopy posture mirroring her own. Quinn rubbed her shoulder absently, aching from the strain of the camera bags she'd lugged around all day.

She hesitated before replying. They'd agreed to have dinner, but that had been hours ago. Maybe Nicole wanted to go home and to bed. She should give her an out. She glanced around, glad to find that they were entirely alone. She stepped closer and touched Nicole's arm.

"Um, if you want to pick up again tomorrow, you could just drop me off—"

Nicole stepped forward and pulled her into a searing kiss. It had more fire and passion than any of their earlier kisses and shook her very soul. Despite the cold, she was instantly warm, almost hot, coming alive with the sensation of Nicole's lips on hers. Nicole pulled her closer with the lapels of her jacket, and Quinn was happily locked in the kiss and embrace.

Moving away, Nicole met her eyes, smiling dopily. "I've been wanting to do that all day."

Quinn's heart was hammering, but she tried to make herself sound coy. "Why didn't you?"

Nicole shrugged, stepping back and letting her hands drop to her sides. "I guess I didn't want to…" She shook her head. "Never mind."

"No, what?"

Nicole bit her lip. "Scare you off, I suppose."

Quinn's stomach dropped a little. Nicole was afraid she'd run away again, and who could blame her?

"I'm sorry, Nicole. I really am."

Nicole frowned. "For what?"

"For that night. When we were kids."

Nicole gave a dismissive wave. "Ancient history. Don't worry about it."

"No, Nicole, it's not. All this time has passed, but now that you're around again, I keep thinking about how stupid I was, how cowardly, how terrible it must have been for you when I left you alone."

Nicole shrugged weakly, her posture a little tight and less assured than before, and she wouldn't meet Quinn's eyes.

Quinn took a deep breath and let it out. She'd been wanting to ask this question for ages but hadn't dared.

"Wh-what did you do? After I left?"

Nicole didn't answer for a long time, and she still wouldn't meet Quinn's eyes. She glanced to the side, searching, as if to the distant past, for an answer. Finally, she laughed weakly and shrugged again.

"I cried a lot. Got drunk on champagne and Sprite. Slept it off wrapped in your dress."

Quinn couldn't help a bark of laughter. "Oh my God! I forgot all about the dress."

Nicole's expression brightened. "You left your stereo, too. I kept them both for a long time. I was hoping you'd ask for them, and we could talk about everything."

"But I never did."

Nicole shook her head and shrugged yet again.

Quinn touched her shoulder, not wanting to do more now that Nicole seemed so vulnerable. For so many years she'd wanted to explain things. But she hadn't, and now here they were, still stuck in the past.

"I am sorry, Nicole. The second the door closed behind me, I regretted leaving you. Then, all the way home, I kept telling myself to turn around, to go back to the hotel. And all spring and summer after that, I tried to make myself track you down, to at least apologize before you left for Chicago."

"Why didn't you?"

"Probably for the same reason you didn't return the dress or my stereo."

Nicole chuckled. "Right. Cowards."

"We were, weren't we?"

They smiled at each other, and Quinn's spirit was suddenly lighter. She glanced around again, waited a beat as a family passed their car, and then she stepped closer, taking one of Nicole's hands.

"I am sorry. I regret what I did very much."

Nicole was silent before she finally let out a long, shaky breath, her expression clearing further.

"Okay."

"And Nicole? I don't want you to hold back now that we're… well, starting this again. You won't scare me off."

"Do you promise?" Nicole asked, her expression troubled but hopeful.

Rather than reply, Quinn stepped into her personal space again and kissed her. She tried to put as much feeling into the kiss as possible, tried to convey every ounce of heartache she'd suffered in the last two decades in the kiss, as well as the excitement of getting to know Nicole again after all these years. She wanted the kiss to suggest that, perhaps now after all this time, they could be something special to each other again.

Nicole blinked dazedly when they drew apart, and Quinn laughed. "Does that answer your question?"

"Uh, yes." Nicole's smile was bright and infectious.

"Good. Now let's go get something to eat before I freeze to death or my stomach eats itself, whichever comes first."

They climbed into the car, and Nicole let it run a bit to warm up. "Where to?"

Quinn was stumped. She hadn't thought this far ahead. Glenwood had some nice restaurants, but she wasn't ready to be out in the world with Nicole, yet. She'd never been a PDA-type person, but the idea of sitting somewhere, not even holding hands, was depressing.

"You know what?" Nicole said, interrupting her train of thought. "How about we pick up a pizza and watch a Christmas movie?"

Quinn laughed, relieved. "That sounds like a great plan."

"Your place or mine?"

"Mine."

Quinn called in the delivery order as they drove. In a town devoid of actual Italians, it had one surprisingly decent pizza place, and their food arrived not long after they'd arrived. She made both of them a Christmas-themed cocktail, mint-forward with a crushed candy-cane rim. Nicole smirked when she took it from her, but she looked pleasantly surprised after she took a sip.

"Nice! It's like Christmas cheer in a glass."

She shouldn't drink too much, but having Nicole here in her space was nerve-racking. With such a small apartment, she so rarely had people over to begin with that having anyone would have made her nervous, but of course this was particularly true with Nicole. She found it hard to relax, hard to sit in her armchair naturally, hard to eat pizza like a normal person. Part of her mind kept drifting to her bed, waiting just out of her peripheral vision. While it could happen tonight, she didn't really think sleeping together was a good idea this early in their relationship. Plus, the notion of it made her stomach twist with anxiety. After all this time, she'd blown that fantasy way out of proportion.

Nicole didn't seem bothered by any of this, eating the pizza like it would be taken from her at any minute. After her third or fourth slice, she leaned back, sighing contentedly, her hands folded on her stomach.

"That hit the spot."

Quinn pushed her first and only partially eaten slice away. Nicole frowned at it, her brow furrowing, and she opened her mouth, as if she were about to ask about it, but Quinn stood and started gathering the dishes, not wanting to explain.

"What movie do you want to watch?" Nicole said, following her into the kitchen with the pizza box.

"I was trying to decide. I have most of them on DVD. Do you have a favorite?"

Nicole shook her head. "Uh-uh. Your place, your choice."

"But you're my guest!"

Nicole shook her head, firmly. "If we do this again, I'll choose, but not tonight. It's up to you."

Quinn flushed with pleasure. The very idea that Nicole would want to do this again with her, spend time with her, made her happier than she could remember being in a very long time.

Still, choosing a movie on what was, though casual, a date, was no small thing. Her choice would say something about her, give something away. Too silly and she'd seem childish, too serious and she'd seem like a snob. But as she'd been asked to choose a Christmas movie, she didn't have much choice in between.

"Okay. How about *Scrooged*?"

Nicole smiled. "My favorite."

Quinn was overly pleased, and while she dug around in her old DVDs for the movie, Nicole washed the dishes and put the rest of the food away. The scenario was all very domestic.

By the time she'd found the film and gotten the DVD player hooked up, Nicole was on the loveseat, one arm draped casually over the back, her legs covered with one of Quinn's crocheted blankets. Nicole had been in her winterwear all day, but now, without her coat on, Quinn could see her lovely red sweater. The gas fireplace was on, and the whole scene was very seasonably cozy.

Realizing she'd been staring, she swallowed and asked, "Can I get you a drink?"

Nicole hesitated. "Sure. I can probably have one more and still drive in a couple of hours, but maybe just a beer, if that's okay. I can't do too many sweet drinks."

She was worried about driving, Quinn thought, pulling a crowler out of the fridge. That meant she was going home tonight. Despite her earlier nerves about sleeping together, she still couldn't help but feel disappointed.

"Has your dad said anything about my mom?" Nicole asked.

Quinn paused, confused. "What do you mean?"

"I'm wondering if they're still dating, or whatever."

"You mean you don't know?"

Nicole was frowning. "Know what?"

"They're on a date right now—well tonight, anyway, I don't know the time. Anyway, like a real date. My dad came over yesterday to show me his new tie. He even got a haircut. And he's taking her to a nice place, this time, not his usual bar and grill."

Nicole's eyes were wide, shocked. "My mom didn't even mention it."

Quinn set the beers on the coffee table, went back to the kitchen for a bowl of pretzels, and came back to sit down next to her. Nicole immediately threw part of the blanket over her legs, and Quinn was forced to scoot a bit closer to her to make it drape properly.

"Maybe she's worried…" Quinn winced at her slip-up.

"Worried? What do you mean?"

She sighed and looked up into her eyes. "Maybe she's worried it will upset you. Her dating, I mean. After your dad and all."

Nicole let out a little scoff of laughter. "Well, she shouldn't be. I'm happy about it. I mean, I'll admit it's a bit, well, weird or whatever, since he's your dad, and we're well…whatever. But I'm glad she's meeting people again, and he seems good for her."

"Does she know that, though?"

"What?"

"That you're okay with her dating?"

Nicole opened her mouth and then closed it, frowning. "I guess we've never talked about it."

"Maybe you should. Tell her what you just said."

Nicole smiled. "I will. I don't want her hiding things from me, that's for sure."

They turned their attention to the TV, and Nicole's arm moved off the couch and onto her shoulders soon after. She glanced up at her when this happened, but Nicole didn't acknowledge what she'd done. Quinn let herself relax into her, the warmth of the room and Nicole next to her one of the most pleasurable sensations she'd experienced in a very long time. She let herself doze through the film, having seen it enough times not to be lost, waking up here and there when Nicole laughed. They grinned at each other a few times throughout the viewing, Quinn recognizing that Nicole was as happy to be here as she was to have her.

The credits started rolling, and Nicole seemed to take that as her cue, pulling her closer and kissing her. Quinn, who had been half asleep for most of the film, was instantly and entirely awake. Nicole pushed her back slightly, and Quinn let herself fall back and nearly prone, Nicole slightly on top of her. The loveseat was too small for either of them to fully recline, but their upper bodies were still flush. Quinn gripped Nicole's shoulders, wanting her impossibly closer, and Nicole's hands began to wander, slightly upward, from her waist. Her fingers brushed the skin on Quinn's stomach, and she gasped. They both pulled apart, breathing heavily and grinning stupidly. Finally, Nicole sat up, pulling Quinn with her.

"Got a little carried away," Nicole said, her smile both pleased and a bit sheepish.

Quinn squeezed her hand. "That's okay. I did, too."

Nicole stood then and Quinn followed, the two of them carrying their glasses and the empty pretzel bowl to the kitchen. Quinn kept a slight distance between them, worried she might throw herself at Nicole if she touched her again. Waiting a while for the next step was better. They were adults, for God's sake, not teenagers.

"I guess I better go," Nicole said, as if thinking along the same lines.

"Hmm," Quinn managed.

"But I'll see you tomorrow after you finish at work? To edit? Maybe you could come to my place?"

"Sure. I'll bring my laptop. Should be there around three or four if that works for you."

"Perfect."

Nicole approached again, slowly, as if holding back, and they kissed briefly and embraced.

"Okay, then. Good night."

"Good night, Nicole."

After she left, Quinn let out a long-held breath and sat back down on the loveseat, literally weak in the knees. She couldn't remember the last time she'd felt like this. She laughed at herself, smiling. If she was this turned on now, what would it be like when they finally slept together? She could hardly wait to find out.

CHAPTER FIFTEEN: NICOLE

Nicole sighed. "Mom, I don't think we need quite so many chips. It's just me and Quinn."

Her mom waved a dismissive hand. "Oh, hush. A good host always offers too much food. Better that, than running out!"

Nicole stopped herself from rolling her eyes and decided to let her mom get on with it, stepping away from the ridiculous and growing spread of food on the coffee table to give her mom room to move around and finish.

Her mom seemed excited, thrilled, even, that Quinn was on her way over. She was putting out enough food for an entire party. Nicole hadn't yet confessed that she and Quinn were seeing each other romantically now, but her mom's teasing had stopped earlier this week, almost as if she sensed it. Nicole wondered if Quinn had told her dad, and if this was why her mom suddenly seemed to know about them, but since her mom hadn't said anything, she didn't, either.

Nicole absently nibbled on a tortilla chip. "What are you up to this evening?"

"I was planning on some Christmas shopping in Grand Junction, but the roads might be iffy later with this cold. Maybe I'll head downtown, poke around in some of the stores."

"Maybe your boy-toy Jack would like to go with you," Nicole suggested, raising her eyebrows up and down.

Her mom rolled her eyes. "Boy toy? Honestly, Nicole. And no. We're meeting for a drink later. I wanted to get him a little gift for the holidays, since we might not see each other until after, but I don't know what to buy."

"How little are we talking here?"

Her mom shrugged. "Well, that's just it. You know how gifts are.

Too expensive, and you look like a jerk. Too cheap, and that's exactly how you seem. Too sentimental, and you're a sap. It's hard."

Nicole grinned. "Seems like you've thought a lot about it."

Her mom swatted her arm. "Oh, you. Of course I have. I mean, what do you get for someone you started..." She sighed. "Well, you know."

"Started dating?"

Her mom still wouldn't meet her eyes, and Nicole stepped closer and waited for her to look up.

"I don't want you to feel bad about dating him, Mom."

"Really? What about your—"

"Dad would want you to be happy. I know he would."

Her mom still looked uncertain, and Nicole pulled her into a hug. They stayed in each other's arms for a long, quiet moment, Nicole's heart lifting with something like hope. A lot of the grief her mom had shared over the last couple of years about her dad had been hard, painful, but this seemed like the next step. Even if nothing came of this relationship, Nicole was genuinely pleased her mom was dating again.

They drew apart, both wiping their eyes.

"Okay, then," her mom said. "Jack and I are dating, and I don't know what to buy him that doesn't scream desperate, late-middle-aged widow."

"You're not desperate, Mom. And Quinn will be here soon. You could ask her for some advice."

Her mom pointed at her. "That's a good idea."

Nicole hesitated, and then, realizing that she was doing exactly the same thing as her mom had by hiding her news, she decided to tell her.

"I'm having a similar problem buying a present for someone *I* started dating."

Her mom's eyes lit up. "I knew it! When did you start?"

"It's new, Mom, and still feels kind of, well, fragile, I guess. We haven't even decided what we are, exactly. I mean, we haven't defined it or anything. I don't want to scare her off, but I also don't want to come off as too...reserved. You know?"

Her mom nodded vigorously. "Exactly!"

They heard a car outside, and Nicole's heart did a dancing jig in her chest. She met her mom's eyes again, which had gone wide.

"Oh. Wow," her mom said. "I see."

"What?"

"You're really into her."

"Is it that obvious?"

Her mom nodded.

"Do you think Quinn knows?"

Her mom rolled her eyes. "What do *you* think?"

Nicole sighed. "Great. Captain Obvious over here."

Her mom squeezed her arm. "Don't think about it that way, Nicole. Most people love knowing how much someone likes them."

"So maybe a grand gesture for Christmas wouldn't be too much, or unexpected?"

Her mom shook her head. "No. Not for her. I can't imagine she's had too many grand gestures in her entire life."

They heard knocking, and both dogs gave a single, halfhearted woof before lying back down again. Nicole wiped her sweaty hands on her jeans and went to open the door.

Quinn seemed to glow in the remnants of the late afternoon sunshine. Yesterday's snow was still sparkling lightly behind her, and her cheeks were rosy from the cold. Her hair, normally a somewhat muted dishwater blonde, radiated like golden halo around her head. She was wearing a very stylish gray peacoat, light and unseasonable, but flattering on her slim, petite frame.

Quinn was grinning when she finally met her eyes.

"Hi," she said.

"Uh, hi," Nicole managed, then moved a step back. "Please. Come on in."

The dogs roused themselves enough to come greet their new best friend, and Nicole used the opportunity to gather her wits as she hung up Quinn's coat for her. The dogs were groaning happily when she turned around, both wagging so hard their whole bodies seem to vibrate with pleasure as Quinn petted them.

"Oh, hi, Annette!" Quinn said as her mom came into the room. She stood up. "I didn't realize you were here."

"Hi, honey. Don't mind me. I'm heading out. I left you girls some snacks so you won't get hungry. Don't let the dogs convince you to share."

"Okay. I won't. Oh! And before I forget, my dad asked me to ask both of you if you want to do something together this Sunday before the holidays."

"Like what?" Nicole asked.

"He suggested skiing, but since I don't ski—"

"Neither do I," Annette said.

"Right. That's what I thought. Maybe you could think of something else?"

Nicole and her mom shared a glance and shrugged.

"Sure!" Annette said. "We'd love to do something. Right, Nicole?" Nicole nodded.

"I'm seeing your dad tonight, Quinn, so we can hash out the plan together. And that will give me a chance to do more shopping for you."

"Shopping? You mean, like gifts? For me and my dad?" Quinn asked.

"Yes! Though I am having a hard time thinking of something for him. I got him a couple of small things already, but I wanted at least one bigger gift."

Quinn grimaced slightly and waved dismissively. "Oh, jeez, Annette. You don't have to get him anything big, or anything at all, for that matter."

"Yes, but, if you had to say in a general category, what would it be?"

Quinn hesitated a while longer before sighing. "Well, he likes to ski, hike, and play golf, in that order."

Her mom brightened. "Perfect! I know just the thing." She walked closer to Quinn and squeezed her hand. "And Quinn, please don't worry. You don't have to get me anything, and neither does your dad. I like giving people things." She glanced at her watch. "Oh, shoot. I need to go if I'm going to have time to pick some things up. Don't work too much, you two. Have some fun, okay?"

Nicole didn't know what her mom meant by that, but it could be read somewhat suggestively, and she had to look away to hide her flushed face.

"We will, Mom," she said. "You, too."

They both watched her leave, and Nicole was soon suddenly hyperaware of the fact that they were alone together again. This had happened last night at Quinn's, of course, but being alone together in her childhood home was different. More illicit, somehow. She'd never once brought a girl over here when one or both her parents weren't here, and she'd brought only a couple of girlfriends here to Glenwood at all. It hadn't even occurred to her to do anything with either one of them while they were here, parents or not.

Once her mom's car disappeared, Quinn turned to her with a shy smile. "Hi again."

"Hi," Nicole said, stepping closer. She pushed a lock of hair behind

Quinn's ear and kissed her lightly. Quinn's eyelids fluttered open, that pink back in her cheeks, a dark hunger in the depth of her eyes. Then, suddenly, she seemed to blink it away, stepping farther away from Nicole and laughing lightly.

"Uh, well, I guess we better—"

"Get to work," Nicole finished for her, more than a little disappointed but trying to hide it. She cleared her throat and indicated the table. "Want some snacks first?"

"Jeez! Look at it all. I don't think I have this much food in my whole apartment."

Nicole laughed. "That's my mom for you. Heaven forbid you ever feel peckish, let alone outright hungry."

After they'd gathered a plate of food, they both settled down next to each other at the dining-room card table. They moved their chairs close enough that they could view each other's computers as needed, doing some of their own editing as well as comparing work from the shared shoots since they'd started this project. An hour in, Nicole offered to get them some wine, and they paused long enough to enjoy most of a glass together before getting back to work. They ate and drank the rest of the early and later evening, and finally submitted their work to John a few minutes after eight.

"Oh, man!" Nicole said, rubbing her eyes. "I'm glad we're done with that for a few days."

"Right? I can hardly believe we get some time off. Well, I have to work at the studio tomorrow, but at least I don't have this to do, too."

"Wow. If I feel like this, you must be totally wiped. You said the studio is closed for the holidays?"

Quinn sighed. "Just Christmas Eve, Christmas, and the day after."

"That's something, anyway."

Quinn shrugged. "It's not usually such a big deal. Off season, it's an easy job except weekends, so I can't complain."

Nicole stood, stretching, and held out a hand to help Quinn up. Both of them groaned and stretched some more, laughing lightly.

"I guess this is what it feels like to be almost forty," Nicole said.

"What, you mean like it hurts to sit too much?"

"Right? Like shouldn't that be the easiest part of life? Sitting? Who knew it could ache this much?"

They stared at each other briefly before they spoke at once.

"Do you want to—"

"Would you like to—"

They laughed awkwardly, and Nicole gestured for Quinn to go on. "Uh, well, I intended to ask if you wanted to go somewhere. Maybe the brewery? It can be kind of crowded on a Friday like this, but we might get lucky if we sit at the bar."

Nicole bit down a pang of disappointment. "Sure! That sounds nice."

Quinn must have caught her brief expression, as she frowned. "Are you sure? What were you going to say?"

Nicole hesitated, chuckling awkwardly, now almost afraid to ask. She gestured loosely at a closed door.

"Well, actually, I was going to ask if you wanted to see my bed-room."

Quinn's eyebrows shot up, and her face seemed to pale. "Oh! Wow. Uh—"

Nicole stepped closer and took her hand. "Hey! I'm sorry. That was really forward. We probably shouldn't, you know…in my childhood bedroom, anyway."

Quinn grinned before a sly expression stole across her face. "Well, we could make out a little, maybe. That's not breaking the rules too much, is it?"

Nicole's mouth went dry, and she shook her head, only managing a weak, "No."

She led her into the bedroom, closing the door behind them and plunging them into darkness, only a dim moonlight leaking in through the window. Almost as if the lighting made them bolder, they were immediately kissing, far more passionately than they had before, their haste and excitement making them both careless and sloppy. Nicole giggled at the awkwardness, Quinn joining her, and then Nicole maneuvered them closer to the bed. They collapsed onto it next to each other, Nicole moving on top of Quinn a few seconds later. She kissed Quinn's lips and chin before moving down onto her neck, and Quinn hissed when Nicole's lips met her pulse point. The sound drove a spike of sheer pleasure through her heart, and Nicole nibbled there again, hoping to hear that same wild response. Instead, Quinn suddenly slid her hands up Nicole's back under her sweater. Her hands were warm, almost hot, and she paused at Nicole's bra.

"Yes," Nicole whimpered.

Quinn unclasped her bra, and Nicole sat up, resting on her forearms as Quinn began exploring her chest.

They froze at the flash of headlights, and Nicole wrenched around, turning wildly toward the window, realizing, as she'd first feared, that the car was pulling into her driveway.

"You have *got* to be kidding me," Nicole said.

They leapt to their feet. She shooed Quinn out of the bedroom, pausing to refasten her bra before joining her in the living room.

"Oh, shoot," Quinn said, laughing. "You have lipstick all over—"

"So do you!"

Quinn rushed into the bathroom, closing the door at the same moment a car door slammed closed outside.

"Shit," Nicole said. She walked to the snack table and grabbed a Santa-themed napkin before scrubbing at her lower face. The dogs were watching her, only halfway interested, and Nicole was dimly aware that the snacks looked suspiciously less ample than they had ten minutes ago.

"I won't say anything if you don't," she told them before giggling, almost hysterically.

Quinn came out of the bathroom then, gesturing wildly for Nicole to replace her, and Nicole managed to slip inside and close the door just as her mom came inside. She could hear Quinn and her mom greeting each other, her heart still racing. She took one look at herself in the mirror and had to slap her hands over her mouth to stop herself from braying with laughter. She had lipstick all over, in places she'd never have expected it to smear and streak. Thank goodness she'd managed to get in here before her mom saw her.

Still giggling, she spent a couple of minutes cleaning up, all the while taking deep, calming breaths to stop the real laughter from leaking out of her. Almost thirty-six years old and her mom had nearly caught her making out with a girl in her childhood bedroom.

Finally clean, she smiled at her reflection, grateful, once again, that she and Quinn had reunited after all these years. She couldn't remember the last time she'd had so much fun.

CHAPTER SIXTEEN: QUINN

On Sunday, Quinn had a nice morning with Annette while Nicole and her dad went skiing. Despite how close it was, Quinn had been to Aspen only once before this, and that had been in the middle of the summer for a photography exhibit. Being here in the middle of the busiest season was entirely different. Thousands of tourists from all over the world filled the streets of the village, many wearing designer clothes that wouldn't look out of place on Fifth Avenue. Many of the cars in the parking lots and at the valet stands were the kind you saw only in movies. Everything, everywhere, screamed money and opulence.

The prices in the shops were astronomical. She and Annette had exchanged looks of outright alarm in the first gift shop they'd visited. They'd laughed together outside on the sidewalk, both joking that they weren't going to be able to buy anything all day, but they still had fun browsing and watching the rich people around them.

They were having a good time. Quinn was surprised by how easy Annette was to spend time with. When they'd planned the day, she'd expected at least some awkwardness. But they'd fallen into an easy rapport right away, chatting like old friends. They had a similar sense of humor, and similar backgrounds, of course, so maybe this was to be expected. It helped, perhaps, that they were both exceedingly pleased with everything, too. While the prices were disappointing, the village was gorgeous. Snow-dappled mountains rose around them, and the entire downtown was decked out in Christmas glory.

The morning passed quickly. Midway, they got ridiculously overpriced coffees and pastries and browsed some more before heading here to the ski lodge to meet the others for lunch. They'd arrived more than half an hour ago, but neither Nicole nor her dad had shown up yet.

Annette was inside the lodge holding their table for lunch, but

Quinn had gone outside to the bottom of the slopes, the whipping wind and snow hurting her face. Earlier this morning, it had been nice, the chill refreshing, the sun bright and friendly. And then, while she and Annette had been browsing the busy shops all morning, the weather had gotten worse and worse. The sunlight had dimmed so gradually, she hadn't realized how dark it had gotten until one of the stores they'd visited turned the lights on inside.

Now she put one hand over her eyes and peered in the direction of the summit, hoping, once again, to catch sight of either her dad or Nicole. Her dad was wearing his new and bright red hat, and Nicole's parka was a brilliant blue, but spotting them was still hopeless. The weather was starting to shift from bad to awful down here, and it looked, if anything, even worse the farther she peered up the mountain. The clouds seemed to have swallowed the summit entirely. Most of the more difficult runs, the runs her dad and Nicole had planned to ski, were at the top of the mountain. The idea that they were up there, stuck in that mess right now, was terrifying.

Suddenly, a loud, pealing alarm and a loudspeaker squawked to life. "Due to the inclement weather, the chair lifts will cease operations in fifteen minutes. All skiers should proceed to the bottom of the slopes immediately."

The message repeated a couple of times before pausing, then began again with a shortened time. By this point, Quinn was cold and nearly numb, and she almost stumbled her way back inside the overheated and now overcrowded lodge. Everyone seemed to be talking at once, voices high and loud and worried. She had to push through the crowds, everyone too self-absorbed to notice her and move out of the way.

Finally, Quinn made her way back into the dining room. Annette's eyes were wide and her face pale, and she stood as Quinn approached, reaching for her hands.

"Did you see anything?"

Quinn shook her head before unwinding her scarf. "No. Did you hear the announcement in here?"

"Yes," Annette said. "I'm scared to death."

Quinn was worried too, but she squeezed Annette's hands as tightly as she could. "Don't be. I know my dad. He's an excellent skier, but he's no hero. He won't chance anything if there's any danger."

Annette's face cleared a little. "Nicole's the same way. She's smart. Careful, not reckless."

"So let's try to trust that they know what they're doing."

Annette leaned back in her chair, her posture and expression still tense, but that panicky wildness had faded a bit.

"I'm going to call my friends that work here, okay?" Quinn asked. "I don't think they're on staff today, but they might know someone that could talk to us."

"Yes. Please do that."

Quinn tried Dane first, but the call went straight to voicemail. She tried Rico next, with the same result. Finally, she sent both a text with information about their situation, hoping one or both would eventually see it.

"Makes me wonder if they're being called in," she said, putting her phone away. "Or maybe they're already on the way. Most phones don't get any service on that road between Glenwood and here."

Annette, clearly only half-listening, was twisting a heavy cloth napkin on her lap. Quinn put one of her hands on top of Annette's, and she jumped slightly before giving her a weak smile.

"Sorry, honey. I'm a worrywart. I don't know wh-what I'd do if—"

Quinn squeezed her hand harder. "I'm scared, too. But let's try not get too worked up yet. They haven't even fully evacuated the slopes yet. They could be here any minute."

Annette's eyes were brimming with tears, but she nodded. She blinked a few times and patted Quinn's hand.

"You're right. Let's get some drinks to help them warm up when they get here."

Quinn glanced around and motioned for the waiter before ordering four hot toddies. As they waited, Quinn avoided Annette's eyes, knowing that if she allowed herself to see her own panic reflected there, this situation would go from bad to worse. One of them had to be calm and collected here, and today that had to be her.

She saw Annette's face light up the second Nicole and her dad walked into the room behind her, and the two of them were up and moving that way a second later. Quinn hugged her dad with fierce, tight panic, and he squeezed her back just as fiercely. He smelled of cold and wind, and when she pulled away to peer up into his face, she was startled by how haggard and windburned he looked. She finally let him go, turning to see Nicole and her mom doing the same, crying lightly as they moved back to look at each other. Nicole, too, seemed worn down. Despite her obvious relief, her face was pinched and almost gray, her cheeks windburned like her dad's.

Annette and her dad moved to embrace, and when they drew apart, Annette gave his shoulders a tight squeeze.

"Thank God you're okay, Jack," she said, and then turned to Nicole. "What on earth happened, honey?"

Nicole glanced at Quinn's dad and then shook her head. "Can we sit down first? I feel like I'm about to fall over."

"Me, too," her dad said.

Annette sprang into action, bustling the two of them over to the table and fluttering about while they made themselves comfortable, taking their outwear to the nearest coat rack and ordering some more hot drinks to follow the ones that had already been delivered. Quinn watched all of this with something like dread building in her stomach. Her dad and Quinn were sharing a lot of worried, almost pained glances. Finally, almost as if she realized she could no longer pretend to be busy, Annette settled in her chair and clutched her drink. Quinn brought hers to her lips, her hands shaking slightly. She was both relieved and terrified.

Her dad finished his drink in one go and pushed the empty mug aside. He made eye contact with Nicole, the two of them communicating a lot in that silent exchange before he began speaking. His gaze moved back and forth between the three of them as he spoke.

"First of all, I want you to realize that we're okay. We're here, and we're okay now."

"But you weren't," Quinn said, almost whispering.

Nicole and her dad shared another long look.

"No," he said. "For a while there, things weren't looking good at all."

"What happened?" Annette asked.

He winced and shook his head. "It came on quick. The storm, I mean. It had gotten a bit darker, yes, but neither one of us paid much mind. It was still warm up there, the slopes were crowded, the whole nine yards. Then everything happened all at once." He paused, rubbing his mouth, seeming to ask Nicole to continue without saying anything more.

Nicole cleared her throat. "We were on a slope together, on our last run before lunch. I wanted to get back here to make sure we could get a table before the rush. When we set off, I saw a couple of flakes in the air, but everything seemed normal. Then this huge gust of wind came through. I saw him on a mogul, a few yards ahead of me, and then he was sliding, super-fast, off the trail, over to the edge of the run and into the woods. Then I couldn't see him at all. We had like a wall of wind and snow between us." She paused and finished her own drink. The waiter, almost as if anticipating this need, appeared at that precise moment and set down new mugs for everyone.

Her dad picked up the story again. "I hit something like black ice, I think, which is pretty unusual in the snow like that, but it can form on rocks if it's cold enough. My skis simply slipped out from under me. The wind was sort of pushing me along. I saw the trees coming, and then..." He lifted his hands weakly and shrugged.

Quinn had unconsciously put her hands over her mouth to hold back the emotion building inside her, and she forced them down and into her lap. Her dad reached out for one, covering it with his.

"I found him at the foot of a tree," Nicole finally said. "But it took a long time. It was so damn *cold*. And the frigging wind was doing its best to push me over or down the slope. But I knew he couldn't be downhill—not when I saw him sliding to the side like that. He was either in the trees or...off the side of the mountain, but I thought there was a good chance he was in the trees. I checked and double-checked them all, but I must have missed his tree twenty times. And the damn wind wouldn't let up. I was so cold and finally about to go get someone to help, and then I finally spotted his hat."

Nicole paused and met her mom's eyes. Nicole's mom had given him a bright red hat this morning. Annette's hands, which had been twisting on the napkin all this while, froze, her body stiff with shock.

"I had to dig and dig to get him out of the snow," Nicole said. "Thank God he woke up when I got the bulk of it off him, 'cause I don't know how I would have dragged him anywhere in that mess."

Her dad shrugged. "I guess I was stunned, the wind knocked out of me, and then the snow over me must have kept me under. I didn't hit my head, I don't think, at least it doesn't hurt or anything. I musta fallen funny. But I would have been in real trouble if she hadn't dug me out."

Quinn jumped to her feet, and her dad did the same a moment later, the two of them squeezing each other. The very idea that she'd almost lost him today was almost too much to absorb. When they drew back, both were teary and happy at the same time, and she squeezed her hands in his.

"Damn it, Dad. You can't do that to me ever again."

He shook his head. "I won't. I'll check the weather report every time I ski." He held up three fingers. "Scout's Honor."

She gently pushed him, annoyed with his flippancy, and then wiped her face before turning to Nicole and Annette. They were also standing again, close together and laughing through tears.

Nicole finally noticed her gaze and gave her a tired grin. Quinn moved around the table and, not caring a bit about anyone else in here, pulled her into a deep, grateful kiss. She peppered her face with quicker, lighter kisses after that, both of them laughing and smiling at each other when she finished.

"You saved his life," she whispered. She could see Nicole wanting to protest, but she kissed her again to stop her. "Thank you."

"You're welcome," Nicole finally said, almost breathless.

Their parents were all smiles when she glanced their way, holding hands as they stood there watching them. Annette's eyes were misty, and her dad's were sparkling, too. Quinn moved slightly away, but Nicole grabbed her hand as they all sat down again, and they kept the connection throughout most of the meal.

The dining room gradually filled to capacity as they sat there eating and drinking far too much. The storm outside the floor-to-ceiling windows looked wild and bitterly cold, the view almost a whiteout.

"So I guess this weather means we're going to have to try to find a place to stay," Annette finally said.

"On Christmas weekend at one of the busiest resorts in the world," Quinn added.

"Is this going to be one of those things where there's only one bed?" Nicole asked, making everyone laugh.

"Doesn't exactly work with four people, especially when two of them are parents of the others," Quinn said.

Nicole wrinkled her nose, and they all laughed again.

"I have no idea what we're going to do," Annette said.

"We could try to wait it out," Nicole suggested.

"That's a plan," her dad said. "This might let up."

"Oh!" Quinn said and reached into her pocket for her phone. "I have a better idea. Let me call Dane again."

After getting through to Dane, Quinn was put in touch with someone who worked there, and the four of them were soon led into the wing for staff housing. They would all have to sleep on bunkbeds, but they would have a bed in a warm place, which was more than a lot of day-trippers stuck in the lodge could say. As they waited for the storm to pass, they relaxed in the staff lounge, playing cards and boardgames.

They drank hot chocolate before switching to some nice wine from the hotel bar and managed to get a table again for dinner, despite the crowds.

Her dad was sleeping in the men's bunkhouse, and he and Annette hung back in the lounge after she and Nicole headed to bed. Several other women were in there already, all of whom were much younger than the two of them, and very curious about why they were there, asking them lots of questions, so that by the time Annette rejoined them, their own moment for a quiet, one-on-one good night seemed to have passed. Nicole sent her a quick wink before climbing into the bunk above hers, and Quinn fell asleep soon after, smiling.

CHAPTER SEVENTEEN: NICOLE

Nicole and her mom sat in front of the TV in the side-by-side easy chairs in a food-induced stupor. Both dogs were piled on her mom's feet, likewise knocked stupid by their overly big meals. Not used to sleeping in a crowded room, she and her mom had left the ski lodge in Aspen quite early that morning, soon after the staff had started stirring and moving about, waking them both. Quinn and her dad decided to stay longer and have breakfast before heading back, and as they had come in their own car, it had made sense to split up. Today was Christmas Eve, after all, and that meant family time.

She and her mom had eaten an enormous brunch and flopped down to watch Christmas movies, their usual ritual for the day. But Nicole wasn't finding the experience as pleasantly opulent as she usually did. Instead, she found herself missing Quinn with a kind of aching, yearning pain, like a toothache she couldn't ignore. Her mind wouldn't settle on the shows they were watching, and unlike the drowsy bliss she'd normally feel, she simply felt bloated.

"You can call her, you know," her mom suddenly said, patting her hand. "I won't be insulted."

"It's Christmas Eve, Mom. She's busy."

"Do you know that for sure? I thought you said she and her dad don't really celebrate."

"They don't decorate, anyway, but, I mean, he comes all the way from Arizona to see her this time of year, so I imagine they do something together."

"Doesn't she have a tiny apartment? What on earth could they possibly cook in there?"

Nicole laughed. "Her kitchen is the same size as yours, Mom. I'm sure she's capable of cooking whatever they want."

They sat in silence a while longer, the film on the TV simply something to stare at, not watch. Her mom was goading her, but Nicole also knew she shouldn't push things with Quinn. While everything had turned out okay yesterday, it had still been a scary experience for all of them. Quinn and her dad deserved a chance to be together and recover.

Her phone rang, and she and her mom jumped. The dogs started barking, and her mom leant down to pat them quiet. Nicole dug around in the blankets until she found the phone, her mom chuckling when Nicole showed her that Quinn was calling.

"Hello?"

"Hi, Nicole. It's me. Quinn."

Nicole chuckled. "Yeah. I know."

She waited through a long pause and then heard a sigh.

"Look," Quinn said, "this will sound kind of weird, but what are you doing today?"

"You mean besides sitting here in my PJs with too much food in my stomach? Absolutely nothing."

"Well, you see, my dad and I decided we might do Wigilia tonight."

"What's that?"

"It's the Polish Christmas Eve dinner. We haven't done it in a long time, not since Mom left. Anyway, we're trying a simplified version since we didn't prepare anything ahead of time. Would you and your mom like to join us?"

"Let me ask." She put her hand over the mouthpiece. "Mom, want to have dinner with them tonight?"

"In her tiny apartment?"

"Yes. In her tiny apartment. The dinner's a Polish Christmas Eve thing, I guess."

Her mom grinned eagerly. "That sounds lovely. Ask her what we can bring."

"My mom says yes," Nicole told Quinn, suddenly feeling foolish, as if she'd had to ask permission. "She also wanted to know what we can bring."

"Um, well, we're having a few vegetarian, fish, and seafood dishes, which is the tradition. Normally there would be twelve things to try, but I'm not sure I'll be able to make that many with such short notice. The number doesn't matter, though, since we're not really religious."

"Does it have to be Polish, or is any kind of vegetarian or seafood thing okay?"

"We're not picky. If you want to bring something, please feel free, but we'll have plenty of food and drink. You're our guests, so just come hungry."

"Okay. What time?"

"Can you get here before four? That way we can watch for the Christmas Star together. That's when we can eat."

"Should we dress up?"

Quinn laughed. "Actually, yes. But not too fancy—something nice."

"Okay. I'm looking forward to it."

"Me, too. See you soon, Nicole."

"Bye."

She filled her mom in, who immediately leapt up to scour the kitchen for something to make. Nicole was still feeling too full to be around food again so soon, so she decided to use the time to take a long, hot shower and dry her hair, which, long as it was, took a while.

After she was freshly clean and wearing actual clothes, she headed down to the local co-op to walk off the rest of the brunch. Luckily the store was still open today for a couple more hours, packed with last-minute shoppers. The very fact that this upscale store could exist in Glenwood now spoke volumes about how much the little city had changed over the years. Everything in the co-op was pricey, but the food was all organic and local, so she was happy to pay the upcharge. She grabbed a bouquet of Christmas-themed flowers, a large ring of cocktail shrimp, and a couple of crowlers of beer from the Glenwood brewery. As she waited in line, she spotted a poppyseed bread that was labeled as a "Polish Classic" and, hoping that was an accurate description, decided to get that, too.

Her mom had baked some cheese and onion enchiladas by the time she came home, and the two of them helped each other get ready, doing a kind of fashion show in the living room while *White Christmas* played for the hundredth time that month on the TV. Nicole settled on fifties-style, pink satin pants and an emerald-green blouse paired with her vintage rose pearls, and her mom went with something even more festive: a bright red skirted jumper over a green shirt, which she paired with a red bauble necklace and earrings. Outfits chosen, they helped each other style their makeup and hair.

Finished, they still had some time to waste before they left, and Nicole spent a few minutes restlessly pacing the house as her mom watched the end of the movie. The dogs' eyes followed Nicole for a while, then, clearly uninterested in whatever she was going through, they decided to ignore her and went back to sleep.

"She did say to come before four," Nicole said, mostly to herself. "And that's like *anytime* before four, right?"

"You're being ridiculous, Nicole," her mom said, shaking her head. "If you want to see her that badly, we should just go. I'm sure she's excited to see you, too."

Nicole shrugged, still uneasy with the idea. "Won't it seem, I don't know, desperate or something?"

Her mom frowned and then gestured to the other armchair. "Sit down, please."

She sounded firm and serious, and Nicole immediately sat. "What?"

Her mom was still frowning, a concerned wrinkle creasing the space between her eyes. She held out her hands and Nicole took them.

"Nicole, I want you to listen to me carefully, okay?"

Nicole nodded.

"There is nothing desperate about wanting to see someone. There is nothing desperate about showing someone how you feel about them. If you like this girl, you don't need to hide that fact from her. Don't play games with this one. Quinn needs you to show her that you care, especially now, here at the beginning. Be as obvious as possible. Do you hear me?"

She'd squeezed Nicole's hands as she spoke, almost painfully.

"Yes, Mom. I hear you."

"Good." She let go, stood up, and turned off the TV. "So are we going, or what?"

Nicole couldn't help nervously checking her watch. With the short drive, they'd still be almost an hour early if they left now. But maybe her mom was right.

"Right. Let's do this."

Nicole had already gathered the various gifts she'd bought Quinn over the last few weeks into a canvas shopping bag. She hadn't meant to go overboard, but that's exactly what she'd done. Every time she was in a store recently and saw something Quinn would like, she'd simply bought it. That had happened a surprising number of times, apparently, as the pile of gifts was sizable. She'd been wrapping them as she bought and hadn't realized, until now, how many she'd gotten. She wasn't sure if she should give all of this to Quinn, in the end, but tonight was the night to give her something if she wanted to do so before the holiday tomorrow. Her mom spotted the bag but thankfully didn't comment, simply adding the gifts she'd bought for Jack and Quinn to it.

They managed to find a single parking space on Grand Avenue a couple of blocks from Quinn's apartment, but it took them some time to navigate the partially shoveled and icy sidewalk to her building. Nicole realized as they approached it that she'd only ever gone through the store to get to Quinn's apartment and wasn't sure how to get inside otherwise.

"Shoot," she said, and explained the problem to her mom.

"I'm sure there's a back door, Nicole. Don't panic."

She was annoyed with what her mom had said, which was, in fact, exactly what she'd started to do, and she cursed her mom's insight. It was aggravating to be around someone who could basically read her mind.

Her mom pointed at an alley that led them around to the back of the city block, and they fought through some small snow drifts to the door, where they saw a mailbox for her business and a doorbell.

Quinn opened the door in seconds, her hair blown back as if she'd run down the stairs.

"Hi," she said, eyes sparkling.

"I hope we're not too early—"

"Not at all," Quinn said.

"I got you these," Nicole said, holding out the flowers.

"They're lovely. Thank you." Quinn held the door open wide with her other arm. "Can I help you carry anything else?"

"No, dear," her mom said. "We'll manage. Lead the way."

The apartment had gone through a major transformation since the last time Nicole had been here. A small Christmas tree stood in the corner of the room, lavishly decorated. Stockings hung on the fireplace, and boughs of actual holly were draped on surfaces around the room. Several poinsettias decorated the various tables, all of which were covered in heavy green and red table clothes. Warm, yellow-white lights strung around the room created a soft, cozy atmosphere.

"Wow," Nicole said, setting her bag of gifts down. "When you go all out, you go all out."

Quinn shrugged, her smile a little embarrassed. "We hadn't decorated in like, ever. It was fun."

"How did you manage to get all of this on Christmas Eve?"

"You'd have to ask my dad. I've been here cooking all day. He's the genius behind it."

They both turned in his direction. He and Nicole's mom were already standing close, talking low and intimately, peering into each other's eyes and grinning stupidly. Her mom had taken the food and the flowers with her, and there they sat, forgotten on the counter as their parents chatted.

She and Quinn widened their eyes at each other in surprised embarrassment and turned their attention to the bag of gifts.

"Oh, wow, Nicole. This is a lot."

Nicole bit her lip. "I know. I'm sorry. I kept seeing things I knew you'd like, and then, before I knew it, I'd bought too much, and I'm not sure—"

Quinn kissed her, and Nicole immediately responded, her body flooding with happiness. She pulled Quinn closer, wrapping her arms around her lower back. They stayed that way, lips locked, long enough that she heard her mom clear her throat from across the room. They pulled apart at the same time, grinning at each other sheepishly. Quinn turned to their folks and pointed at the mistletoe hanging a few feet from them.

"Sorry," she said. "But it's tradition."

Everyone laughed, and Nicole used the time it took to put her gifts under the tree to gather her senses again and cool off. She saw some other gifts, some with Quinn's name, some with her dad's, but also a couple with Nicole's name on them, and some with her mom's. Her stomach gave a funny, thrilled leap at the sight of them all. The last couple of Christmases had been more than a bit subdued. The one right after her dad had died had been downright dour, in fact. Last year had been a little better, but still sad and a little lonely. Her grandparents were all long dead, her aunts and uncles basically strangers, so it had been a while since they'd had a celebration like this. Seeing all of it— the gifts, the decorations, the food—and having people to spend the holiday with, was making her feel, for the first time in a long time, that things were finally better. Her dad would have wanted this for them.

When she stood, she had to wipe a stray tear away from her eyes, but the others were so wrapped up in the activity in the kitchen, no one had seen her. She stayed there, just watching the three of them laugh and talk together, her mom and Quinn giggling like old friends. Jack couldn't seem to keep his eyes off her mom, and while this was the first time she'd seen someone who wasn't her dad showing interest like that in her, Nicole was entirely happy about it.

The doorbell rang, startling everyone, and Quinn dashed out the door again to let Molly, Rico, and Dane come in. They all spent the next twenty minutes choosing drinks and getting food and gifts settled and unpacked. Quinn and her dad were very happy with the poppyseed cake.

"Where on earth did you find one?" Quinn asked.

"In the co-op."

"It's perfect. I didn't have time to make one today, and I haven't had it in ages. Thank you."

"You're welcome."

Quinn almost kissed her then. Nicole could see it in her eyes and in the slight step her way, but after a nervous glance at her friends, she smiled again before turning back to the others. Even without the kiss, Nicole's heart was hammering as if the kiss had happened, and she had to wipe her sweaty hands on her legs. She caught Molly's eye. She had apparently witnessed this exchange and was squinting at her, as if trying to figure something out, but Nicole played innocent, smiling back until she looked away. She wasn't about to give away the secret if Quinn wasn't ready to tell her friends yet.

Once it started getting dark outside, Quinn made everyone go to the front windows, encouraging them to look up into the darkening sky above the buildings across the street. Nicole was standing close enough to Quinn that she linked their hands together, and Quinn glanced up at her before peering outside again, squinting against the glare from the streetlights.

"How will we know it's the Christmas Star?" Rico asked, his eyes shaded with one hand and face flat against the window.

"We pretend it's whatever star we see first," Quinn explained.

"Do I get a prize or something?" Dane asked, pointing. Everyone followed the direction of his finger, and while Nicole was fairly certain he was pointing at Venus, not a star, that was apparently good enough, as Quinn and her dad relaxed and moved away from the windows, everyone following suit a moment later.

"No, no prize," Quinn said. "Though you can be the first person to get the *opłatek*, if you want."

"The what, now?" Dane asked.

Quinn laughed. "It's a Christmas wafer. We had to make do with a fake one this year since we decided so late, but Dad and I will explain it."

Quinn's dad Jack moved into the kitchen and pulled out a large flatbread cracker. "So, uh, basically, we go around the room and tell each other something. You can admit a fault, if you want, or say something nice, and give the other person some kind of specific best wishes if you know they want something, like a new job, say. You have to try to talk to everyone."

"Right," Quinn added. "And when you finish, the person listening takes a small piece of your cracker and eats it. Then you switch. Both people have to eat a piece of the other person's cracker, or the good wishes won't come true."

"We can demonstrate, if you'd like," Jack said.

Everyone nodded, and Jack held his cracker out, smiling at Quinn.

"Merry Christmas, Quinn. I know we haven't done this in far too long, and that's my fault. I hope you'll forgive your old man. I want to say that I love you, I'm proud of you, and I hope that this upcoming year brings you every happiness."

They hugged and gave each other a quick kiss. Quinn broke off a small piece of his cracker and ate it.

"Thank you, Dad, and Merry Christmas. It has been a long time, but I understand, and you don't need to apologize. Let's just plan to do this every year from here on out. I love having you here, and I hope that this year we can see more of each other than usual. I love you."

He broke off a piece of her cracker, ate it, and they hugged again.

"So that's it!" Quinn said. "No skipping! Try to talk to everyone. Grab a cracker and get started."

Nicole and the others glanced at each other, a little uneasy, but once they began, Nicole found it painless to say nice things to everyone. She told Quinn's friends how much she'd enjoyed meeting them, and they said similar things to her. Talking to Jack was awkward, but as she was so pleased with the way he was treating her mom, she found it easy to compliment him. After him, she and her mom were paired, and she immediately teared up.

"You go first," she told her.

Her mom's eyes sparkled a little, too, and she laughed. "I don't know why I'm getting emotional."

"Me either," Nicole said, laughing.

"Well, then," her mom said, clearing her throat. "Basically, I'm so very glad you've been here all month, Nicole. I wish you could be here more often, but I'm also so darn proud of your accomplishments. And I'm so happy about Quinn. She's really lovely, and you two are wonderful for each other. I love you, and I want the best for you this year."

"Oh, Mom," Nicole said, crying now. They hugged long and hard. Nicole took some of her mom's cracker and ate it.

"Okay. Well, Merry Christmas, Mom. I love being here with you, too. I want to come back here and live here full time, and I'm hoping that I can make that happen in the next year or two."

"What? Really?"

"Yes. And I'm so glad about Jack. I love seeing you so happy. I love you, and I want the best for you this year."

Her mom was crying now, too, and they spent a long while in each other's arms, both of them whispering encouragements and laughing at the scene they were causing. Finally, they drew apart, and Nicole realized that the only person left for the exchange was Quinn.

They approached each other slowly, both a little hesitant. Nicole suspected that her makeup was a mess, but Quinn was smudged herself. They grinned at each other.

"Hi."

"Hi," Nicole said, chuckling. She took a deep breath before meeting Quinn's eyes.

"I like you a lot, Quinn. I want this, whatever it is, a lot. I think I've wanted to be with you for most of my life. I hadn't seen you in so long, but it almost feels like everything since was just a kind of break. You already mean a lot to me, and I want to make this work."

Quinn was clearly shocked, her mouth slightly open, and Nicole had to force her to take a piece of cracker from her. Quinn took a tiny morsel, chewed it, and swallowed, shaking her head.

"Wow. You just…said that."

"Mm-hmm. And I meant it."

"Well, I like you too, Nicole. I hope that's not a surprise. I don't want to keep you guessing. I want you to know it. And I want this, too. I want to be with you."

They kissed then, long enough that a chorus of hoots and hollers erupted from Quinn's friends, and they smiled into the kiss before drawing apart.

"I guess everyone knows, now," Quinn whispered.

"I guess they do. I don't mind if you don't."

"Why would I mind?" Quinn said.

They kissed again, and the others were polite enough not to mock them this time. Nicole could have stayed there, kissing Quinn by the Christmas tree, for the rest of the night.

CHAPTER EIGHTEEN: QUINN

Quinn wiped her eyes with a tissue before grinning at herself in the bathroom mirror. Earlier today, when her dad had suggested celebrating Christmas Eve for the first time in decades, she'd been happier than she could have imagined. Then Nicole and her mom had shown up, and then her friends, and that happiness had soared even higher. And Nicole had said what she said—that this meant something to her, that she wanted this, and Quinn realized she'd never known this kind of joy, possibly ever.

They'd eaten dinner right after the *opłatek* exchange, everyone sitting higgledy-piggledy on whatever chairs they could find. Quinn had brought some upstairs from the studio to supplement her meager seating, but no one seemed to mind eating in random places around the room, and everyone, including her, had eaten far too much and had a few too many glasses of wine, the laughter and voices rising louder and louder so that her tiny apartment nearly sounded like a nightclub. Quinn had finally excused herself to clean herself up a bit, knowing that her makeup was a complete mess, but also needing a few minutes to center herself in a quiet space.

Smeary makeup wiped away and cleanly reapplied, she grinned at her reflection, relief squeezing her heart with pained hope. Maybe this thing with Nicole was going to work out after all. Some part of her had been stuck in something like anxious dread ever since they first kissed, which meant she'd been holding back. She knew that about herself and wasn't exactly proud of it, but she also hadn't been able to do anything about it until now. Then Nicole said what she said, and now, standing here and able to reflect on it, she believed Nicole had meant every word. She could let this happen between them and be happy about it.

Quinn opened the door carefully, peering out before stepping into the living room. She was happy her friends knew about the relationship now, but the knowing glances and smirks coming her way were still embarrassing. Molly had been trying to corner her and get the details since the kisses she witnessed, but so far Quinn had dodged her. It didn't seem right to get into it here, when Nicole was, at best, a few feet away at any given time. Molly could be inappropriate, too, and she wasn't about to explain their love life in front of her dad and Nicole's mom.

"Were you hiding from me?" Molly said, so close to her ear that Quinn couldn't help but shriek.

Quinn swatted at her arm. "Jesus! You scared the hell out of me."

Molly laughed, her dimpled, all-American smile gleaming with teeth so straight and wide and white she could have been a toothpaste model. "That was the plan. So, were you?"

Quinn opened her mouth to deny it but ended up laughing. "I guess I was."

Molly linked her arm with Quinn's, drawing her toward the open loveseat.

"Don't worry, Quinn. I won't embarrass you in front of your dad. But you better goddamn believe you're telling me everything the next time I see you. And I mean *everything*."

Quinn winked at her. "It's a deal."

Her gaze strayed over to Nicole, who was chatting with her dad and Annette in the kitchen. Rico and Dane were playing a rousing round of dominoes nearby, so she had a hard time hearing over their antics, but she could see everyone's grinning faces in the kitchen. Her dad seemed happier than she could remember seeing him in a long time, and the fact that Nicole had a little something to do with that filled her with a happy warmth. She didn't have a camera nearby, but her phone functioned in a pinch, and she snapped a few shots of the three of them.

Nicole's gaze wandered her way, searching the room, and they made eye contact, Nicole's grin widening broadly. Annette and her dad noticed, and they smiled her way, too, and then Molly elbowed her.

"Ouch!"

Molly's frown twitched with amusement. "Stop making heart-eyes with your lady. It makes us singletons jealous."

"You don't have to be single, you know," Quinn said. "Toni would say yes."

Molly rolled her eyes. "How many times do I have to tell you? She's my boss. It wouldn't be professional."

"Good excuse."

Molly chewed her lips anxiously. "Do you think she'd go for it?"

"Yes." Quinn shrugged. "I see the way she looks at you when you're not watching. She's attracted, at the very least."

"I mean, what would I even say?"

"Gee, I don't know. You could just say, 'Hey, Toni, do you want to go on a date?'"

Molly rolled her eyes. "Oh, come on. It's not that easy."

"Or you could kiss her. That's what I did with Nicole."

Molly's eyes brightened, and she turned toward her, excited. "You did what, now?"

Quinn's dad tapped his wineglass with a fork, effectively silencing the room.

"I wanted to say to all of you how very happy I am to share this evening with you. Merry Christmas." He held up his glass, everyone raising theirs toward his before they all took a long sip.

"Anyway," he said, "it's starting to get late, and as I understand it, the other gentlemen here have to work in the morning."

Everyone booed.

"Quinn and I traditionally open presents tonight, Christmas Eve, and as I believe everyone brought their gifts with them, I wondered if you would like to share that tradition with us here, tonight, before we wrap up."

"Was that a pun, Dad?" Quinn asked.

He winked. "You know it. So? What do you all say?"

Everyone cheered and clapped, and Quinn moved to stand up to help him. Her dad waved her back down in her seat, and as Nicole and her mom pulled up chairs, he began passing out gifts. It took quite some time to distribute everything, but by the time he was done, everyone had a small pile of gifts in front of them. Quinn's, however, was anything but small, her collection dwarfing the rest, nearly all of them labeled by Nicole's elegant handwriting.

Nicole was watching her, anxious, so Quinn mouthed, silently, "It's okay. Thank you," and saw her visibly relax.

"So do we do this one person at a time or all at once?" Dane asked.

Quinn's dad, seeing her sizable pile, lifted his shoulders. Normally, they did it one person at a time, but he was giving her a chance to avoid having everyone watch her open this enormous pile.

"Let's do it all at once," she said, and soon everyone was tearing into their gifts.

Quinn opened the presents from her friends first while they opened hers to them. In addition to the smaller gifts like cookies and miniature booze bottles she gave everyone, she'd bought Dane and Rico a fondue set, as they were always waxing poetic about eating it during their ski vacation in Switzerland last year. They'd bought her a yearly membership in a Colorado beer-of-the-month club, and Rico had knitted her a lovely purple and white matching scarf, hat, and mitten set done in a charming unicorn pattern. She'd bought Molly four tickets to a home game for the Avalanche in Denver next month, and Molly squealed so loud and so high, Quinn was afraid her wineglass would shatter. After several rounds of hugs and thank-yous, she opened Molly's gift to her: a full-day package at a new spa here in town.

She paused then to watch her dad and Annette smiling and laughing over their own gifts, and for Nicole and her friends to open theirs to each other. She opened her gifts from Annette next, all of which were birding-themed, including a nice watercolor of a nuthatch from a local artist. This choice was amusing, in a lot of ways, as Quinn had done something similar for her, giving her an updated bird field guide as well as a small, framed print of that kingfisher she'd snapped a couple of weeks ago. Her dad, as always, had gifted her the annual trip she took to Arizona to visit him in the spring—flight and airport shuttle—and she'd given him, also as usual, an annual subscription to several of his streaming services and magazines. These weren't exactly personal gifts, but she and her dad liked giving each other useful things like this, so it worked for them.

Finally, she was left with the pile of gifts from Nicole, and Nicole was left with hers. Quinn had told herself all night not to compare the quantity of things Nicole had given her with her own gifts, but now, seeing the enormous discrepancy, she couldn't help but feel disappointed in herself. Nicole was clearly nervous, too, biting her lip and wringing her hands slightly, and she wished, then, that they'd arranged to do this exchange privately.

"Say!" Molly said, slapping her thighs and standing up. "I'm beat. Aren't you beat, Rico and Dane? Because I sure am, and you drove! We should get going." Her tone had that phony jolliness Quinn had overheard her use at work.

Dane and Rico peered up at Molly, obviously confused, and then Rico's expression cleared, and he stood up, stretching and yawning dramatically. "Boy—you're right! I am beat!"

Dane, still lost, opened his mouth to complain, and then Rico gestured, more obviously, toward the door, tilting his head none-too-secretly in Quinn and Nicole's direction.

"Oh!" Dane said, standing up. "I mean, yes! I'm beat, too."

"Same," Annette said, standing. "Jack, do you think you could drive me home?"

He stood to join her, and Quinn had the chance to thank Molly and Annette quietly before they left as they hugged good-bye. After a flurry of gathering gifts, taking leftovers, getting dressed, and finally leaving, she and Nicole were left, blissfully alone. They smiled at each other, both a little shy, and then Nicole gestured at the door.

"That was nice of Molly."

"It was nice of her. She's the best."

"I like your friends a lot."

Quinn grinned, reached out for her hand, and squeezed it. "Good. I'm glad. They like you, too. They're your friends now, too, you know."

Nicole nodded, her gaze moving away, seeming to avoid the remaining presents. Finally, she focused in on the kitchen and asked, "Do you want some wine? There's some left in that last bottle."

"Yes," Quinn said, a bit desperately.

Nicole chuckled and moved to pour the last of it into two new glasses. They drank it down quickly, standing there in the kitchen. Nicole was clearly as anxious as she was, her face a little pale, her posture rigid. Still, the wine did the job, and Quinn allowed herself to relax with the extra libation.

"Look, Quinn—"

"Nicole, I—"

They both chuckled.

"You first," Quinn said.

Nicole sighed. "I wanted to say again that I'm sorry—for getting you all those gifts. I didn't realize how many there were until we were on our way here. I should have…sorted them or something, before coming here."

"You're apologizing? For buying me presents?"

Nicole chuckled falsely and then shrugged. "I guess I am."

Quinn moved forward in one big step and pulled Nicole's face closer to hers before kissing her with every ounce of her passion. As the kiss continued, she recalled every missed opportunity between them, all the times they could have been kissing, could have had this. All those years avoiding each other, all those lonely Christmases they'd had, when, in the end, what they'd needed was each other.

"Wow," Nicole said, breathing heavily.

Quinn grinned and pointed at the mistletoe, which hung several feet away, nowhere near them. "It's tradition. And now I don't have to feel bad about getting you fewer presents."

"No. You don't. Not at all. Should we open them now?"

Quinn shook her head. "No. Let's wait."

"Why?"

Quinn kissed her again, briefly, before pulling her toward the bed. "We can open them in the morning."

Despite her bravado, Quinn was trembling, and when she reached for the buttons on Nicole's shirt, her fingers didn't cooperate like they should. She fumbled at one briefly, and then they both giggled before Nicole took over, unbuttoning her shirt enough to shuck it off all at once. If Quinn had thought it had been hard to function when Nicole had a shirt on, she could hardly think now that her shirt was off. She was wearing a gorgeous lace and satin black bra—the kind of thing Quinn had rarely seen in real life. The piece was so pretty, and so perfectly designed for Nicole's style, it looked as if it had been made just for her. Her breasts were larger than Quinn's, larger than she'd expected, really, and so incredibly delicious in their creamy splendor she could hardly believe her eyes. Quinn forced herself to move her hand to cup one of Nicole's breasts over the soft satin, and Nicole's head rolled back, her mouth opening in a gasp.

"Not fair," Nicole said, her voice broken.

"Hmm?" Quinn asked. She had barely heard what Nicole said, her entire being centered on the breast in her hand.

"You still have a shirt on," Nicole said, grinning wickedly.

"Then take it off," Quinn whispered, that bravado from earlier still within reach.

As if she'd been waiting for permission, Nicole suddenly steered her forward until the back of Quinn's knees hit the mattress of her bed. She sat down heavily, looking up at Nicole, who was quickly shucking off her pink pants, only to reveal a pair of panties that matched her bra in style and glamour. Quinn had dressed up for the evening, and while she didn't own anything like Nicole's lingerie, when Nicole pulled her shirt off and over her head, her eyes blazed at the sight of Quinn's chest.

"Much better," Nicole said.

Nicole knelt down, pushing Quinn's legs open, and moved closer, her face even with Quinn's chest. Nicole moved to unclasp Quinn's simple bra, waited for Quinn to nod her consent, and then removed it, letting it drop onto the floor next to them. She examined Quinn's breasts for a long moment, and Quinn had to fight a wriggle of embarrassment as she waited for Nicole to stop staring. Finally, Nicole looked up to meet Quinn's eyes.

"Much, much better," she said, and then leaned forward and took one of Quinn's nipples in her mouth.

Quinn groaned, arching into her, and Nicole's hot hands were suddenly on her back, dragging her closer. Nicole's mouth was doing wonderful, unworldly things to her, and every time Nicole sucked, a little harder each time, it felt as if her soul was draining into the sensation. She threw one arm over her face, biting her arm to keep from calling out, but Nicole, seeing this, moved it gently away.

"I want to hear you, Quinn," she said, that wicked grin on her face again.

Quinn's chest was heaving from her runaway breath, and she bit her lip before nodding.

"Okay."

Rather than move back to her nipple, however, Nicole's smile broadened, and she reached around to unclasp her own bra, letting it drop to the floor. Quinn's breath caught in her throat at the sight of her exposed, dusky nipples. Almost without thought, Quinn bent forward, but Nicole stopped her with one gentle hand.

"Uh-uh. Not yet. It's your turn first."

Quinn groaned in frustration, and Nicole laughed, the tension breaking for both of them. Quinn smiled, a bit sheepish from her own desperation.

"Now scoot back," Nicole said, "so I can pull your skirt off."

Quinn didn't hesitate, and the two of them managed to slip it down and off her legs in seconds. Again, Nicole paused, her fingers hooked into the top of Quinn's underwear, and Quinn nodded as enthusiastically as she could.

"Please," Quinn said, the sound almost a whimper.

Nicole's lips lifted slightly, and she slipped the underwear off, tossing them backward into the room a moment later. Nicole knelt there in silence, her eyes rooted on the space between Quinn's legs, and Quinn heated with longing. Her earlier embarrassment had vanished, leaving her only hot, desperate.

"Please, Nicole. Please," she said again, not bothering to hide the fact that she was begging now.

Nicole ran the fingers of both hands lightly over Quinn's thighs, up and down a few times, and Quinn sank back onto her elbows. Nicole grabbed the underside of Quinn's thighs and pulled her closer to the edge of the bed, and then, after parting Quinn's labia with her fingers, she leaned in. She stroked the length of Quinn a few times, her tongue broad and flat, before finally stopping on her clit and gently sucking on it.

"Oh my God," Quinn said, throwing her head back.

She squeezed her eyes shut, the pleasure sharp and bright enough that she was momentarily giddy. Nicole's fingers moved closer to her opening, and she nodded before speaking.

"Please, please, Nicole. Inside."

Nicole slipped one finger inside and Quinn almost sat entirely upright before she made herself relax again, back onto her elbows. The sweet torture continued, and Quinn was dimly aware of her own rasping gasps and moans over the rushing roar of the blood in her ears.

She knew she wouldn't last long, but when her orgasm built and then crested seconds later, its power blindsided her. For several throbs, as the pleasure pulsed through her, she could only freeze in place. Then her body, by instinct, began to undulate with it and with Nicole. Nicole pulled her closer, hands back under her thighs, the two of them moving together as Quinn's pleasure crested and continued. Finally, Quinn let out a single, raspy yelp and collapsed backward, boneless and spent.

Soon Nicole was up on the bed with her, and she helped Quinn scoot backward until they were on the pillows together. Quinn nestled her head on Nicole's shoulder, and Nicole pulled her closer until they were flush, legs on that side linked together. They lay there in perfect, silent bliss, and Quinn let herself rest long enough to calm her racing pulse.

"I've wanted that for almost as long as I can remember," Nicole suddenly said.

Quinn moved enough to prop herself on one elbow so they could look at each other.

"Me, too," she said.

Nicole's answering smile was almost too much—a mix of hope and happiness that pierced her heart. Quinn leaned forward to kiss her, trying to convey how blissfully happy, how perfectly, wonderfully excited and overwhelmed she was with everything that had happened these last few weeks. When she moved back, Nicole's eyes were sparkling, and Quinn chuckled.

"Hey, none of that," Quinn said.

Nicole blinked rapidly and shook her head. "No, not tonight."
Quinn grinned at her. "And certainly not now."
Nicole looked confused, her brow furrowed.

"Not when it's your turn," Quinn said. Nicole's answering smile was enough boost to her confidence to begin, and Quinn leaned in for the next kiss.

CHAPTER NINETEEN: NICOLE

When she woke up the next morning, Nicole was surprised by the harsh brightness of the sunshine streaming in through the windows. The apartment was east-facing, and maybe she shouldn't have been so surprised, but it almost seemed as if the sun was literally right outside the window. She rolled away from the light to face Quinn, who was still asleep. The sight of her there, her naked shoulders exposed, her hair mussed, was one of the most beautiful things she'd ever seen. She'd wanted this kind of relationship with Quinn for so long that she found it hard to believe it had finally happened. She continued to watch her, the sunlight outside occasionally flashing off a passing car.

Quinn, as if sensing her gaze, finally began to stir, her dark lashes fluttering before she finally opened her eyes. She squinted a moment before smiling at her.

"Good morning."

"Morning."

They both grinned stupidly at each other, and Quinn's cheeks turned a rosy pink.

"Last night was…really something," she said.

Nicole lifted an eyebrow. "Good something or…?"

"You know," Quinn said, pushing her shoulder slightly.

Nicole leaned in for a quick kiss. They stayed there in bed for a while longer, smiling at each other, before, finally, Quinn rolled onto her back, stretching, the sheets slipping down to reveal a flash of her breasts. She caught Nicole staring at them and pushed her again.

"Perv."

"Takes one to know one."

Quinn got up first, pausing, shyly, before walking, fully naked, over to her wardrobe and pulling out two bathrobes—one a short cotton affair, the other a full-length flannel. She held the cotton one out for Nicole.

"Sorry. I only have the two robes."

"Sure," Nicole said, slipping it on. It barely hit mid-thigh. "You just want to see my butt."

Quinn chuckled. "Of course I do."

While Quinn took a shower, Nicole checked her phone, relieved to see a message from her mom.

Merry Christmas! No need to rush home. I'll have dinner together around five or five thirty this evening. Please let Quinn know that her dad wants them to have dinner with us if that's okay with her.

Quinn came back into the living room, her hair wrapped in a towel, and Nicole showed her the message.

"That sounds nice," Quinn said, smiling.

Nicole sent her response and put her phone back in her purse.

"Although you know what that probably means," Quinn said.

"What?"

"That my dad stayed the night with your mom."

They were both quiet before giggling.

"Good for them," Nicole said.

"No kidding."

"It's about time."

"For real."

They both laughed and stepped closer, embracing and kissing lightly. Quinn smelled fresh and minty, and she'd brushed her hair. Nicole knew she must look a mess.

"I should get cleaned up. Also, do you have an extra toothbrush I could use?" Nicole asked.

"Oh, yes, sorry, of course. Let me show you."

When she finished in the bathroom, Nicole was tempted to put her clothes back on. The apartment was warm enough, but she did feel a bit self-conscious waltzing around half-naked. Still, Quinn had put her robe on again after her shower, so Nicole decided to stay that way, too. She'd already caught Quinn staring at her legs a few times in the last ten minutes, and that could only mean good things if she kept them uncovered.

When she came out, Quinn was in the kitchen mixing pancake batter, and the scent of coffee filled the room with a heady bliss. Quinn had Christmas-themed mugs out for them, and Nicole poured them both a cup.

"How do you take yours?" Nicole asked.

"Splash of cream."

Nicole had the same, and they stood there sipping their coffee for a long while before Quinn turned back to their breakfast.

"Do you like them big or small? The pancakes, I mean."

"Oh, whatever is easier. No preference."

She watched Quinn work, the sleeves of her flannel robe rolled up her forearms. Despite the shower, Quinn's hair was still mussed, and Nicole was both embarrassed and turned on by a hint of a love bite on Quinn's neck. She stepped closer to her, wrapping her arms around her from behind, and kissed her there again. Quinn shivered in her arms.

"You keep that up, and we'll never get anything to eat."

"That's okay," Nicole said, deepening the kiss before nibbling a little lower. She heard Quinn turn off the burner, and then she was spinning around and back in her arms, kissing her back.

"Bed. Now," Quinn said.

Much later, they were finally eating their cold breakfast and drinking fresh coffee, their robes now switched out of fairness, according to Quinn. Nicole, of course, had wanted to look at Quinn's legs, too, so she didn't object, even though the flannel robe was much too hot.

"Should I put on some music?" Quinn asked, gesturing at her Bluetooth speaker.

"Yes, absolutely. Anything but Christmas music."

"Why not?" Quinn asked.

"My mom has been listening nonstop since I got here. Reminds me of working retail."

Quinn laughed. "That's for sure. Okay, no Christmas music." She pulled out her phone, scrolled for a while, and then grinned at Nicole. Soon, 90s lady rock started playing, and they both shared a smile at the opening bars to a well-known song by the Cranberries.

"One of my favorites," Nicole said, bobbing her head.

"Me, too."

They were sitting apart, Quinn on the armchair, Nicole on the loveseat, almost as if by mutual agreement, though neither of them had mentioned it. If they sat together, they'd end up back in bed again and never get to the pancakes or anything else, let alone make it to her mom's for dinner.

Nicole set her plate down on the coffee table, feeling, finally, as if that big emptiness in her stomach was full. Though she'd eaten her weight in food yesterday, their last meal had been almost eighteen hours ago.

Quinn, clearly thinking something similar, was blushing lightly, and she smirked as she set her plate down, too.

"Guess we worked up an appetite," she said.

"I wonder how?" Nicole replied, and they grinned at each other. In that moment, Nicole wanted more than almost anything to go to her, kneel down in front of her, and pick up right where they'd left off. Quinn's eyes flared with surprise, as if reading her thoughts, and she broke eye contact, clearing her throat and rubbing her hands nervously on the arms of her chair.

"Uh, well, we should, um—"

"Open presents!" Nicole said, almost desperately. She laughed and regulated her tone a bit. "Sorry. I mean we should open presents. I want you to see what I got you."

Quinn stood up, and Nicole had the distinct pleasure of watching her bare legs as she gathered their presents, still piled near their seats from the night before. Quinn moved both piles to the coffee table in front of the loveseat, but then hesitated before going over to her wardrobe, opening it, and pulling out an enormous wrapped present. She brought it over to Nicole and handed it to her a little sheepishly.

"I almost didn't give you that one," she explained, sitting down next to her.

"Why?"

She shrugged. "I'll explain it after you open it. But open the others first, okay?"

Nicole grinned. "Okay. In that case," she reviewed the pile in front of Quinn, dug around, and pulled one out, "open that one last, too."

They decided to go one person at a time, since only the two of them were here.

Quinn had bought her several locally sourced gifts. Nicole unwrapped a bottle of a gin from a nearby distillery, a gift card to the Glenwood Brewery, and a nice matching red scarf, mitten, and hat set made from Colorado wool. Quinn also gave her two books about Doc Holliday, one a biography, the other a fictionalized version of his life. They both agreed to wait on the final present until Quinn had opened hers.

"Thank you, Quinn," she said, hugging her and bussing her lips. "I love all of it."

"Really?"

"Yes. I really do. Now open mine."

Like her own, Quinn's gifts were mainly local. Nicole had bought her some locally made clothing—two scarves, some thin merino wool gloves for outdoor winter photo sessions, and several pairs of novelty socks that were either camera, wildlife, or mountain themed. She'd also gotten her a gift card from a local photography print shop Quinn used, and one from a frame shop for the same reason. She'd kept the amounts for both modest, but there was enough money to get one nice print and frame.

"Wow, Nicole," Quinn said, slipping the gift cards back in their envelopes. "That was a good idea. And I like the clothing, too."

"Even the socks? I kind of went overboard. I love socks so much. Maybe I was sort of buying them for myself, too."

Quinn shook her head. "I love them. It'll be nice to wear them. It will make me think of you."

They both grinned and kissed again, and the longer they kissed, the more that low warmth she'd been suppressing for the last stretch of time together started to rise to a steady heat.

Quinn pulled back first, laughing weakly.

"I don't know how I'm going to get through dinner tonight without wanting to take your clothes off all over again."

Nicole laughed, weakly. "We'll make sure we sit apart. No touching."

Quinn smiled. "Right. No touching."

They both scooted apart, as much as they could on the loveseat, and then gave each other goofy grins.

"Last one," Nicole said, pointing at the two remaining presents. "You first."

Quinn pouted but nodded before opening the last gift. It was probably clear from the long velvet box what Quinn was going to find inside, and her eyes met Nicole's briefly before opening it. Nicole had given her silver-and-aquamarine earrings and a necklace. They were made from Colorado silver and gems by an artist in a nearby former mining town. Nicole had driven there to look for something for her mom, had found a nice pair of earrings for her, and had almost left before this set caught her eye. The color of the gemstone was the same as Quinn's eyes. She'd stared at it long enough that the salesperson had come over to her and convinced her, without much struggle, to buy the whole set. She'd been tempted to return it several times in the last two weeks, or give it to her mom, who would also love it, but she'd decided, in the end, that this was just the kind of thing she'd wanted to find for Quinn.

Quinn hadn't reacted to the gift yet, sitting stiffly, and Nicole's stomach clenched with dread the longer Quinn simply sat there, staring at it. Finally, she looked up with tears in her eyes.

"Oh, Nicole," she said, whispering. "They're beautiful."

"It's your birthstone. And—"

"The Colorado state gem. I know. Thank you. It's always been my favorite."

"You like them?"

A single tear fell from one of Quinn's eyes before she launched herself at Nicole and squeezed her in a hug. She pulled away, both cheeks tear-stained now. "No, silly. I love them."

Nicole relaxed and wiped her brow. "Whew! I got worried there for a minute."

"You shouldn't have," Quinn said, wiping her eyes. Her expression fell. "Though I wish you'd opened mine first. It's going to be a letdown after this."

Nicole rolled her eyes and pulled the large present into her lap. Like the velvet box, the shape made it clear what she'd find when she ripped off the paper—framed artwork—but when the picture was revealed, she was still pleasantly surprised. The print was a professional-grade copy of Quinn's photograph of the otters. She'd admired them before, and that version was still hanging on Quinn's wall, but this was clearly a higher-quality print and frame job.

"Stupid, right?" Quinn asked, her face pale, her expression almost scared.

Realizing that she needed to get this completely and totally right, Nicole waited until Quinn's eyes met hers before responding.

"Are you kidding me? Quinn—I love it. No one ever gives me photographs, and this one is so wonderful. I love their expressions, and I love the contrast of the water and the animals with the snow. It's really beautiful."

She set the framed work down and hugged Quinn firmly.

"I love it," she said into her hair. "It's one of the nicest things anyone has ever given me."

Quinn pulled back, her expression wide and surprised. "You mean it?"

"I do. You couldn't have gotten me something I'd love more. I hope—"

She realized she'd nearly said too much. She'd almost told her that she hoped their place together would have lots of their art on the walls. She chuckled to cover her near slip and finished instead with, "I mean I hope you know I love your work."

Mazzy Star started playing on the Bluetooth, and Quinn jerked her head that way before peering up at Nicole.

"Do you remember?" she asked. "When this song played at the hotel, in our room?"

This exchange was as near as they'd gotten to actually talking about that night since that brief exchange at the ski resort, and suddenly Nicole did remember. This was the song that had been playing when Quinn left her there in their room, alone.

"Yes," Nicole finally said, almost breathless. The memory explained, now, why Quinn had been so quick to turn this same song off when it played in the car a couple of weeks ago. It reminded her of that awful night.

Quinn smiled up at her, her eyes tear-stained again, and when they kissed, this time neither of them bothered to slow things down or pull away, moving, soon after, back to the bed. It didn't make up for that lost night all those years ago, but now it almost seemed as if they'd finally and entirely moved past it.

CHAPTER TWENTY: QUINN

As she and her friends climbed up the hill, dragging two toboggans, Quinn couldn't help but notice how many children were here this morning. She should have expected there would be a million kids trying out their new sleds the day after Christmas, but the idea simply hadn't crossed her mind. The kids' parents and some other family members were here, too, making theirs the only group that differed from everyone else's. If it bothered Nicole or her friends, they weren't letting on, but Quinn found herself somewhat reluctant to stand too close to Nicole. She was also worried that Dane and Rico might give themselves away. Nicole, as if sensing this dilemma, threw her concerned glances, and Quinn tried her best to wave it off. The past two days had been absolute bliss, after all, and the last thing Quinn wanted to do was bring anyone down.

Last night at Christmas dinner, for example, she'd been happier than she could remember being. Nicole had been worried that her mom would tease them for spending the night together. Quinn had been a bit embarrassed to be around her dad, too, knowing that he was aware that Nicole had stayed over, but both of their parents had been completely lovely about it—greeting them as if the day was like any other, not the most important one Quinn could remember in years. Her dad had also been clearly and gloriously happy—far more than she could remember seeing. In fact, seeing him and Annette together, obviously wrapped up in each other, was almost as wonderful as her feelings for Nicole. The four of them had a nice dinner, played cards, watched the end of a Christmas movie, and then, when Nicole casually told her mom she was going back to Quinn's, both of their parents had once again been entirely casual about it.

She and Nicole had another incredible night together, and now they were going sledding with her best friends. So no, she absolutely didn't want to ruin any of that with her own anxiety. If Nicole and the others didn't mind that the five of them stood out, she would try not to mind herself.

Still, when Nicole held out her hand near the top of the first hill, Quinn didn't reach for it. Nicole frowned and stepped closer, speaking low enough that the others couldn't hear her.

"Is something the matter?"

Quinn shook her head. "No. I'm sorry. I'm just not used to..." She gestured, vaguely, at the crowds around them. "Being in the open, I guess."

Nicole's brow creased. "What? You mean like out? In front of strangers? You kissed me when we were in Aspen—at the restaurant, I mean."

Quinn shrugged and shook her head. "I know, but that was different. Everyone there was an adult, and I was so relieved that you and my dad were okay. I don't know if I would have done it, otherwise. But here? In front of lots of families, kids? We might...I don't know. Offend someone, I guess."

Nicole shrugged. "Who cares? And anyway, no one is going to notice us. They're all wrapped up in their own lives."

Quinn quelled a surge of frustrated nerves, and she turned away from Nicole to hide her expression. Her friends were horsing around in the snow, both Molly and Rico trying to drag the massive Dane to the ground and into a snowbank. They were laughing and nearly hysterical, and Nicole chuckled next to her as they watched them. Again, Quinn told herself to let go of her nerves. They'd been having such a good time, and everyone but her was enjoying this.

"Okay, okay," Nicole said, approaching the others. "Break it up, you guys. We haven't even gone down a single time yet, and it took forever to get up here."

"It took forever because you chose the highest hill!" Dane said.

"And me and Dane had to drag the sleds!" Rico added. "If we'd chosen one of the other hills, we could have used the tow-line."

Nicole held her hands up in a sign of defeat. "You're right, you're right. But now that we're here, maybe we can actually go sledding? Please?"

Rico peered down the hill and shook his head. "No way. I'm gonna walk down."

Molly laughed. "What? Why?"

"Too steep."

Molly laughed again. "Are you kidding me? Aren't you like almost a professional skier?"

Rico shook his head. "That's different. I'm in control when I'm skiing. I've never sledded like this."

"Ridiculous," Molly said, shaking her head.

"It's okay, honey," Dane said, pulling him close with one arm and kissing the side of his head. "You go down and take pictures of us."

Molly rolled her eyes. "Fine. But Dane—you're with me on the big one. I want to go fast. Nicole and Quinn, you can have the smaller one for yourselves."

She said this as if she were doing Quinn a favor, but as the four of them settled on the toboggans, still waiting for Rico to get back to the bottom, Quinn couldn't help the bubble of nerves roiling her stomach. Nicole's arms and legs were wrapped around her from behind. Anyone watching them could see that they were together. They wouldn't be sitting this way if they weren't.

Nicole's chin was on her left shoulder, her breath ghosting her ear. Quinn closed her eyes, trying to enjoy the sensation, but her anxiety was getting worse the longer they sat here. Friends wouldn't sit like this, would they? Not this long, anyway.

"You're stiff as a board," Nicole said. "Are you nervous?"

She was, in a way, though not in the way Nicole meant. "A little."

"Don't be. I was going down this hill when I was a kid. I'm sure I can get us safely to the bottom. Keep your feet up and relax—I'll steer with mine."

Quinn tried to do that, closing her eyes again and taking deep breaths. She and Nicole were cuddling on a sled in one of the most beautiful places in the whole world. The piercing sun in the bright, cloudless mountain sky was like a halo, shining down on a perfect, fresh layer of snow. People were laughing, joking around much like her friends had been doing. Kids were squealing with joy, and parents and grandparents were snapping memories on their phones and cameras. Beyond all the beauty, happiness, and joy around her, she'd just had two days of incredible sex with the woman of her dreams. And Nicole had been accepted by her best friends as if she'd always been part of their group. Nothing could be better.

She opened her eyes and made herself release some of her concern, a real smile rising to her lips. If someone had a problem with the two of them, she needed to learn how to care less. She'd never been this happy. She turned awkwardly in the sled and pulled Nicole into a loose hug.

"Thank you for being here today. I know you and your mom usually go to the springs—"

Nicole kissed her temple—the only part of Quinn she could reach from behind her.

"Of course! And this is super fun. Mom and I can swim later, whenever we're done here. You and the others can come too, of course. My mom likes everyone."

Quinn's mind flashed back to Nicole's curves in a swimsuit, and she had to suppress a shudder of longing.

"Sounds nice. A soak in the springs after this would be perfect."

"Mmm," Nicole said, resting her chin on Quinn's shoulder again. The humming seemed to reverberate throughout Quinn's body.

"Rico signaled!" Dane said. "He's in position at the bottom."

"I wish I could have given him a better camera," Quinn said, thinking of the collection she'd started of Nicole and Nicole with her friends and family. The Christmas photos from her phone had turned out okay, but cameras were always better.

"That's okay," Nicole said. "It doesn't have to be a good photo."

"You guys ready?" Dane asked.

"Ready!" they all shouted.

All four of them laughed most of the way down. Dane and Molly were right next to them almost the entire time, and then they had to swerve rather dramatically around a child that spilled off his saucer right in front of them. Quinn was too focused on the hill in front of their toboggan to watch what happened, but she could hear Molly laughing and judged, correctly as it turned out, that everything was fine. Nicole was, as she'd claimed, an expert, making small corrections as they sailed down the hill that seemed as smooth and natural as someone steering a car. They came to a soft stop a few feet from Rico, who was still taking pictures with his phone. He paused before laughing and pointing up behind them. She and Nicole turned and saw Molly and Dane several feet from their upended toboggan. Dane's feet were pointed up the hill, and he was spread-eagle on his back. Molly was sitting up, laughing hard, her face pink from the cold snow bath they'd clearly undergone.

"Are you guys okay?" Quinn shouted, hands cupped around her mouth.

Molly waved a hand at them, seemingly weak from laughter. Dane lifted one thumb and then dropped it back into the snow.

When they finally made it back down, dragging the toboggan behind them, the five of them decided that, despite having only done one single run, they'd take a break for refreshments. The warming hut only had very small and nonalcoholic hot drinks, but Molly had a little bottle of Irish crème liquor in her pocket from Christmas Eve. She shared a splash in everyone's cocoa. They spent the greater part of the morning there at the hut, getting a cocoa and chatting and laughing between the three other runs they did.

"I'm starving," Molly said as they bought their fourth mini cup of cocoa.

"Same," Dane and Rico said.

"We should go back to town for lunch," Quinn said.

"But we barely did anything today!" Nicole said. "What, four runs, total?"

"You on some kind of schedule, or something?" Molly asked.

Nicole laughed and shook her head. "Not exactly. We can always come back some other time, I guess."

"Nicole and her mom are going to the springs after this," Quinn explained.

"Did you want to come with?" Nicole asked everyone.

Quinn and her friends exchanged glances before everyone shrugged or nodded.

"Sure," Dane said. "Sounds nice, actually. It's pretty out today with the sun and all, but I'm kind of cold anyway."

"I'm freezing," Rico said, shuddering. "You all have been exercising, at least, but standing around in the snow is chilly-willy."

"The springs would definitely be great after lunch," Molly said, rubbing her shoulder. "It was funny, but that first fall kind of hurt."

"Great," Nicole said, smiling widely. "I know my mom will be happy to see everyone again."

Quinn's heart lifted. Her friends had every excuse to dodge and do their own thing, but they wanted to join them. It meant a lot to her that they all got along like they did. She couldn't remember a time when she'd dated anyone that even wanted to meet her friends, let alone someone that genuinely clicked with them like this.

A couple hours later, after a light lunch and some time apart to get ready, everyone was in the hotter thermal pool with Quinn's dad and Nicole's mom. All seven of them were lined up in the heated jet seats. Quinn was sandwiched between her dad and Nicole, and when she leaned forward a bit, she could see all her friends beyond Nicole, eyes closed and enjoying the hot, soaking massage. She closed her eyes again, leaning into the bubbling jets. She couldn't remember the last time she'd been this relaxed. Being here, surrounded by the people she loved the most, was an extra bonus.

Nicole suddenly stood and moved away, farther into the pool and away from the jets, her swimsuit-clad chest and shoulders exposed. She waved a hand in front of her face and panted dramatically.

"Way too hot," she said, unnecessarily.

Nicole's mom Annette also stood up and moved closer to her daughter, waving a hand in front of her face.

"I agree. I can't take this hotter pool for very long."

"Wimps!" Quinn said, laughing.

Nicole and Annette stuck their tongues out at the same time, making everyone laugh.

"Anyone want to go to the cooler pool with us?" Nicole said, gesturing. She was giving Quinn a hopeful smile, but Quinn shook her head.

"Maybe once my jets turn off. I want to get extra cooked before that."

"Same," her dad said.

"Me, too," Rico said, sliding closer to Quinn.

Molly and Dane, however, joined Nicole and her mom, and Quinn watched them walk away together, up and out of the thermal pool and into the cooler swimming pool nearby.

"She looks great in that suit," Rico said.

Quinn laughed at him, and he winked.

"It's true," he said. "Not a lot of women can pull that gothy, vampy look off so well, even in a swimsuit. She's nice, she's smart, and she's very pretty."

Quinn was strangely flattered, as if Nicole's good looks and personality spoke well of her, somehow. She squeezed Rico's hand under the water and bumped his shoulder with hers. He was always the quieter of the couple, but that meant that when he said something, people tended to pay attention and, in her case now, believe him.

"She is, isn't she?"

"You got a real catch there, honey," her dad chimed in, clearly overhearing their entire exchange.

"Thanks, Dad."

The three of them sat there in the hotter thermal pool a while longer, Quinn wondering, a little less than idly, how long she and Nicole needed to stay before they could excuse themselves and go back to her place. Nicole might look very good in a swimsuit, but now Quinn knew she looked even better without one.

CHAPTER TWENTY-ONE: NICOLE

"I think you're getting better at this," Nicole said as Quinn finally made it to the bottom of the ski slope.

Quinn came to a wobbly stop, paused, frozen in place for a long moment as if uncertain of her balance, and then stood entirely upright, balancing her entire weight on her ski poles, still shaky. Her face was strained with anxiety, and another few seconds passed before the corners of her mouth pinched into a tight, false smile. Nicole moved closer, careful to avoid crossing their skis.

She had been giving Quinn informal ski lessons for the last hour. Initially, Nicole had suggested that Quinn enroll in one of the beginners' courses, but all of them had been filled with kids, and Quinn had been too embarrassed to join them. Nicole had talked her into trying to ski with her coaching, and after a few fake and short runs without poles to practice stance and balance, they'd just done the easiest green with poles together.

"Are you okay?" Nicole asked.

Quinn shook her head. "I mean, I didn't die, but I also didn't like that one bit."

Nicole grimaced. "I'm sorry, Quinn. I shouldn't have forced you to try. I know you weren't that jazzed about it."

Quinn shrugged and shook her head. "No—that's not it, Nicole. It's not your fault. I could have said no. Like I said, I've always wanted to know how to ski. But I guess I'm too much of a fraidy cat."

Nicole shook her head. "That's not true. It's actually pretty scary. I mean, jeez, you're basically sliding down a snowy hill on two pieces of wood. But you will get better if you want to keep trying."

Quinn's expression showed her disbelief, and Nicole's stomach twisted with guilt. Quinn had clearly gone along with this to please her, and she shouldn't push her limits further.

The weather today was brisk, but with an occasional gust of warmer wind that forecast snow. Today was incredibly sunny with the bright blue sky, blindingly bright on the snowy slopes. Despite the warm breeze, Quinn looked cold, miserable, and eager to stop. Nicole decided that she needed to give her an easy out.

"What say we get a drink?" Nicole asked. "Warm up a bit?"

Quinn dropped her shoulders, obviously relieved, and then she checked her watch. "I'd like to, but do we have time?"

Nicole checked hers. They were meeting with John, the city's tourism commissioner, this evening. Quinn had worked this morning at the studio, so they hadn't gotten to Aspen until almost one, a little over two hours ago.

"We have enough time for a quick one if we hurry," Nicole said. "Let's return our skis first, though."

This was luckily easier than she'd anticipated, the crowds strangely absent today, and soon they were seated inside the lodge, at the very table they'd been with their folks a few days ago. With the windows dampening the lovely sunshine a bit, they had a gorgeous view of the ski slopes rising outside their window.

Quinn took a long, deep swallow of her Irish coffee, her eyes closed. She hummed happily, and Nicole was struck, once again, by how much she liked being with this woman. It didn't hurt, of course, that she was pretty and smart and successful, but she was also a lovely person. They had such a nice, easy time together. And Quinn's friends were super sweet, her dad seemed to like Nicole, and Nicole's mom was basically in love with Quinn. And now Quinn was here, trying something that clearly made her very anxious, just so she could spend time with Nicole today. The sun was making her hair seem extra light and luminous, and when she opened her eyes, Nicole was stuck once again by how blue those eyes were—startling, even.

Quinn wrinkled her nose playfully. "You have that look on your face again. I thought we were past that."

"What look?"

Quinn rolled her eyes. "You know—that one." She made a blank expression, widening her eyes and opening her mouth stupidly before shaking her head as if dazed.

Nicole snorted and decided to pretend she didn't know what she meant. "No, I don't. You'll have to tell me."

Quinn's cheeks reddened, and she opened her mouth, hesitating before saying, "You look like you're struck completely dumb by the sight of me."

Nicole leaned forward across the small table and took both of Quinn's hands in her own. "That's because I am—every time I look at you. My friends in high school used to say that I was hit by the stupid stick when I saw you in the halls."

Quinn laughed. "And you are now? Still?"

Nicole nodded. Quinn's glance darted away, and it took everything in Nicole's willpower not to grab her and kiss her senseless right then and there. Quinn's modesty was unearned. She would clearly never see herself the way others saw her, which was a terrible shame, but Nicole could try to show her anyway. She leaned forward for a sensible, public kiss, but Quinn moved back abruptly, pulling her hands from Nicole's.

"What—" Nicole said.

"Can I get you ladies anything else?" their waiter asked.

"Uh, no," Quinn said, blushing furiously. "Just the check, please."

He walked away, and Nicole jerked a thumb in his direction. "Worried he'll report us?"

Quinn shook her head, frowning. "I'm sorry, Nicole. I'm not used to being open like that. Out in public, I mean."

Nicole remembered that Quinn had been nervous about this yesterday, too, when they'd been sledding with their friends. Nicole had dismissed it at the time, and Quinn had seemed to get over whatever had bothered her, but with the sleds and later the hot springs, the two of them hadn't been affectionate at all beyond some light, non-physical flirting. Quinn was clearly embarrassed now, troubled even, and Nicole realized in an instant that she shouldn't brush Quinn's feelings off so lightly this time.

"Hey," Nicole said, leaning closer and lowering her voice. She was careful not to reach for her hands again, despite her instinct to do so. "We don't have to do anything you're not comfortable with. I'm sorry I didn't listen to you yesterday."

Quinn shook her head. "No, Nicole. That's not right. You should be able to act any way you want to. It's me. I've never…been open like you are when I'm dating someone."

"Never?"

Quinn shook her head. "No. Not at all. Certainly not in Glenwood."

"If you don't mind me asking, why?"

Quinn shrugged, her eyes still not meeting hers. "I guess I was afraid of what other people in town might think if they saw us. They might, I don't know, boycott the store or something."

Nicole could understand this reasoning on some level. When she'd lived in Glenwood as a kid, the town, like a lot of Colorado then, had been pretty conservative. But the demographics of the state had shifted a lot in the last twenty years, and so had Glenwood itself. Colorado was rather firmly liberal now in a lot of areas, and even Glenwood Springs was more progressive than it had been. She'd noticed a number of stores and restaurants with rainbow stickers in the window, and a lot of queer tourists over the last few weeks, and no one had seemed bothered in the least by the sight of anyone holding hands in the streets.

But of course, all of this was much easier to see as an outsider. Nicole had left and only came back periodically, which made the changes in town that much starker. Quinn would always find it harder to recognize these changes because she'd been here in the middle of them. Quinn looked extremely uneasy right now, and Nicole recognized the need to phrase the next thing she said very carefully.

"Listen, Quinn—this goes both ways, okay? Do you remember when we first kissed? Up at the cemetery?"

"Of course."

"And you wanted to wait to tell your friends?"

"Yes."

"I was fine with that. Really. Did I want to tell them? Of course I did, but that wasn't what *you* wanted. And I was totally okay with that. But then later, when you were comfortable, you *did* tell them, because you knew how important it was for me to be open with our friends. Do you see what I mean? Things have to go both ways."

Quinn hesitated before letting out a long, shaky breath. Some of the tension seemed to ease out of her shoulders. "Okay. I believe you. I guess I was worried you'd...get sick of catering to me, or something. It's stupid."

"It's not stupid, Quinn. You're allowed to have feelings and opinions. You're allowed to be nervous at the start of a relationship."

"It's, well—I'm sure you've dated all sorts of women who will do anything in public—"

Nicole frowned. "I don't know what kind of life you think I've led, but that's not true at all. And anyway, those other women don't matter. You're the woman I'm with now, Quinn."

Quinn squinted at her for a couple of seconds, her gaze roaming over her face. Finally, she smiled, genuinely this time.

"Okay, Nicole. I believe you. And thanks."

"Sure thing, hon."

"Hon?"

"Should it be baby, instead?"

Quinn almost sneered and shook her head. "No. That's gross. Too…infantilizing or something."

"Okay. How about 'sugar'?"

Quinn pretended to think about it. "It's fine. Whatever you want."

"Okay, hon."

The check came then, and they paid and made their way back to Nicole's car. They'd gotten lucky despite arriving so late in the day— the car was close to the lodge, which meant that by the time they were driving out of Aspen, they still had plenty of time to make it to their appointment with John.

"Why did he want to meet so late in the day again?" Quinn asked.

"I guess it was the only time he could fit us in. With the holidays, he probably had some catching up to do, or at least that's what he suggested yesterday when I called."

When they'd sent him their photos last Friday, they'd decided to send everything sorted together by theme. That meant that John would see their work blended, anonymous to a certain extent. Nicole wasn't sure what the process today would be like—whether he would choose which photos to use now, or if he was reviewing with them at this point, but she was still glad they had decided to attempt to remove some of the bias that might come up if they submitted separately.

As they drove, the sun was setting, but a light orange glow in the sky from the sunset gave off enough light to illuminate the snowy, pine-covered hills around them. The road was clear of snow, the traffic was light, and they drove into Glenwood with enough time to pick up three takeaway coffees before parking at city hall. The building was already closed for the day, but John had told her to come around back to the delivery entrance and call him when they arrived. He appeared almost at once, as if he'd been waiting for them, and they followed him upstairs into the boardroom where they'd met him just over three weeks ago.

Thinking back on that meeting, Nicole had to smile. She'd been so anxious to be here, next to Quinn, that she had barely been able to focus on anything John was saying. Sitting next to her again, after all that time, had been far more unnerving than she could have ever anticipated. And now here they were, friends again and lovers, and the interim between that moment three weeks ago and now seemed both very long and almost as if they'd just been here.

John seemed bedraggled and worn, his suit wrinkled, the top two buttons on his shirt undone, and his tie loose and crooked. He took the coffee from Quinn gratefully and sat down, indicating two chairs to his left. He'd set up a large, flat-screen monitor that was almost as big as a television across from the three of them. He had a laptop hooked so the monitor showed what was on his screen.

"Okay, ladies! I think I've got this right now. I'm not the tech-savviest, so my assistant set this up. Basically, we're going to look at everything together, and I'll tell you what I think and start a list of what to use. If we need to do some reshoots, we'll make a separate list, but from the quick review I gave them last night, I don't think we need any. Sound good?"

They both agreed, but Nicole was suddenly nervous. It didn't matter how long she'd been in the business, she was always anxious when her work was reviewed. It had something to do with the nature of art itself, as far as she could tell. It went from something private, almost intimate, when you were creating it, to something public. Quinn looked similarly anxious, lips thin, her hands gripped together on the table, almost twisting on themselves.

It took a moment for John to find and open the first batch of photos he wanted to review, but he finally started with the folder labelled "Animals." Nicole could recognize her own, clearly lower-quality work mixed in with the various shots of the elk and then watched as photo after photo of various birds and animals Quinn had shot scrolled by. Nicole had seen some of these, of course, when they had sent their photos last Friday, but she was still blown away by the quality and quantity of Quinn's shots. Some of the animals featured here were species Nicole had never seen in the wild, despite a lifetime of living almost exclusively in the state.

John was making little sounds in his throat as he scrolled through them, pausing on each photo for a couple of moments and making a note with each on a legal pad next to him. Almost all of this specific folder was Quinn's work, and Nicole couldn't have been prouder of her. Her work was gorgeous. John hit the end of the folder and left the screen on a stunning shot of a colorful bird mid-flight. The detail on the feathers and the bird's gleaming, beady black eyes were incredibly beautiful, and possibly one of the best wildlife photos Nicole had ever seen. He turned toward them, eyes wide.

"Wow. Just wow. We've got an incredible panel of animals here. I don't see any need to add to this, so we're done in this category. If either of you manages to get something we missed in the next couple of weeks, I'm happy to slip it in later, but we can safely focus elsewhere with the time we have left. These are absolutely breathtaking. They're even more stunning here on the big screen. The two of you are incredible."

Nicole gestured broadly at Quinn. "It's almost all her this time, John. Only a few of mine were in there."

John read from his legal pad. "Let me guess: shots A011, 16, 21, 25, 36, and 40?"

Nicole double-checked her notes. "You're exactly right. Those are mine."

John grinned. "No offense to you, but yes, it was obvious one of you was the expert here. The quality doesn't compare."

The two of them finally looked at Quinn, whose face was contorted with warring emotion. She seemed, on the one hand, incredibly proud. She was fighting an enormous grin, basically, but every time she met Nicole's eyes, that grin faded a bit and her brow contorted. She reached out and touched Nicole's hand.

"I'm sorry, Nicole."

Nicole shook her head. "We always knew that your animals were better than mine by a long shot. You don't have to feel bad, Quinn. This is obviously your strength." She gestured at the screen. "That little bird is one of the most beautiful things I've ever seen. Don't feel guilty. Feel proud."

Quinn's eyes teared up a little, and she leaned closer, pulling Nicole into a tight hug. She stayed there in her arms long enough that Nicole saw John shift in his chair, uncomfortably, and when they moved apart, he appeared puzzled.

He shrugged and faced his laptop again, this time opening the folder for the fake wedding. There were far more photographs in this folder, and it took much longer to get through them. Despite positioning themselves in different parts of the venue, she saw a lot of overlap between Quinn's photos and her own. John paused far longer on several shots, going back and forth between similar photos several times until he found the ones he preferred, apparently, and made a note. Finally, he made it to the end of the folder and swiveled his chair their way again.

"These are also excellent. I think the Sunlight Resort will be extremely pleased with the way they turned out. You highlight the beauty of the lodge and the ski slopes and surroundings, and the guests came out well, too. You'd never know the wedding was staged." He paused, meeting their eyes. "I also know that the two of you submitted these blindly, and I can totally respect that fact. I would call this category finished, since I think you got all the shots we need. So, if you're satisfied to have me make the choices, we can leave it there and move on."

"That sounds good—" Nicole said.

"No," Quinn said. "I'd like to know which ones you chose."

Nicole stared at her, frowning. "What? We agreed—"

Quinn glared back at her, her expression dark. "No, Nicole. You decided that for both of us. I'd like to know."

"But—"

"Uh," John said, standing up. "How about I give the two of you a moment to discuss. My wife texted a bit ago, so I should call her."

He nearly ran from the room, and she and Quinn were left alone.

"What is this about, Quinn? I thought you wanted unbiased results."

Quinn shook her head. "Listen, Nicole, I get why you wanted to do that. And you're right. I think we should let him choose blindly. But I also want to know, for my own sake, if he's choosing any of my work."

"Why?"

Quinn's expression darkened further. "I know you're trying to protect my feelings, Nicole—"

"What? That's not remotely true!"

"But I want to know. I need to know if I'm any good. That's all there is to it."

Nicole couldn't help a stab of something close to dismay. They'd discussed this very scenario together and decided that making the entire process anonymous was better for both of them, so they could avoid situations like this, when someone might get upset or even defensive. Nicole hadn't been hurt by the wildlife photos because she wasn't, herself, a wildlife expert. She'd expected that John would choose Quinn's photos. What she hadn't wanted was some kind of competition with the other categories, and that's exactly what Quinn seemed to be asking for now. Quinn still looked hard, stubborn, and Nicole could tell there would be no dissuading her, not here, not now, anyway, which meant she couldn't do anything about it, no matter how terrible this could be.

Nicole sighed. "If that's the way you want it, Quinn, then fine."

"Fine."

They sat in, for Nicole, frustrated silence until John returned, and his happy expression fell at the sight of their dour faces. He cleared his throat, clearly uncomfortable again, and sat down.

"So you want to know?" he asked them.

Quinn nodded at once, and Nicole did after a long, awkward pause.

She'd been dreading the outcome, because as she'd partly expected, and as was revealed as he read through his list, most of the photos he chose were Nicole's. Nicole had hoped that the ratio would be closer to half and half, and they could put this whole thing behind them, but in the end, he chose about forty of her shots and twenty of Quinn's. Not all of these would actually be used. In the end, the Sunlight Mountain Resort would have the final say in what they wanted, but that discrepancy meant that far more of Nicole's photos would likely end up on the city website and on the resort's website and brochures than Quinn's.

Quinn was rigid next to her, and pale, her hands now clasped on the arms of her chair as if the room were shaking. John watched her, too, appearing troubled and worried, and he and Nicole shared a long, silent glance, an entire conversation exchanged in that moment. He seemed to know what had happened without her explaining.

"Er, uh, should we go on?" he asked. "We could meet again tomorrow—"

"I want to finish this," Quinn said, her voice low and angry, almost a growl.

"Quinn, I think we should—"

"What? What do you think?" Quinn snapped, looking at her for the first time in the last several minutes. Her eyes were red, clouded with tears.

Nicole shrugged, weakly, raising her hands. "We don't have to do this, you know. We could let him choose."

"Now I *know* you're trying to protect my feelings," Quinn said, her voice still harsh with anger, hurt. "I don't need saving. Okay?"

Nicole could hardly believe what she was hearing. Not even an hour ago, everyone had been happy, excited even, and now Quinn was acting as if she'd been betrayed, deceived somehow. Beyond this, Quinn was acting this way in front of what amounted to a colleague—a kind of boss, even. Her behavior was incredibly immature and unprofessional. Beyond her own hurt, Nicole was beginning to fight a rising anger, not entirely at Quinn per se, though she certainly wasn't innocent here, but at the whole situation. They could have easily avoided this problem by simply letting John choose without them here. She should have foreseen this exact situation, and maybe, on some level, she had when she'd insisted on sending the photos blind. Maybe Quinn was right. Maybe, if she was being honest with herself, she had wanted to protect Quinn's feelings.

"Fine," Nicole said, leaning back into her chair, unable to hide her own anger. "Please go on, John."

The process for the rest of the photos followed along the same lines. It took a long while to get through each of the folders—half an hour to forty-five minutes in most cases. After each folder was finished, Quinn would insist on knowing which photos John had chosen, both of them hearing, every time, the vast discrepancy between Nicole's photos and her own, almost always a ratio of about 2 to 1 and, in one case, almost 3 to 1. In some instances, the results were even worse. They had both taken photographs alone, after all, since they had divided most of the list. John wanted some reshoots of some of the photos, and all the reshoots he requested were from Quinn's solo shoots.

As the evening turned late, Quinn seemed to close in on herself more and more, hunching up in her chair, refusing to look at Nicole or take the hand Nicole offered a few times, cringing away when Nicole tried to lean closer. Even John seemed cowed, clearly more and more reluctant to continue as the night wore on.

When they did finally finish, the three of them sat in stunned silence, as if after a shared trauma, which is exactly how it seemed to Nicole. She could no longer even look at Quinn, afraid that if she did, she'd burst into tears. She could only sense her there to her right, frozen in place like a sentinel.

John was talking quietly, gravely even, as if to spooked children. He reminded them that they had just over two weeks to finish the rest of the shoots and reshoots. He gave them a list of the ones they had to take, as well as some optional ones should they find the time. He also gave them their press packets for the New Year's Eve ball this weekend. After that, he basically rushed them out of the building, clearly glad to be rid of them.

The street was dark and silent, the air piercingly cold at this late hour.

"Here," Quinn said, shoving her copy of the list at Nicole. "You take it."

"I have my own," Nicole said.

"I don't need it," Quinn said, and when Nicole still didn't take it, Quinn threw hers on the ground and turned and started walking away.

"Quinn!" Nicole said, leaping forward and reaching for her arm.

Quinn rounded on her, eyes blazing, and yanked her arm free. "Don't touch me!"

Nicole froze, so hurt and startled she had no response. She saw Quinn's rage falter, her brow furrowing briefly with concern, but that hard anger came back into her eyes all at once.

"Things were always going to work out like this, Nicole," Quinn spat. "Once I saw your name in that folder three weeks ago, I don't know why I even tried."

"Quinn—"

"I need to be alone. Okay? I can't be near you right now."

She turned and started walking away again, and Nicole called after her.

"You're talented, too! You know you are! This isn't fair!"

Quinn didn't respond, still walking away.

"Damn it, Quinn! Don't do this to us! I don't care about any of it! I don't care about anything but you! Don't you understand?"

Quinn still didn't respond, fading, eventually, into the dark, cold night. Nicole let out a long, frustrated groan, wanting, more than anything, to erase the last few hours of their lives.

CHAPTER TWENTY-TWO: QUINN

Quinn sat behind the front counter of her Old West photo studio sewing a small patch in the seat of a pair of trousers. They were fashioned to look like they were from the nineteenth century, though they included a zipper and elastic for modern-day comfort. Over the years, she had become something of an expert at repairs like this. When she'd worked for her dad, he'd fixed a lot of the props at the studio himself, but he'd always hired out the clothing repairs. Quinn had seen one of the bills and, wanting to see if she could learn how and save them some money, she'd taken some tailoring and sewing classes at the community college. Now, except for more serious issues, she could fix almost any of the props, most of which needed monthly if not weekly repair, especially now that they'd been so busy with the holiday crowds.

Yesterday, she'd come down here to the studio from her apartment in the middle of the night—long before the store opened—to work. After everything that had gone down with Nicole and John over at city hall, she couldn't sleep at all, but her insomnia had its advantages. Not only could she repair the props that needed it, the tedious, nitpicky work itself kept her mind gloriously free of thought. Between repairs and the overabundance of holiday tourists once she'd opened that morning, she'd kept busy all day. She even allowed some latecomers to enter a couple of minutes before closing time, something she never did, just so she could use up part of her evening. By the time she'd stumbled upstairs, she'd been so exhausted, she simply collapsed in her bed.

This morning, even though it was Saturday, their busiest day any week, let alone during the holidays, she'd sent her assistant Kim home for the day when she showed up. She did this in part out of guilt—Kim had worked a lot lately to cover for her, and she'd earned it. But Quinn also sent her home because she couldn't force herself to make small talk with her employee. She could fake friendliness with customers—that was second nature at this point, regardless of her mood—but if Kim stayed, she'd end up spilling everything, possibly even crying in front of her, and that couldn't happen.

Moreover, Quinn had wanted to use the store's business to keep her mind occupied, and it had worked for a while. She'd been slammed all morning, but now in the late afternoon, the studio was strangely empty. Most weekends were busy all day all winter, especially around Christmas and New Year. She kept poking her head outside, wondering where everyone was, but even the streets were empty. There were no big sporting events on TV today, as far as she could tell, and the news was blissfully light, so she could only imagine that everyone had decided, as a collective, to take it easy back at their hotels. Three customers had even called to cancel their evening appointments. Strange. Still, she'd had enough repairs piled up from the holidays to stay busy. Until now. So she sat, completely motionless for the first time in thirty-six hours. Memories of city hall, of that awful, terrible evening, started to bubble up, and she couldn't think of any way to distract herself.

It had been high school all over again. Eighteen years ago, she'd been an asshole to Nicole over more or less the same thing, and she had blamed Nicole for something that had everything to do with her, Quinn, and nothing to do with Nicole. Nicole's talent had won her that scholarship, while Quinn's lack of confidence had meant she hadn't even tried. And now, Nicole's talent had simply meant that John preferred more of her photos over Quinn's. Simple as that.

Yet Quinn had acted as if Nicole had betrayed her, personally, somehow. She could remember her anger, and she'd known in some part of her heart and mind that her rage was misdirected, but she hadn't been able to control her hurt at the time. Even now, when she pictured sitting there in that boardroom, listening as John chose Nicole's photos over and over again instead of hers, asking her and her alone for reshoots, that same frustrated rage threatened to boil over. Now, even when she could recognize how awful and petty and immature she had been, she couldn't help but feel, in some, not-so-small part of her, justified in her anger. The shame of recognizing this fact made her sick.

"You're a goddamn asshole, Quinn Zelinski," she whispered to herself.

Tears threatened, and she stood up quickly, scanning the room for a project, any project, she could turn her attention to for a while. She couldn't be idle and alone with herself, or she'd completely lose it.

The sleigh bells on the door saved her, and she spun that way, a wide, customer-service smile in place, but saw only Molly.

One look was enough to see that something was wrong. Molly had dark, exhausted rings around her red-rimmed eyes. Her usually sunny complexion was pale, almost gray, and her hair was greasy and lank. Alarmed, Quinn took a step toward her, arms opening, but Molly threw up her hands to hold her back.

"I need to say something to you," Molly said. Her tone was dark, angry and low, voice shaking slightly.

Quinn stopped at once, realization sweeping through her with something like horror.

Molly cleared her throat a couple of times, her eyes shifting to the ceiling. She blinked rapidly a few times, obviously trying not to cry. She swallowed again, and her expression hardened.

"You're a goddamn asshole, Quinn," Molly said.

Quinn, remembering her own whispered curse minutes ago, didn't disagree. She was already blinking away her own tears, her heart squeezing painfully. When Quinn didn't speak, Molly frowned and continued.

"Nicole came to me. I don't know that she meant to, or if she sort of stumbled my way—it doesn't matter. She came into the brewery yesterday, after lunch. She told me she wandered around all night, and then she'd come in to get a drink. I don't know if she forgot I worked there or if she came there to find me, but I'm glad she did. I asked Toni for the day off and took Nicole back to her mom's place.

"Her mom was a wreck. She'd been calling Nicole all night and morning. She even called the cops. I guess Nicole sent some kind of scary message to her at like midnight. Her mom was afraid Nicole had hurt herself."

If Annette knew, that meant her dad knew, Quinn thought. Quinn hadn't called him since the day after Christmas, and she was struck, again, with something like horror, by how selfish and self-centered she was. He came here twice a year, and she'd basically forgotten his existence for the last three days. The idea of upsetting him, of worrying Annette, and hurting Nicole…

She was crying now, the tears flowing down her cheeks. If the sight of this reaction moved Molly at all, she didn't show it.

"Nicole didn't want to talk, at first," Molly said, her tone still angry, hurt. "Then, finally, after some coffee and some food, she told us everything, Quinn. Everything."

"Oh?" Quinn asked, speaking for the first time. She was starting to feel light-headed, and she stumbled on her way to one of the chairs clients used for their photos, sitting down on it all at once, almost limply.

"Yeah," Molly said. "She told us how awful you'd been to her. How you'd basically been a complete jerk about your work. She didn't word it that way, but her meaning was clear. Annette and I were up half the night calming her."

A faint echo of Quinn's anger at Nicole threatened to flare up again, but one look at Molly's face was enough to force it back down deep inside, hopefully for good. Molly still looked angry, upset, and Quinn felt that awful pinching pain again. She had so few close friends, and now she'd managed to dive-bomb the one that meant the most to her, possibly the best friendship she'd ever had.

"Is she…is she okay?" Quinn said, her voice breaking briefly.

"Who? Nicole? The woman's whose heart you broke? Is she okay? Is that what you're asking me right now?" Molly nearly shouted at her.

Quinn sobbed, hiding her face in her hands. The shame and pain were suddenly far too much to take, even sitting down. She sobbed for some time, and although she didn't expect or anticipate it, suddenly Molly was there, pulling her into a rough hug.

"I'm so mad at you," Molly said between her own sobs.

"I do-don't blame you," Quinn said, crying into her friend's hair.

Molly pulled back, kneeling in front of her, but left her hands on Quinn's shoulders. She waited until Quinn met her eyes before asking, "Why? Why did you do that to her, Quinn? Why?"

Quinn could tell by the tension in her hands that Molly wanted to shake her, and that only made her cry harder. Quinn buried her face in her hands again, but this time, with Molly rubbing up and down her back, she was able to calm down faster. When she finally looked at Molly, she appeared more disappointed than angry.

"Why, Quinn?" she asked again, almost gently.

Quinn shook her head. "I can't explain it, Molly. I was so angry. I've never been that angry in my life except…" She thought of that moment in the hotel room in high school. She shook her head and continued. "And it kept happening. Photo after photo, and John kept picking Nicole's work over mine, and I got more and more upset."

Molly still looked confused. "Nicole said you two had planned to avoid any hard feelings by submitting blind. Why didn't you let them stay anonymous? Why did you insist on knowing whose photos were chosen?"

Quinn swallowed and shook her head, squeezing her eyes shut against the shame threatening to take over again. Thinking back, she couldn't explain that choice. They could have avoided all of this if they'd done what they'd planned. Sure, she might have found out eventually, once the photos were posted, but she wouldn't have needed to find out right there in that small room. Nicole had been reluctant, very reluctant even, to change their plan, and that attitude had fueled her determination to know one way or another at the time. She'd suspected, rightly, that Nicole had guessed what would happen. Neither of them had been surprised by the outcome—John had clearly preferred Nicole's work, and Nicole had obviously expected that he would. Even thinking about it now made her angry all over again. Molly was still expecting an answer, but Quinn couldn't tell her any of this. It would prove exactly what she clearly suspected: that Quinn was a complete asshole.

She took a deep breath. "I don't...I don't know why I did that."

Molly's brows furrowed further. "So you had no reason for it? Cause that's what we couldn't figure out. Me, Annette, and Nicole, I mean. Why don't you know?"

Quinn tried to think back again, remembered being upset at the idea of Nicole hiding things from her, and that was as far as she got. Even that seemed like an incredibly stupid reason to do what she'd done.

She shook her head. "I can't explain myself, Molly. I don't know why I insisted on knowing, and I don't know why I got so upset. I felt so...betrayed, I guess. That she was so much better than I am."

Molly squinted at her, frowning and almost sneering. "Jealousy? That's it?"

Quinn tried to shake her head, but she couldn't deny the reality of the entire scenario. As with the scholarship, her anger had been rooted in jealousy. That was basically at the heart of it.

Molly, as if reading her thoughts, moved back to her feet. Her expression shifted, once again, to disappointment, and she shook her head.

"When you told me that old story about you and Nicole, when you were kids, I mean, I used to feel sorry for you. But I don't this time, Quinn, and I'm starting to wonder if I was wrong about the past, too. You can't go around blaming other people for your shortcomings. That's not fair, and it's not right. No one deserves that, least of all Nicole. The only thing I've ever heard from her about your work is how proud she is of you."

Quinn remembered then, for the first time since it had happened, how delighted Nicole had been with her animal photos, how pleased she'd been with Quinn's talent. The memory almost made her sick. Nicole was the better person, obviously. Quinn's insecurities had led her here, once again. She couldn't be proud of Nicole's talent, because it made hers seem the lesser. The recognition of that fact now, in all its ugly truth, made her feel like the world's biggest piece of shit.

"Listen, I need to go," Molly said, gesturing vaguely at the door. "Toni was nice enough to give me yesterday off last minute, but she'll have kittens if I don't show up again for one of the busiest nights of the year. I'll see you around, I guess."

She turned to go, and Quinn, suddenly coming back to herself a bit, called out, almost desperately, "Wait!"

Molly turned, brow furrowed, clearly frustrated.

"Do you think I can fix this, Molly? Is it too late?"

Molly raised her hands in a broad shrug. "I don't know, Quinn. If you'd seen her yesterday, you'd know what I mean. She was a goddamn wreck. She's a little better today, but not great." She started to turn away and then looked back. She hesitated for a long time. "And honestly? I'm not sure you deserve her."

Quinn felt as if she'd been kicked in the stomach, and she watched, silently, as Molly left without saying another word. In the last forty-eight hours, she'd somehow managed to ruin the best friendship and relationship of her life, all because of her petty, immature, asinine jealousy.

She cried for a while, finally deciding that unless she called Kim in to take over, she should close the shop for the night. She made a hasty handmade sign to hang on the door claiming illness, locked up, turned off the lights, and headed upstairs to her apartment.

The Christmas tree and all the other decorations were still here, and she was swept up in the memories of the holiday, less than a week ago, first with her family and friends, and then with Nicole alone. They'd all had such a great time together. Her dad had been happier than she could remember seeing him. Her friends had a great time too. And her time with Nicole had been some of the best moments of her life.

No, she couldn't stay here, not right now. She grabbed her keys and heavy coat, nearly racing out the back door, and started walking, away from downtown and into a nearby neighborhood, not going anywhere but somewhere else. She walked through the neighborhood by her elementary school, pausing and staring at it blankly and long enough that she started getting cold. She turned back on Tenth, passing the historical museum, wondering if she should go inside to be somewhere, anywhere. She decided to move on, finally stopping when she spotted a bench at the bus stop on Grand. She'd just seen the bus pull away, so she knew she'd have it to herself long enough to decide what she wanted to do.

She sat there, watching the light traffic pass by idly, her mind in such turmoil she couldn't seem to make it calm. Her watch showed that hardly any time had passed since Molly more or less stormed out of her studio, yet it already seemed like hours. How on earth was she going to get through the rest of the day, let alone the rest of her life?

A sob caught in her throat, and she swallowed it, suddenly angrier and more disgusted with herself than she'd allowed herself to recognize before. What was her plan here? To let things with Nicole end like this? Without a fight?

No, goddamn it, she told herself, standing up and slapping a fist into her other palm. She was not going to let one mistake ruin her life again. She was going to make things right with Nicole, with her dad, with her friends, with Annette, with everyone.

The question was, how?

CHAPTER TWENTY-THREE: NICOLE

Nicole stretched and then groaned, her head pounding. Last night, she and her mom had decided to share another batch of Christmas margaritas, and they'd had enough of them that a second pitcher had seemed like a good idea. This morning her blinds were drawn, thank goodness, but even the small amount of light hurt her eyes. She threw an arm over her face and then groaned, the pressure enough to make her headache sing again. Sadly, she knew of nothing better for a hangover than to get up and do something about it.

She swung her legs out of bed, sitting up all at once, and her stomach lurched fitfully. She swallowed the mouthful of saliva that came with her nausea and waited it out, eyes shut tight. Damn tequila, she thought. She promised herself never to drink that much again, knowing, in her heart, that she was lying to herself. Her mom's margaritas were just that good.

Images of Quinn bubbled up then, but she brushed them away as fast as she could, not willing to let herself dwell on her right now. A lot of the grandstanding she'd spouted last night had been a direct result of the liquor, but she did remember promising, on her mother's name, to forget the name Quinn Zelinski and move on with her life. She didn't think she'd actually ever *forget* her, but letting herself get pulled back down into that awful, horrible morass the other night was not something she wanted again, either. If it hadn't been for her mom and Molly, she didn't know what would have happened. And she did feel better. Two days of wallowing was enough. She was still hurt, heartbroken, but she wouldn't let it break her, either. Starting today, she was moving on.

When she stumbled out of her bedroom and into the living room, she saw that the curtains had been drawn out here as well. Her mom was tully reclined in her armchair, nearly lying flat, a folded rag over her eyes. She was in real clothes, different from what she'd worn last night, so she must have gotten up at some point earlier this morning. The dogs lifted their heads, one of them snuffing at her in a half-bark, half-growl, and then they too laid their heads down again, as if nursing their own hangovers. She remembered watching them eat a lot of junk food last night, so maybe that wasn't much different. The whole household was suffering today.

"Is that you, Nicole?" her mom asked, voice scratchy.

"No. It's the tooth fairy."

"Ha, ha. How are you feeling?"

"Like ass."

Her mom sighed, removing the rag before kicking her recliner upright again. She groaned, hand to her forehead, and then stood up, unsteady.

"Okay," she said, "New rule. No more Christmas margaritas."

"Agreed."

"Until next year."

Nicole laughed and gestured at the bathroom. "I'm going to take a hot shower and get some pain relievers in me, see if I can steam some of this out of my head."

"Okay. What do you want for breakfast? Or almost lunch, I guess, considering the hour."

Nicole's stomach gurgled unhappily at the idea of food, and she waved a hand dismissively. "Nothing. Or toast, maybe. Dry. And hot tea, please."

Her mom looked as if she wanted to argue, then paled before nodding. "Yes. I think you're right. Toast and tea sounds like just the ticket."

The shower helped, and by the time Nicole had brushed her teeth and dried her hair, the ibuprofen was starting to kick in, and she felt about a thousand times better. Her reflection looked better than it had, too. Yesterday and the day before, she hadn't been able to meet her own eyes in the mirror. That crushing, awful pain had been there, too raw and open to avoid. Now, however, she simply seemed a bit tired, more careworn than usual. That heartache had retreated to something inside, internal. She was proud of this progress.

When she came out into the living room, her mom was sitting at the little table, a plate of dry toast and a cup of sweet, hot tea waiting for her. She sat down across from her and nibbled delicately at the toast, waiting for her stomach to revolt, but it held. Her mom was watching her, smirking.

"What?"

Her mom laughed. "Nothing. I haven't gotten that drunk in a long time. And I don't know that I've ever seen you like that. You were really funny, though I barely remember what you were saying."

Nicole remembered her mother laughing, but not what she'd said to make it happen. "Yeah. But drinking like that was a bad idea."

"Fun while it lasted, though."

"Sure. But not worth this."

"No."

They were quiet again, and Nicole could see the questions in her mom's eyes. She didn't want to talk about Quinn anymore, but she also didn't want her squatting like a toad between them, either.

"It's okay, Mom. We can talk about her."

Her mom sighed and shook her head. "I'm so sorry, hon. I know I pushed you, and I shouldn't have. Not after what she did to you last time, when you were kids. I should have…I should have known this would happen again."

Nicole set her tea down and took her mom's hands, waiting until their eyes met.

"You have nothing to apologize for, okay? All of this is on Quinn—every bit of it. I don't want you to feel bad, you hear me?"

Her mom's eyes filled before she blinked the tears away. She took a long, shuddering breath before speaking. "I do. I'm just so sorry it turned out this way. I thought…"

"Me, too. And we were both wrong. But that doesn't mean we have to feel guilty or bad about it, certainly not you. I want to move on with my life and try to forget it ever happened."

"Okay, Nicole."

Her mom still looked devastated, and the heartache that had threatened Nicole for the last hour welled up inside, this time, however, warring with a deep-seated rage. She hated that Quinn had done this to her, certainly, but she also hated how much she'd hurt her mom. Her mom had only wanted the best for both of them, and she'd let Quinn into her heart, too. She was heartbroken at the loss, too.

Her mom sighed and then shook her head, dismissively. "So, what are you going to do with yourself today?"

Nicole sighed also. "I should be working, or at least making some phone calls to set up some stuff, but I guess it can wait. It's tight, but I'll be okay if I use every day I have left after today. I'll have ten days and ten different shoots to finish by the eleventh, and then there's the ball tomorrow."

Her mom's eyes went wide. "Oh my gosh! I forgot all about the ball."

According to the press packet Nicole had been given, as well as some of the details John had shared with them in person at the beginning of all this, the Elks had run a small New Year's Eve ball at their lodge for as long as anyone could remember, but this was the second year they'd teamed up with some other charitable organizations to host a much larger event in one of the grand ballrooms at the Hotel Colorado, the same hotel where her mom had worked, and the same ballroom where Nicole held her Non-Prom all those years ago. The Elks had asked the city tourism board to help promote the event by including them in this tourism campaign, in part because all the charities were Glenwood-based. So far, the Elks had managed to get fairly impressive ticket sales for the ball this year and last, but they were hoping that with some promotion they might be able to sell out and possibly grow the event in coming years.

"What are you going to wear?" her mom asked.

"Nothing special. I'm supposed to blend in. I have an all-black affair that kind of makes me invisible."

Her mom frowned. "Well, that's no fun."

"Are you going?"

Her mom hesitated before speaking. "Jack bought us tickets."

They hadn't talked at all about Jack and what their relationship might mean now that she and Quinn had broken up. Her mom had been avoiding the topic, and to be honest, so had she.

Her mom, seeing something of this in her expression, continued, almost babbling. "But I don't have to go. I mean, if it will upset you or something."

Nicole cut her off with a gesture. "No, Mom. That's not fair to either of you. You should go and have fun. You and Jack have nothing to do with me and Quinn."

This was partially bluster on Nicole's part, and she could tell her mom knew this from her uncertain expression. After all, if her mom and Jack stayed together, that would mean that she and Quinn would have to interact with each other again—maybe not anytime soon, but eventually. Right now, that seemed utterly impossible.

Her mom bit her lip, clearly worried. "Do you think she'll be at the ball?"

"Who, Quinn?" Nicole asked, then snorted. "I doubt it. She basically quit the other night. I can't imagine that she'd show her face, not after all that, not after the way she acted in front of John. He might have already fired her—who knows?"

All of this had come out rougher than she'd meant, and her mom was squinting at her, almost wary. Nicole didn't want to become angry or bitter, either, so she forced herself to smile.

"So, let's forget about all that for now. What say we take a walk somewhere? Maybe get you those birds before the New Year?"

Her mom slapped her forehead, dramatically. "Damn it! You're right! I only have today and tomorrow to get five more."

"Just five?"

The last time her mom had mentioned her bird list, she'd still had ten birds to find by New Year. Her mom wouldn't meet her eyes.

"Jack and I saw some down by the river the other day. He has a real eye for spotting them."

The pain and anger threatened again, so to distract herself, Nicole suggested that they change for their time outside. She dressed as warmly as possible, with silk long underwear underneath her fleece-lined pants and a thick wool sweater. She almost grabbed the hat Quinn had given her without thinking, then flinched away from it, pain stabbing her heart. She had to sit down, suddenly weak, and she sat on her bed for a long moment, taking deep breaths and trying not to cry. She'd been fooling herself from the moment she woke up. All her feelings were too raw, too recent, and too horrible to simply forget. Quinn had hurt her as deeply as she could be hurt, worse than when they were kids, and worse than any girlfriend since. But she would never let her mom see something like that again, and she would never, ever let someone do that to her again. And she wouldn't let the pain take her back under again, not now, not when her mom was waiting for her.

She stood, grabbed the red scarf, hat, and mittens Quinn had given her, and threw them in the corner of the room out of sight, reminding herself to donate them somewhere. After a few minutes digging around in her clothes, she found her old hat and scarf, and met her mom back in the living room, a wide, fake smile plastered on her face.

"Shall we?"

Her mom had been looking at her phone, frowning at it, in fact, but she looked up as Nicole came in. At the sight of her, her mom's expression faltered, but she grinned again, held up a folded map, and shook it slightly.

"Yes—let's go. I have some ideas about where we might look."

They drove to three different parks around town. Her mom had been to all of them before to birdwatch, she explained, but like anywhere, each park and the birdlife there was different every time she visited. She usually sat somewhere near the center of the park in silence before starting to look for birds, but Nicole suggested that they sit, instead, near the edge of the first park to avoid upsetting the birds at all. This worked at the first park—right away her mom spotted a Townsend's Solitaire hiding among the pine boughs of a large tree near the center of the park. They sat there another thirty minutes before moving on to the next park. They didn't catch anything new there, but at the last park, her mom saw a Canada Jay—rare enough here in the state that she hadn't seen one since she started her list.

Her mom took out her phone to add both birds to her app, and it took her long enough that Nicole almost offered to help her. Her mom was frowning at her phone again, and Nicole wondered, briefly, if she was texting with someone. She was sitting in a way that Nicole couldn't see her screen, but she was typing more than a bird app merited. Nicole decided not to mention it, however, since she was probably texting with Jack. Maybe her mom didn't want to bring him up and remind her of Quinn. Finally, her mom put the phone away, smiling brightly.

"I don't know about you, but I could use a break. How about some fancy coffee?"

"Sure! That sounds nice. Where should we go?"

"I'll show you. Then, when we're done, we can go to the river trail. There's one more place I want to check for birds."

River Blend Coffee, like the brewery, was on the ground floor of the Hotel Denver, and the late morning sun was so warm, they decided they would stay and drink their cappuccinos on the patio outside at the café. They chatted about a lot of light nothings—some shows they were watching, the way the town had changed in the last twenty years—all surface-level topics, but important nonetheless. Nicole had been here in town almost a month now, and for so much of that time, she'd either been busy shooting photos or with Quinn. She regretted the latter now, wishing she'd spent more time with her mom, but promised herself that once this job was over, they'd be together the entire weekend before she went home.

Home, she thought, wincing. She'd hardly given her place back in Fort Collins a thought the entire time she'd been here. She missed her friends there, of course, but that was the extent of her regret. Even her usual work held little appeal now. She loved it, but removed from her everyday life like she'd been the last month, nothing back home seemed to matter to her as much as it once had. She could happily stay here in Glenwood and never look back.

They were almost finished with their coffee when Molly walked by, obviously on her way to work, based on her polo and apron. She was digging around in the apron, oblivious to everything, and when Nicole called out to her, she leapt into the air and let out a little squeak.

"Jesus!" she said, hand on her chest. "You scared the hell out of me."

"Jumpy much?"

Molly shook her head. "Sorry. I'm super late for work again, and my mind is elsewhere. Sorry I can't stop and chat!"

"That's okay. I'll try to catch you later."

"If you're hungry, come on in for a late lunch!"

Nicole and her mom made eye contact, and her mom raised an eyebrow.

"What do you think?" she asked.

Nicole shrugged. "I could eat. I feel a lot better now that we've had some fresh air and good coffee. It's up to you."

Her mom stood. "Let's go in, then. They have great soups."

Molly had already disappeared inside by the time they'd bussed their table at the café and gathered their things. A long line of people waited to be seated in the brewery for lunch, but despite the sizable crowd, Nicole spotted Rico and Dane seated at a small, four-person table near the front window. They had seen her first and waved her and her mom over. The men stood to hug them both, then offered to share their flight of beer while they waited for their server to come back.

"Uh, no," Nicole said, grimacing at the offered beer. "Kind of overdid it last night."

"Hair of the dog?" Dane said, holding up a glass a bit higher.

The smell was enticing, and Nicole and her mom took a careful sip.

"Nice. I think I'll get one," her mom said, and they all laughed.

The server arrived soon after, fast considering these crowds, and they all ordered food and drinks.

After he left, Rico and Dane shared an uneasy glance before Dane said, "We, uh, heard what happened. I'm sorry Quinn treated you like that."

"We were really upset with her," Rico said.

"Are upset." Dane glared at him.

"Yes," Rico said. "Are upset. And super sad for you."

Nicole's face was suddenly hot, and her eyes were burning. These were Quinn's friends first, and between them and Molly, she was surprised to have their support like this. She didn't want anyone to have to take sides, but she appreciated that they were upset with Quinn, too.

She swallowed the lump in her throat and managed, "Thanks."

Dane, seeing her becoming emotional, looked a little panicky, and then his expression brightened. "Say. Before I forget, are you going to the ball tomorrow?"

"I'm doing a photo shoot there."

His face fell, but his smile returned a second later. "Well, even so, you have to let our friend in town do your hair. Amanda's an incredible stylist, and she's always complaining that she never gets to style long hair anymore. When we told her about you, she asked—"

"Demanded, more like," Rico said.

Dane laughed. "Okay, she *demanded* that we tell you to go in." He pulled out his wallet and handed her a business card. "Call her and schedule something for tomorrow. She'd love the chance to do something fancy."

"What are you wearing?" Rico asked.

Nicole's mom pointed at him. "I asked her that this morning! She told me she wants to be invisible."

The men sneered at Nicole, looking so appalled she could only laugh.

"Come on, guys. I'm working. I'm supposed to blend in."

Rico shook his head. "No, no. Don't you have anything nicer you could wear?"

"Well, I guess I do, but—"

"No buts," he said. "You're getting your hair and makeup done, and you're dressing up."

"I'm getting my makeup done, too?"

He ignored her, turning to the others to ask their opinions about colors of clothing and styles for her hair. Her mom was thrilled with the idea, and Nicole listened as the three of them made plans without once asking her for her input. Seeing her mom so excited made her give up any notion of protesting. If it made her happy, she had no reason to say no.

CHAPTER TWENTY-FOUR: QUINN

Seeing them come outside of the brewery, Quinn hid around the edge of the building, waiting until Nicole and her mom got in Nicole's car. Quinn ducked and crouched behind a mailbox as they drove away, hunched up to avoid being spotted. She'd been waiting outside for over an hour now. Molly had been able to send some updates via text, but as she hadn't been sitting there at the table with Dane and Rico when Nicole and her mom came in, she had only been able to give Quinn vague updates, at best.

Still, the initial stage had worked out as they'd planned, though there had been two scary moments. One had been when Molly had baited Nicole and Annette to go into the brewery. Quinn had been able to watch the entire scene from across the street, so she'd seen when Molly had overacted. She'd pretended to be super surprised to see Nicole and her mom there outside the café, but her whole performance had been over-the-top and far too dramatic. Yet apparently Nicole had bought it, and she'd gone along with the invitation and met up with Dane and Rico inside, as planned.

Nicole's mom Annette had been the scariest part of it all. None of this would have worked if she hadn't agreed to come to the café and then the brewery to begin with. Quinn herself hadn't been brave enough to call or text her, so she'd asked Molly to contact Annette this morning. Molly told her that Annette was reluctant to get involved, and Quinn and her friends more than half expected that she and Nicole wouldn't show up at all, especially when Annette wouldn't confirm that she was coming. But then, after what had seemed like a thousand years of waiting, they'd spotted Nicole's car driving by, and the plot Quinn and her friends had hatched began.

Last night, after she'd gotten back to her apartment from her depressing walk, she'd spent a couple of hours trying to think up a means of winning Nicole back. Whatever she did, it was going to have to be more elaborate than a humble apology. Showing up at her house and begging wouldn't be enough. Quinn halfway expected that if she had tried, Annette wouldn't even let her inside. Eventually, stuck for ideas, Quinn called her friends, pleading with them to help her, and they'd come through for her. All of them were disgusted with the way she'd treated Nicole, Dane almost hanging up on her, but she'd managed to convey her desperation over the phone, and the three of them had visited as a group late last night.

Rico had thought of the New Year's Eve ball, and then planning was just a matter of putting the rest of the pieces in place. Nicole would already be there, taking photos, so even if Annette ignored Molly's invitation this morning, and the whole scheme to get Nicole dressed and gussied up fell through, at least Nicole would be in the room already. Once that piece fell into place, however, they needed to decide what they would do or, more accurately, what Quinn would do, once Nicole was there. Those ideas took Quinn and her friends well into the wee hours of the morning, and even then, Quinn wasn't sure she would be able to pull things off on time. It didn't help that today was a Sunday and a holiday weekend, so when Quinn started making phone calls this morning, she hadn't gotten anywhere. But some time remained tomorrow before the ball, and Quinn had made peace with the idea that if she tried as hard as possible to get her plan in action, she would be able to show Nicole how much she cared, and she had to believe that would count for something.

The idea that her plan might not work, that Nicole would turn her down anyway, made her sick to her stomach, and she forced herself to dismiss the very idea. It had to work. If it didn't, she wasn't sure how she could continue her normal life. She would have to take a long leave of absence from work, at the very least, close the studio and run away for a while. Maybe visit her dad long-term or something. She shook her head. No, she told herself. That wouldn't happen. This would work. It had to.

Molly and the guys were waiting for her inside at a table by the windows, and she sat down, eager to hear how things had gone. Molly had only pretended to come in to work—her presence here entirely for show to get Nicole inside. Her boss Toni had been willing to play along.

Once she sat down, Dane pushed a beer her way, and Quinn took a long, grateful swallow.

"I still don't understand why you didn't have Annette bring her here to begin with," he said. "Why go through that whole thing with the coffee shop outside?"

Molly grinned, rubbing her hands. "When I texted her this morning, Annette told me they were drinking last night, so she knew she would have had a harder time explaining why she wanted a beer."

"Ah—gotcha. Did Annette know you were going to bump into them like that?"

Molly shook her head, her grin even wider. "No. But she played along, just like I knew she would."

"So, it all worked out?" Quinn asked. "Nicole agreed to everything? To get her hair done and dress up, I mean?"

"Yes!" Dane said. "Annette helped there, too. I think Nicole was going to put her foot down about it, but Annette was so excited, she seemed to sort of cave."

Quinn relaxed, smiling. Having Annette's support in all of this was a pleasant, entirely unexpected bonus. Last night, when Molly had told her more of the details about her time over at Annette's place, when she took Nicole home after she'd shown up at the brewery the other day, it had sounded like Annette might never forgive her. And true, in the grand scheme of their plan, it didn't matter how Nicole was dressed or what she looked like tomorrow, but if the spotlight was going to be on *her*, she'd want to look her best, and she suspected Nicole would, too.

The four of them sat there, quietly sipping their beers. Quinn stared outside at the bright winter day, suddenly nervous. She'd been wanting to ask her friends something, but it took her a long time to force it out. She met Dane's eyes.

"How was Nicole? I mean, how did she look? Could you tell?"

He and Rico shared a look, Rico lifting one shoulder, uncertain. Dane tilted his head back and forth, clearly not sure what to say.

"A little pale, I guess," he finally said.

"Tired," Rico added.

"But definitely better than Friday, when I saw her," Molly said.

Quinn's stomach clenched with something akin to grief, and she put her face in her hands, suddenly too sad to see their expressions anymore.

Dane rubbed his hand up and down her arm. "It'll work, honey. I really think it will."

Quinn looked at him again and tried to smile. "I hope so."

Her friends shared a worried look, and Quinn's eyes welled with tears. Regardless of what they'd said last night or what they said now, they had the same doubts she did. They might do all this work, and nothing would come of it. She might try as hard as she could, only to have Nicole, rightly, turn her down.

"Hey," Molly said, slapping the table. "No more doubts, okay? If we fall down that rabbit hole, we might as well give up now, right?"

Quinn tried her hardest to believe her. "You're right."

"So, let's move on to the next steps, okay? First—the easy part. What are you wearing?"

Quinn shook her head. "Does it matter?"

Molly's eyes widened dramatically. "After all this work to get Nicole dressed up? And you're asking if it matters?"

Dane and Rico were clearly insulted, too, lips peeled back as if in disgust.

"Well," Quinn said, backing down. "Rico's friend is doing my hair and makeup already, so I guess a nice dress would be a good idea."

"Not a nice one, a new one," Molly said, standing up. "Come on. We're going shopping."

Quinn shook her head. "Don't be ridiculous. There's no way I'm finding a new dress on the Sunday before New Year's Eve. Where would we even look? What's open?"

"I don't care if we have to drive to Denver, girly. We're getting you something nice, and you're not arguing with me about it."

Quinn looked at Dane and Rico, hoping they would back her up here, but they agreed with Molly.

"You have to knock her socks off," Dane said.

"Totally. You need to look ready to eat," Rico said. Everyone grimaced, and Rico laughed. "Sorry, I mean, uh, kiss and make up."

"You're all ridiculous!" Quinn said.

"Get up, lady," Molly said. "We're going."

"We'll, uh, stay here," Dane said.

"You just want to finish my beer," Quinn said, frowning at him.

"Not at all! I mean, I'll finish it—it's an insult to leave good beer like that behind. I think, you know, you might want to save some of your feminine mystery. You know, for the big reveal tomorrow night."

He was being a lazy ass, but she didn't argue, and in the end, it didn't take a three-hour drive to Denver, or even an hour and half to Grand Junction, to find a dress. She and Molly decided, almost on a whim, to check out a bridal rental place in town that was miraculously open. They expected the worst, only to be met with several nice options, including a velvet one in dark maroon that draped Quinn's body, exaggerating her modest curves. With the jewelry Nicole had given her at Christmas and a pretty, dark silk scarf, she predicted that she would, indeed, knock Nicole's socks off, as Dane had put it. Assuming Nicole would look at her or listen to her at all. At several points during the dress shopping and coffees afterward, Quinn could feel a tempting well of deep despair opening inside her. If this didn't work, she honestly didn't know what she would do.

She and Molly spent the rest of the afternoon calling various people involved in the New Year's Eve ball, finally getting through to everyone they needed to talk to late in the evening. In what seemed like the third or fourth miracle of the day, everyone they talked to had not only been willing to listen to her, but they had also enthusiastically agreed to help her. It seemed, in fact, that everyone liked a long-shot love story.

Now with all the moving parts in place, with only a couple of specific details to attend to tomorrow, she and Molly could ostensibly relax. Neither, however, could quite manage it. Quinn knew why she was anxious, but Molly seemed overinvested on her end.

"Why are you so worked up?" Quinn finally asked.

Molly's gaze met hers and darted away. "I-I was wondering..." She shook her head. "No. It's stupid."

"What?"

Molly sighed and rubbed her face, dragging her fingers down it a moment later and stretching her skin. She let out a groan of frustration.

"I was wondering if I should ask Toni to the ball."

"What? Of course you should!"

Molly's eyes brightened, and then she shook her head. "No. I mean, even if I could work myself up to it, she's working. It's New Year's Eve, for God's sake. It's like the busiest night of the year. *I* barely got off, and I asked months ago. She would have needed to ask someone to cover for her ages ago, like I did."

Quinn turned to face her as fully as possible on the loveseat, grabbing her hands and squeezing them.

"How long have you worked there again?"

Molly frowned. "You want to make me feel old?"

"Ha! No, Molly. But how long?"

Molly counted on her fingers, squinting. "Jesus. It's been almost five years."

"Okay. And how many times have you helped someone out at work? Covered a last-minute shift, went in for them on your day off?"

Molly's cheeks colored and she shrugged. "I don't know."

"Plenty." Quinn answered for her. "And you almost never ask for anything in return."

Molly wouldn't meet her eyes, and she shrugged, halfheartedly. "So?"

"Soooo," Quinn said, shaking their joined hands. "That means it's time to call in all those favors. You've got years of goodwill on your side, Molly—use it. I'm sure there's someone you can guilt or charm into covering for Toni."

Molly's eyes brightened with hope again, and that was enough for Quinn to push her to start making her own series of phone calls. It didn't take long at all before one of the assistant managers agreed to take Toni's shift. Quinn was pretty sure everyone the two women worked with knew about their flirtation, since their attraction was obvious to everyone who saw them. Like her own luck with the organizers at the ball, the people Molly worked for loved a love story.

"Now you just have to ask her to go with you," Quinn said.

Molly laughed, but she looked anxious, her body tight and hunched in on itself. Quinn squeezed her hands again before standing up, dragging Nicole up with her.

"Come on, then. Let's go to the brewery right now. No chickens allowed."

In the end, Quinn watched the entire thing with Dane and Rico, both of whom were still there, ostensibly to watch the game.

Toni agreed to the date at once, lifting Molly into a tight, body-clenching hug, and most of the restaurant, patrons and staff, burst into applause. She and the guys hugged, all of them similarly affected and wiping away happy tears.

Now Quinn had to hope that she was seeing a preview of tomorrow night when she asked Nicole to forgive her. Anything else was unthinkable.

CHAPTER TWENTY-FIVE: NICOLE

Nicole peered down at herself. "What do you mean?"

Her mom was still shaking her head. "Uh-uh. No way. You're not wearing that. It's too plain."

Nicole surveyed herself in the mirror. Her suit was black and somewhat austere, but functional for work events. Her shoes were plain black leather flats. She'd worn this same outfit at the faux wedding a couple of weeks ago, and her mom had complimented her at the time. In fact, it had been unusual for her to wear it then, since she usually tried to blend into the background. She'd only chosen it because she wanted to dress up a bit for Quinn and because the fake wedding had taken place during the day, which meant more people would see her. She'd planned, today, to wear what amounted to black pajamas, but Dane, Rico, and her mom had convinced her to dress up, and this was what she had.

"What's wrong with it?" she asked.

Her mom sighed and stepped up behind her in the mirror, putting her hands on her shoulders.

"When you were a teenager, and all you wanted to wear was black, I never complained, did I?"

Actually, compared to a lot of her friends, both of her parents had been incredibly decent about her fashion choices as a teen. They let her choose to look and dress however she wanted with almost no grief.

"No, you didn't complain," Nicole said. "But what's that got to do with anything?"

"I want you to keep all those years in mind as I tell you this, honey. Black is not the only color in the world."

Nicole laughed. "I know that, and you know I wear more colors now. And anyway—you're the one that wanted me to get dressed up, and I don't have anything else with me. What were you expecting, a ball gown?"

Her mom frowned. "Couldn't you at least wear a different-colored shirt?"

Nicole's silk shirt was also black, paler than the black of the blazer and slacks, but still black.

"What color do you suggest?" Nicole asked. She used all sarcasm she could inject into her question, but her mom either missed it or chose to ignore it.

"You always look so nice in red, honey. Do you have a nice red shirt?"

Nicole met her mom's eyes in the mirror. She didn't understand why her outfit was so important to her. Nicole would be working all night, and no one but her mom and friends would notice her shirt, but for whatever reason, her mom was very worked up about it. She turned, pulled her into a tight hug, and inhaled deeply, as if she could absorb her warmth.

"Sure, Mom," she said, moving back. "I can wear a red shirt if you think it'll look better."

Her mom's eyes brightened. "It will. Oh, this is going to be so much fun! I haven't been to a fancy ball in about a million years. I should go get ready myself."

Nicole watched her leave, smiling and holding her tongue. She didn't remind her that she would be working, so the ball wasn't going to be that much fun for her. Nicole had no reason to bring her down when she was so excited.

The ball was going to be in the Hotel Colorado—the grandest place in town, where celebrities and presidents stayed when they came through. Her mom had worked almost her entire career at the Hotel Colorado in various positions, rising from front desk to assistant general manager by the time she retired. Nicole herself had worked at the hotel occasionally as a teen, acting as a fill-in, mostly, for the regular staff during busy times. Nicole had always loved working there and loved visiting her mom at work—any excuse to go to a place that no one she knew would ever be able to afford. When she was growing up, in the off-season, her mom had occasionally been able to get free or significantly reduced hotel packages for the family, and she and her parents would spend a weekend in a lavish suite with over-the-top meals included. It didn't matter that the hotel was only a few blocks away from their little house. It was a world away from home in every other way that mattered. Nicole had always loved to pretend that they were the kind of family that could afford that sort of vacation on their own.

She'd chosen to throw her celebratory Non-Prom there all those years ago because of this connection. Her mom had helped her get a discount on the space rental, and since everyone in town knew the hotel was the nicest place in town, the ballroom had leant the celebration a kind of formality and opulence it might not have otherwise had. Still, that night had tainted her feelings for the hotel ever since. And now, as her more recent experiences with Quinn threatened to bubble up all the time and crush her heart even more than it already was, she needed to be careful not to think about any of that tonight.

She quickly changed her shirt, pleased, despite everything, with her appearance. Her mom was right—the red suited her.

The doorbell rang, and she checked her watch. Damn. Dane and Rico were early. In the living room, the dogs stood at high alert, both growling with rumbling menace at the door.

"Back," Nicole told them, though of course the dogs ignored her. She was forced to drag them both away, and they stood a few feet behind her, still growling. When she opened the door, the two men came inside, and both dogs ran for the kitchen at high speeds, yipping and terrified.

"What did we do?" Dane said, pouting. "I love dogs."

"Don't worry about it," Nicole said. "They're just big fraidy cats, and they hate everyone but my mom." And Quinn, she thought, but didn't say.

"You look nice," Rico said, but his tone wasn't enthusiastic.

"You sound like my mom," Nicole said. "I don't have anything fancy with me, okay? This was the best I could do on short notice." She realized, then, that both men were in quite lovely, matching gray suits with purple paisley ties. "You two, on the other hand, look incredible."

They both preened briefly, and everyone laughed.

"So, are you ready?" Dane asked, checking his watch. "Amanda's waiting for you."

Amanda, their friend and stylist, had been so enthusiastic when Nicole had called her yesterday, she seemed a bit unhinged.

"You're actually early, guys," Nicole said. "I don't even have my equipment ready."

Dane clapped his hands. "Well, chop, chop! Amanda is practically drooling to get at you."

Nicole still didn't know what to make of that reaction, but she didn't argue, heading into her bedroom to start gathering the various cameras, lights, and tripods she would be using tonight. She'd had to rethink the whole shoot once she accepted that Quinn wouldn't be there. She and Quinn had originally planned, much like the wedding, to shoot at different angles and places around the room, but as she was going to be working alone, she would need to do everything herself—a lot of work for one person.

The recognition that she'd be alone, while not a new one, took the wind out of her, and she sat down heavily on her bed, squeezing her eyes against possible tears.

"Damn it, Quinn," she whispered.

It took her a moment to get herself together again, but when she came back into the living room with some of her bags, Dane and Rico were joking with her mom, everyone too wrapped up to notice her. She smiled at the sight of them—happy that, like her, her mom had made some new friends in these nice men. Even if Nicole didn't end up moving here, at least she knew more people around to keep an eye on her mom while she wasn't here. All three genuinely seemed to like each other, and that made her like her new friends even more than she already did.

Her mom was wearing an actual evening gown—sapphire-blue and off the shoulders, draping to the floor. Her mom's makeup and hair were far more elaborately styled than they'd been in ages, possibly ever. She was also wearing a beautiful necklace Nicole had never seen before. Had her mom and Jack, like Quinn and herself, exchanged some of their presents privately? She dismissed that intrusive memory as quickly as she could and stepped toward her mom, gesturing up and down.

"Wow. You look…wow. I'm blown away."

"Isn't she incredible?" Dane asked. "Rico and I were just telling her."

"You are," Nicole said.

"Thanks, honey. I wanted to take full advantage, so I did."

"Jack'll never know what hit him," Rico said, winking.

Her mom laughed and then gestured at the men. "They were explaining what their stylist friend plans to do with you, so maybe by the time I see you later, you might be up to snuff, too."

"Wait, what?" Nicole asked, frowning at her friends.

"Uh, wow!" Dane said, dramatically checking his watch. "Look at the time. We better get going if we want to have time for dinner after you get your hair and makeup done."

He elbowed Rico, not in the least covertly, and Rico said, "Oh, yes! I mean, of course! We should go."

Her mom, Dane, and Rico looked strangely guilty, and no one would meet her eyes. All of them seemed to be hiding something from her. She was about to press them on it when her mom's phone rang, cutting off her train of thought.

"See you later, dear," her mom said, taking the phone back into her bedroom.

"Let me help you with those bags," Dane said, lifting one off her shoulder.

"Me, too," Rico said.

Soon she was left alone in the living room, and she knew then, without a doubt, that something was up. She used the next minute or so to get the rest of her photography equipment and to settle herself. If she wanted some kind of hint, she would have to keep pretending that she was entirely oblivious. She didn't know Dane or Rico very well yet, but she'd been around them enough to recognize that one or both of them would eventually let something slip if they weren't on their guard.

Dane and Rico drove her in their old jalopy, and she wondered, not for the first time, why they'd insisted on driving. It sort of made sense, in a way, since after her appointment with the stylist, the three of them were joining Molly and Toni for dinner before the ball, but Nicole could have easily driven herself, and the guys wouldn't have had to wait for her to get her hair done. That earlier suspicion grew stronger. They were trying to herd her around from place to place, directing her and keeping her from something.

When they finally made it to the small salon, Amanda, the stylist, was so excited to start, Nicole was once again struck with the sense that something was entirely off here. No one would ever be this excited to do hair. She was practically bouncing in place when they walked in the door and let out a long and very high-pitched squeal.

"Oh my God, oh my God, oh my God!" Amanda said, racing toward her and pulling her into a hug. She drew back almost at once, grimacing. "Oh! I'm so sorry. That was weird. I'm Amanda."

"Nicole," she said, shaking her hand.

"I'm sorry I got so excited when I saw your hair. Rico was right— it's glorious."

"Oh?"

Amanda laughed. "Only people with glorious hair don't see it. You wouldn't believe how rare it is for me to see something like yours. I can tell you take great care of it."

"Thanks?"

"Sit, sit," Amanda said, gesturing at the single barber's chair.

"Should I change my shirt?" Nicole asked, sitting down. "I brought one just in case."

"No. That's okay," Amanda said. "You won't get dirty or anything. I'm styling today, and we can put a smock on for the makeup." She turned to the men. "Guys? Think you could go get us some coffees? Pretty please?"

Her friends left, and Nicole watched them through the mirror, fighting a desperate longing to join them. The last thing she wanted was to be left alone with this nut.

Soon, however, Nicole had relaxed and was enjoying herself. Amanda, surprisingly, became nearly silent as she worked, which Nicole preferred. She also gave Nicole one of the best head and shoulder massages she'd ever had. All the tension from the last couple of days seemed to leave through this woman's skilled fingertips, and Nicole almost nodded off once or twice, snapping awake and shocked with herself. She was never like this with a total stranger. Amanda smiled at her in the reflection both times this happened, as if she'd expected it and didn't hold it against her.

By the time her friends came back—having taken far longer than getting coffee would merit—her hair was nearly done. Amanda had chosen an elaborate series of braids, woven through with red flowers and beads that miraculously matched her shirt.

"Oh, good," Amanda said, opening and closing her hand at the coffees. "Gimme."

Rico gave them both a coffee, and the four of them sat or stood there sipping them. Nicole hadn't wanted one before, but after her near nap, coffee was a nice pick-me-up.

"We got you this, too, Nicole," Dane said, reaching into a bag. He pulled out a boutonniere, the red spray roses very much like the flowers in her hair.

She frowned at it, feeling, once again, as if something was happening behind the scenes that she wasn't aware of. First, her mom asked her to wear a red shirt. Then, Amanda had flowers for her hair in almost the exact same color. Then, the guys came back with a boutonniere that nearly matched. Sure, they'd seen her shirt earlier, but the flowers didn't look like the kind of thing you could pick up in a shop at the last minute. It would have had to have been ordered ahead of time.

"What the hell is happening?" Nicole asked.

Rico and Dane shared a startled, guilty look, and Nicole was certain, then, that her suspicions were right.

"Uh, what do you mean?" Dane asked, looking anywhere but at her.

"You know exactly what I mean," Nicole said, trying to keep her voice calm.

He and Rico shared another look and then one with Amanda. Whatever they were planning was all so elaborate, even the stylist was involved.

"Could it be enough to say that it's a surprise?" Dane finally asked.

She stared at him for a long time. He looked scared but also hopeful. He obviously wanted her to play along with this plan, whatever it was. And since her mom was involved, too, she could only imagine that it all came back to her, somehow. Maybe her mom was going to surprise her with something later, at the ball, or after. She could only hope after, since she would be working all night, but that was the only explanation she could think of.

She sighed. "All right. Surprise it is. But don't ever let anyone ask you to surprise someone again. You're all terrible at it."

Dane, Rico, and Amanda cheered, and Amanda soon got back to work. Still, the entire time Nicole sat there, being primped and pampered, she couldn't shake the deep-seated worry that something more was happening, something beyond a simple surprise. And the jollier and sillier everyone else acted, the more and more she suspected that she wasn't going to enjoy it in any way.

Still, if it made her mom happy, she wouldn't resist. She'd hated seeing her mom so upset the last couple of days, and anything she could do to help cheer her up was good enough for Nicole.

Unless...But no. This couldn't be about Quinn. Quinn would never think to do anything like this for her.

Her eyes stung, but luckily the others were too wrapped up in a discussion of some reality show she'd never heard of to notice. By the time they were ready to leave for dinner, Nicole had mostly forgotten about Quinn, now curious about the surprise waiting for her later tonight.

CHAPTER TWENTY-SIX: QUINN

Quinn had been hiding for hours, now, here at the Hotel Colorado, first to help set things up, then simply staying because she was too anxious to do anything else. Amanda had dropped by earlier this evening to do her hair and makeup before leaving—to do the same for Nicole—but since then, Quinn had been entirely on her own, basically pacing around the hotel room she'd rented for the night. She'd tried to eat and drink some water, knowing she would be up for hours yet, but she couldn't make herself. All she could do was pace and fidget.

She'd planned this whole thing so late, only one very expensive hotel suite had remained, but she was glad for the extra space to ramble around in. The room had a balcony view, but she was so scared of being seen that she peeked through the curtains only once or twice, even after Nicole was safely inside downstairs, setting up the shoot for the ball. Even when the ball began, when no one would see her in the halls even if she left her hotel room, she stayed there in her suite, alone.

Finally, just before nine thirty, she heard a soft knock at the door. She raced to it, peered through the keyhole, and then opened the door as quickly as she could. She expected her dad, but he'd also brought Annette.

"Oh, honey," Annette said, opening her arms.

Quinn sobbed and threw herself into them, hugging her tightly. She didn't want to let herself cry, not really, but she couldn't stop a few tears escaping. Annette hugged her back just as fiercely, and Quinn heard a few muffled sobs, as well. Finally, they drew apart, and Annette took her hands.

"Come on, dear," she said. "Let's go inside for a moment. You look like you need a chance to calm down." She turned to Quinn's dad. "Could you make us a cocktail, hon? Just a little one, for the nerves."

"Sure thing," her dad said, and disappeared in the direction of the mini bar.

She and Annette moved over to the loveseat in the sitting room and sat down, Annette taking her hands again. Her expression was warm, with a slight hint of something like pity, and Quinn had to stifle a sob again.

"Why-why are you doing this?" Quinn asked her. "Why are you helping me?"

Annette peered at her long and hard, appearing almost angry now. Then that softness seeped into her eyes again, and she smiled, patting Quinn's hands.

"I won't lie to you, dear. I was very upset with you. Angier than I've been in a long time. Not that that's saying much, since I don't let myself get angry very often, but I was pissed as hell at you for how you treated my girl."

A tear rolled down Quinn's cheek, but she let it stay there.

"So why?"

"Because," Annette said, "everyone deserves an extra chance. Maybe even more than an extra chance, in your case, considering your history. And I could tell from the way Molly described it that you wanted to make it up to her."

"I do," Quinn said, as seriously as she could.

Annette nodded. "I know you do, dear. And maybe, selfishly, I want to help you, because helping you means helping Nicole, which also means helping me."

Quinn understood this, and she squeezed Annette's hands briefly before wiping her eyes, trying to be as careful as she could with all the makeup she was wearing. Annette was watching her again, that slightly wary anger there in her eyes again, and Quinn chuckled nervously.

"How do I look?" she asked.

Annette smiled then, genuinely, and pulled her into a quick hug. "You look amazing, Quinn. Nicole will never know what hit her." She paused, clearly considering whether to continue. "You know, early this month I told Nicole that she needed to go all out for you—to show you what you meant to her. And now I know that she needs that, too. What you're doing tonight is a good step to making it up to her."

Quinn licked her lips, suddenly very anxious again. "Do-do you think she'll take me back?"

Annette lifted one shoulder. "I don't know, Quinn. I really don't. But I will say I'm rooting for you. Both of you."

They hugged again, and some of the tension Quinn had been holding inside all day melted in Annette's arms. She was struggling against tears again, but these felt more like happy tears than before.

Her dad saved them by coming in with a small tray with glasses and a cocktail shaker. She and Annette wiped their eyes again before standing up to join him. He poured them three small martinis and then held his glass up.

"To second chances," he said.

"And third chances," Quinn added.

"And to as many chances as it takes," Annette said.

They clinked glasses and drank, Quinn tossing hers down in one long gulp, sputtering slightly when she swallowed.

"Shall we?" her dad said, holding out an arm.

She met his eyes, and he smiled at her. She smiled back and took his arm, holding hers out for Annette.

"Let's do this," Quinn said.

The three of them took the elevator together down to the lobby. Quinn was suddenly worried again that Nicole would see her before everything started, but Annette assured her that she was far too busy to think of anything but the photo shoot. Molly, Toni, Dane, and Rico were waiting for her near the doors to the ballroom, and all four cheered when they finally saw her.

"You look like a million bucks," Molly said.

"Thanks," Quinn said. "I feel like I'm about to fall to pieces."

Molly gave her a quick hug. "Don't. All you can do is try, right? And this is one hell of a way to try."

All her friends and her dad and Annette said something similar, and for the moment, she had hope. Maybe this would work, and she and Nicole could welcome in the New Year together.

Then the assistant MC opened one of the ballroom doors, and Quinn's nerves skyrocketed again.

"Are you Ms. Zelinski?" he asked her.

She could barely nod.

He handed her a microphone and pointed at a spot on the grip. "When you hear your cue, just push that button there and you'll be on."

She nodded again and took it from him, hands shaking.

"You'll do great," he said, seeing her nerves. He looked as if he wanted to say something more, but suddenly the band, which had been playing all this time, fell silent. "Good luck," he said, and disappeared inside.

"Distinguished guests, ladies and gentlemen, and all the rest of you!" the MC said from inside. Some light laughter followed this. "Please pardon the interruption, but we have a special request from a long-term resident of our fair city. Her story was so, well, touching, that we absolutely had to help her. Please enjoy this short presentation."

Quinn knew what was happening behind the closed doors in front of her. Inside, the lights were being dimmed even further, and a large, movie-style screen was dropping down behind the band. All was going according to plan. She took a deep breath and closed her eyes, waiting for the music to start. Finally, Mazzy Star's "Fade Into You" began to play. Quinn opened her eyes and pushed her way through the ballroom doors.

Everyone was staring at the movie screen, where a series of photos were being displayed, one after another. All of them were of Nicole—Nicole and her friends and their families, or of Nicole and her. Most of them had been taken over the last month, but she'd found some older pictures of them from when they were kids, and every once in a while, one of those appeared—the two of them looking ridiculously young. The older ones were always group shots, since even then she'd been too much of a coward to get one of just the two of them, together, but the newer ones were an homage to their time together the last few weeks. Photos of their trip to the brewery, the hot springs, the cemetery, ice-skating, sledding, holiday time with their friends and parents, and everything else that had happened this month cycled through on the big screen.

Quinn spotted Nicole almost at once. She was standing, stock-still, near the stage by the band, camera in hand. Her attention, too, was rooted on the photos, but even from here, Quinn could see her expression. Quinn took another deep breath, let it out, and turned on her microphone.

"Nicole," she said.

Nicole wrenched her attention away from the screen, peering desperately around the room before finding and settling on her. Most of the rest of the crowd turned her way, too, parting for her as she approached.

"Nicole," she said again. "First of all, I want to apologize. But beyond an apology, I want to offer you this." She indicated the photos on the screen. "A glimpse of our life together. Something I tried to throw away, as if it didn't matter to me. As if *you* didn't matter to me."

Nicole was still frozen in place, and Quinn had to swallow a lump in her throat before continuing.

"But you *do* matter to me, Nicole. You're the most important thing, the most important person in my life. Everything I said—everything I did was because of my own insecurities, my own jealousy. Of you. Of your incredible talent. Because you are talented, Nicole—one of the best artists I've ever known. But *your* talent doesn't hurt mine, and I know that now. And I'm so sorry I thought otherwise. It was never your fault, Nicole. Everything fell apart because of me."

Nicole still appeared shocked, and she was still motionless by the stage, her camera clutched to her chest. Quinn was about ten feet from her now, having walked the length of the ballroom as she spoke, and the entire crowd of New Year's guests surrounded them, watching. It took Quinn much longer to find her voice again, swallowing hard several times, and she could feel loose tears coursing down her face, but she made herself continue.

"I wonder, Nicole, if you could ever find it in yourself to forgive me. I'll do whatever it takes to show you, to *prove* to you, that you mean everything to me, if you'll give me another chance."

After a pregnant pause, with everyone waiting, watching, Nicole broke into a heartbreaking, beaming smile. She raced forward, swinging the camera out of the way at the last moment, and the two were in each other's arms seconds later. The entire room erupted into cheers and applause, and Quinn's heart felt as if it might stop working from happiness. Most of the crowd was still watching as they kissed, but Quinn was soon able to forget all of them in the blazing warmth of Nicole's lips and arms. By the time they drew back, however, still clasped tight, the band had started again and the lights had brightened a bit. Everyone was dancing around them, pretending not to notice.

"You did all this for me?" Nicole asked, tears streaming down her face.

"Yes, Nicole. All for you. I'm so sorry—"

Nicole kissed her, hard, and then drew back with an almost audible pop. "I forgive you."

"Just like that?"

"Just like that."

The band switched to a slower song, and Nicole moved back enough to offer her a hand. Quinn laughed and took it, and they were soon moving into a dance, the camera still awkwardly hanging from Nicole's shoulders.

"I'll have to get back to work after this," Nicole said, sighing.

"No, you don't," Quinn said, grinning. "I hired another photographer for the rest of the night."

Nicole laughed. "Really?"

"Yep! I want you all to myself."

Nicole laughed again and hugged her, briefly. "Thank you. That's really nice."

"It's just selfish," Quinn said, grinning at her.

"Well, selfish or not—I'm glad. Now I get to look at you in this dress all night."

"And I get to see you in this suit," Quinn said, running her hands up and down the lapels. "You look incredible."

Nicole smiled. "I guess now I know why everyone wanted to get me dressed up."

"Now you do."

They danced a while longer before Nicole wanted to stop to put some of her equipment away, especially the camera that was slung around her shoulders. When they moved off the dance floor, however, family and friends swarmed them, everyone congratulating them. She shouldn't be surprised at this point, considering all that Annette had done to help with everything, but she was still more than pleased to see how excited and happy Annette was with their reconciliation. Quinn thanked everyone again and then told Nicole how all of them had helped set things up.

"It's the nicest surprised I've ever had," Nicole said before hugging nearly everyone in turn.

"You two deserve it. After all you've been through, you're meant to be together," Annette said.

"Thanks, Mom," Nicole said, hugging her again.

"Thanks, Annette," Quinn said, and hugged her, too.

"I mean it," Annette said to her, almost whispering. "You belong together. As long you remember that, I won't worry about either one of you, ever again."

Quinn kissed her cheek and then let her friends pull her and Nicole back onto the dance floor. The music had picked up, and they all ended up having a great time out there for the next couple of hours. Almost as if no time had passed, midnight was closing in, and everyone was given a class of champagne or sparkling juice to toast in the year.

"Ten!" everyone shouted. "Nine! Eight! Seven! Six! Five! Four! Three! Two! One! Happy New Year!"

She hugged and kissed all her friends, her dad, Annette, and, right as the band began playing "Auld Lang Syne," she and Nicole stared at each other. Nicole held out her hand, and she took it, letting Nicole pull her away from everyone else. Nicole ran her fingers along the edge of her jaw, sending shivers throughout her body, and then kissed her, very lightly.

"Happy New Year, Quinn," she whispered.

"Happy New Year, Nicole."

"I can't wait to get you back to your place after this."

"I have a room upstairs."

Nicole's answering smile was broad, and the next kiss made everything they'd gone through the last few days melt away in the heat of their passion.

"Even better," Nicole finally said.

Quinn could only agree.

EPILOGUE

Nicole slid the box into place and then stood up, groaning. She hadn't realized until she started this move that she'd accumulated so much crap. She'd lived in her apartment here in Fort Collins for almost ten years, so she shouldn't be surprised, but she'd always prided herself on being a kind of minimalist. She tossed, recycled, or donated things all the time, and she wasn't a collector or sentimentalist for stuff of any kind besides camera equipment. But when they started packing her apartment last week, she and Quinn realized the time they set aside wouldn't be enough if they wanted to get back to Glenwood in time for Christmas.

Nicole's mom and Quinn's dad had driven up with Molly a few days ago to help, and then Dane and Rico had come yesterday. Nicole also had some very nice friends here in Fort Collins who were only too happy to come by and put things in boxes for her in return for some local beer and pizza. Some people might think that her friends were getting a little long in the tooth for free food and drink as an incentive, but it had worked like a charm. Her friends and family had come over every afternoon and evening the last few days.

Finally, the moving pod had been dropped off last night, and today, Saturday, almost everyone she knew had come again to help load it. Today had, in fact, turned into a kind of party, with everyone taking breaks to eat the food her friends Jai and Stuart were serving in her apartment complex's courtyard.

Nicole was currently standing at the back of the pod by the sliding door, taking boxes from her friend Maddie and placing them, Tetris-style, on top of others and around her furniture. Her friends and family had formed a kind of human chain to bring the boxes down the stairs and directly to her here at the pod, and between all of them, they were making short work of it. In fact, the only real holdup was her, since she had to find a place to put the various boxes she was being handed.

She turned, like a robot, to take the next box, only to find her friend Maddie grinning at her. The others in the chain had already wandered away, leaving the two of them alone.

"That was the last one!" Maddie said.

"Really?"

"Really. Though I still can't believe you're moving. I barely even see you for the last twelve months, and now you're leaving us behind."

Nicole laughed and held out her arms for a hug. All her friends had said something similar to her over the last few days, but they didn't hold it against her, either. After she and Quinn had finished their work for the city last January, Nicole had been forced to go back to her so-called "real life" here in Fort Collins. But she'd driven down to Glenwood Springs at least once a week, more often when she could work remotely. She and Quinn continued, all the while, to plan for Nicole's move, but moving wasn't as easy as simply wanting to do it.

Then, Nicole's work had suddenly gotten busier—she was offered a last-minute show in Denver throughout the summer and fall—and the move to Glenwood had been postponed even longer. Between her trips to Glenwood and Denver, she'd barely spent any time in her apartment in Fort Collins or seen her local friends here for the last year.

Then, about a month ago, during the last week of Nicole's Denver show, something astonishing had happened. Quinn had driven into Denver to tell her that'd she'd been hired on assignment for *National Geographic* and would be leaving for Australia and Southeast Asia for the next year, possibly longer.

Quinn had been in equal parts terrified, excited, and worried. She told Nicole she was terrified to screw things up, excited at the chance of a lifetime, and worried about what it meant for them here and now, still so near to the beginning of their relationship. Further, she was going to have to figure out what to do with the Old West Studio in Glenwood for the duration. Her assistant, Kim, was still in graduate school and couldn't work there full-time during the school year.

In terms of their relationship, at least for Nicole, it hadn't even been a question. She told Quinn she was going with her and putting her own work on pause. They planned to spend the next year and more traveling together, and Nicole would be paying her own way out of her savings, acting as a kind of assistant wherever she could. Nicole had no illusions that she would take her own photos beyond those for personal use, though she was bringing some of her own equipment in case inspiration struck. They'd be spending some time in cities, after all, and she might find enough material for a show of her own when they returned.

So, considering that she'd be away for over a year, and that she and Quinn planned to move in together when they came back to the states, she'd decided to move out of her place in Fort Collins before they left early in the new year. They were leaving her things in storage until they were home again, and they'd be looking for a new place together in Glenwood when that happened.

Nicole and her friend Maddie finally let go of each other, both teary. They chuckled and wiped their eyes, stepping back and surveying the pod.

"It looks good," Maddie said. Her voice was gruff with emotion. "I'm surprised you didn't use a U-Haul."

Nicole pushed her lightly, and they both forced a laugh. Nicole worried she might start crying for real if they went on like this.

"So, how's married life treating you?" Nicole asked, if only to change the subject. Maddie and her fiancée Ryann had gotten married last Valentine's Day.

Maddie beamed. "It's great. You'll know soon enough, I guess, with your shotgun wedding."

Because Quinn was using a special kind of work visa for her trip, it made more legal sense for the two of them to get married before the trip. She and Quinn were keeping the entire thing very low-key. This Thursday, the day after Christmas, they had an appointment with the county clerk in Glenwood. Only their folks, Molly, Dane, and Rico would come to the courthouse with them. She and Quinn were pretending, for now, that it was all some legal convenience, but Nicole was over the moon about it, and Quinn was, too. They wanted a bigger celebration, later, when they came back, but Nicole was still thrilled with this smaller affair, too.

Maddie, as if reading her thoughts, said, "You *have* to have some kind of big party when you get back, to celebrate all of these changes."

"For sure," Nicole said. "We'll have a big homecoming, wedding reception, and moving bash then. You and Ryann will be at the top of the guest list. It'll be the biggest, queerest party of the year."

"We'll be there," Maddie said, her eyes wet again.

Nicole cleared her throat and gestured at her building. "We should go join the others. If we're not careful, Jai and Stuart will eat and drink everything."

They closed and locked the pod together and wandered around the outside of the building to the back courtyard. It was only a few days before Christmas, but the weather was almost warm. A couple of heat lamps had been set up back here, and the picnic tables that were a feature of this courtyard had been draped in red-and-green-checkered tablecloths. Some nice, seasonal flower arrangements in red, white, and green sat in the middle of every table, giving the entire space an appropriate, holiday festival feeling. How her friends had managed to arrange all this without any warning was beyond her, but the sight of it almost made her tear up again. Everyone that had been part of the moving chain was here, as well as some of the others that had been helping Quinn clean inside. All in all, perhaps thirty people had gathered here.

Nicole and Maddie were greeted with a lot of shouts and clapping, everyone's chipperness likely the result of the libations coming from a tapped pony keg set up near the grills. Nicole's friend Erin ran a brewery in the nearby town of Loveland, and she could be counted on to bring the best of the best when she came to a party. And this was exactly that—a party. Nicole hadn't planned to have anything like a going-away get-together, mostly because she hadn't had the time to plan one, yet she'd ended up with one anyway, and one far classier than she could have planned. It touched her deeply to know that her friends would think to put something together like this for her without asking.

Nicole spent a few seconds searching for Quinn and finally spotted her with the rest of the Glenwood contingent—their parents, Molly, Toni, Dane, and Rico. Maddie's wife Ryann was with them, too, chatting with Quinn and her mom. After greeting several people, she and Maddie made their way over to them, and Quinn stopped, mid-sentence, to kiss her. Their parents and friends nearby clapped and hollered at them when this happened, and they broke their kiss with a laugh.

"All done?" Quinn said, quiet enough that only Nicole could hear her.

"All done."

Quinn smiled broadly and pulled her into another kiss, ignoring the further catcalls from their friends and family.

"I'm glad," Quinn finally said. Her hands were still looped around Nicole's waist.

"Me, too," Nicole said, realizing as she said it that she *was* glad. She was also a little sad to be leaving all these lovely people behind, and she loved her work, and she'd miss her mom when they were abroad, but this was also the first step in her new life with Quinn. Soon they would be married, and then they'd be on the trip of a lifetime, sutured together for the next year.

Quinn, as if realizing that everyone was watching them, stepped back, grinning at the others, cheeks burning red. Nicole's eyes blurred again, and her mom, seeing her face, was smart enough to change the topic.

"Your friends are so nice, honey," she said.

"For real," Molly said. "I don't even know this many people. And all these people just showed up to help you move. Amazing."

Her mom nodded. "First, they help you move, and then those lovely men over there arrange this party for you. These are wonderful people, Nicole."

Nicole peered in the direction of the grills, where her friends Jai and Stuart were distributing food. Jai was manning the grills, and Stuart stood next to her friend Erin, helping distribute beer from the keg.

"Ah!" Nicole said. "So this party was their idea."

"We helped, too," Maddie said, pulling Ryann closer with one hand.

"Thank you guys so, so much," Nicole said. "It's one of the nicest things anyone's ever done for me."

"This was the least we could do," Ryann said "We're going to miss you so much." Her eyes caught on something behind Nicole, and she said, "I'm sorry, but could you excuse us for a moment? My friend Alex just showed up, and I think that's her new girlfriend. I haven't met her yet."

"Of course," Nicole said, hugging her and Maddie before they left. She watched them walk away and then greet two women she didn't recognize. Then, as Nicole surveyed the rest of the courtyard more, she spotted several more people she didn't know at all. Somehow, almost like her Non-Prom all those years ago, this afternoon had turned into a major celebration for friends and strangers alike.

Her mom moved closer to her, linking an arm around her waist.

"Getting to meet so many of your friends makes me feel better, somehow," she said.

"Oh?" Nicole asked.

"I mean, I've been up here a few times to visit you, and I've been introduced to some of these people before, but seeing them all here, together, makes me feel better about you living up here by yourself all those years."

"What do you mean?"

Her mom shrugged. "I always worried you were, I don't know, a little lonely."

Nicole hugged her mom with one arm. "Me? Lonely? I was worried that *you* were lonely all by yourself like that in Glenwood."

Her mom laughed. "Not me. I have lots of friends like this, too. Too many, even."

By this point, Dane and Rico had wandered away to talk to Jai and Stuart, and Quinn, Molly, and Toni were standing some distance away, both laughing with Quinn's dad.

Quinn's dad had come, as usual, for the holiday season, but this time he'd be staying in Colorado, as he'd offered to watch over the Old West studio while Quinn was gone. This was a major relief for Quinn, since she hadn't wanted to close it for any length of time, and his stay was also a boon for their parents, since they could spend more time together this year. Her mom had been to Arizona a couple of times this year, but having him there in Glenwood would, of course, be better on all counts. He was, ostensibly, staying at Quinn's place, but both she and Quinn suspected he'd stay over at her mom's more often than not.

Molly, Toni, Quinn, and Quinn's dad had moved away from them, ostensibly to give them privacy, and Nicole took the opportunity to watch Quinn—her fiancée!—with some of the people Quinn loved best of all. Quinn was practically glowing with happiness.

"You've got a good one there," her mom said, squeezing her again.

"I know. I feel like the luckiest person alive. I'm also glad you'll have Jack to keep you company this year."

Her mom grinned at her. "Me, too."

She and her mom moved closer to the others, and the six of them chatted for a while longer before Nicole was literally dragged away by some of her other friends. For the next two hours, she was called from group to group, and while she was glad to get a chance to say thanks and good-bye to everyone that had helped her the last few days, she kept glancing around the crowd, searching for Quinn, who was always somewhere else, chatting with small groups of her local friends. With her small business to run, Quinn had managed to come up to Fort Collins only a couple of times this last year, and she hadn't met very many people here before today. Nicole was glad her friends were excited to get the chance to meet her or get to know her better, but she also wished the two of them had thought to stay together all afternoon.

Nicole was standing near the keg, and her friend Erin caught her peering around at the crowd.

"Just go," Erin said, waving her hand.

"What?"

Erin rolled her eyes. "It's obvious you're looking for your girl. I give you permission to leave me alone. My wife is around here somewhere, and I have a beer. And we'll talk later tonight."

Nicole squeezed her hand, mouthing her thanks, and darted, as quickly as she could, around the edge of the crowd, pretending not to hear people calling her to them. Quinn spotted her at the same time Nicole found her, and, like Nicole, she excused herself from the small group of people she was with. They met halfway, embracing and kissing again. Nicole lost herself in the kiss so much that if people cat-called them, she didn't hear it. When they drew apart, Quinn's eyes were shining, and Nicole worried, once again, that she might start crying herself.

"I love you so much, Quinn," she said instead.

"I love you, Nicole."

"I'm so glad I get to spend the rest of my life with you."

Quinn sighed, happily, leaning into her, and nuzzled into Nicole's neck. "Me, too. I'm so happy, I can hardly believe it."

They drew apart and smiled at each other, and from the way Quinn's eyes clouded with fondness, she knew she was giving Quinn that look again—that dopey, dazed look she'd given her most of their lives. Quinn's grin broadened, and Nicole's heart did a happy leap. Quinn's happiness would always delight her more than anything else.

"Should we get back to your party?" Quinn asked, gesturing.

Nicole sighed. "I guess we should. But let's stay together this time, okay?"

"Sure." Quinn said, then hesitated before smiling slyly. "Although..."

"Although what?"

"Everyone's so busy, they might not notice if we left for a little while."

Nicole frowned. "Why would we do that?"

Quinn rolled her eyes. "So we can go upstairs to your apartment."

Nicole remained confused a while longer, and then she got it. "Oh. Oh! Yes. I think we should do that."

They grabbed each other's hands and giggled as they ran inside. They were halfway up the stairs before Nicole realized something and stopped. Quinn, on the steps above her, looked back and down at her, seeming confused.

Nicole sighed. "I just remembered the mattress is already packed in the pod."

They'd planned to stay with Erin and her wife Darcy tonight before driving to Glenwood tomorrow morning.

Quinn cocked an eyebrow. "Why is that a problem?"

Nicole laughed, and they continued, making it inside her apartment and locking the door behind them in record time.

About the Author

Charlotte was born in a tiny mountain town and spent most of her childhood and young adulthood in a small city in Northern Colorado. While she is usually what one might generously call "indoorsy," early exposure to the Rocky Mountains led to a lifelong love of nature, hiking, and camping.

After a lengthy education in Denver, New Orleans, Washington DC, and New York, she earned a doctorate in literature and women and gender studies. She currently lives with her wife, son, and their cats in a small city in Wisconsin.

Charlotte is a two-time Golden Crown Literary Society "Goldie" Winner for *Gnarled Hollow* and *Legacy*, and a finalist for a Lambda Literary Award for *Gnarled Hollow*.

Books Available From Bold Strokes Books

A Haven for the Wanderer by Jenny Frame. When Griffin Harris comes to Rosebrook village, the love she finds with Bronte de Lacey creates a safe haven and she finally finds her place in the world. But will she run again when their love is tested? (978-1-63679-291-0)

A Spark in the Air by Dena Blake. Internet executive Crystal Tucker is sure Wi-Fi could really help small-town residents, even if it means putting an internet café out of business, but her instant attraction to the owner's daughter, Janie Elliott, makes moving ahead with her plans complicated. (978-1-63679-293-4)

Between Takes by CJ Birch. Simone Lavoie is convinced her new job as an intimacy coordinator will give her a fresh perspective. Instead, problems on set and her growing attraction to actress Evelyn Harper only add to her worries. (978-1-63679-309-2)

Camp Lost and Found by Georgia Beers. Nobody knows better than Cassidy and Frankie that life doesn't always give you what you want. But sometimes, if you're lucky, life gives you exactly what you need. (978-1-63679-263-7)

Fire, Water, and Rock by Alaina Erdell. As Jess and Clare reveal more about themselves, and their hot summer fling tips over into true love, they must confront their pasts before they can contemplate a future together. (978-1-63679-274-3)

Lines of Love by Brey Willows. When even the Muse of Love doesn't believe in forever, we're all in trouble. (978-1-63555-458-8)

Only This Summer by Radclyffe. A fling with Lily promises to be exactly what Chase is looking for—short-term, hot as a forest fire, and one Chase can extinguish whenever she wants. After all, it's only one summer. (978-1-63679-390-0)

Picture-Perfect Christmas by Charlotte Greene. Two former rivals compete to capture the essence of their small mountain town at Christmas, all the while fighting old and new feelings. (978-1-63679-311-5)

Playing Love's Refrain by Lesley Davis. Drew Dawes had shied away from the world of music until Wren Banderas gave her a reason to play their love's refrain. (978-1-63679-286-6)

Profile by Jackie D. The scales of justice are weighted against FBI agents Cassidy Wolf and Alex Derby. Loyalty and love may be the only advantage they have. (978-1-63679-282-8)

Almost Perfect by Tagan Shepard. A shared love of queer TV brings Olivia and Riley together, but can they keep their real-life love as picture perfect as their on-screen counterparts? (978-1-63679-322-1)

The Amaranthine Law by Gun Brooke. Tristan Kelly is being hunted for who she is and her incomprehensible past, and despite her overwhelming feelings for Olivia Bryce, she has to reject her to keep her safe. (978-1-63679-235-4)

Craving Cassie by Skye Rowan. Siobhan Carney and Cassie Townsend share an instant attraction, but are they brave enough to give up everything they have ever known to be together? (978-1-63679 062-6)

Drifting by Lyn Hemphill. When Tess jumps into the ocean after Jet, she thinks she's saving her life. Of course, she can't possibly know Jet is actually a mermaid desperate to fix her mistake before she causes her clan's demise. (978-1-63679-242-2)

Enigma by Suzie Clarke. Polly has taken an oath to protect and serve her country, but when the spy she's tasked with hunting becomes the love of her life, will she be the one to betray her country? (978-1-63555-999-6)

Finding Fault by Annie McDonald. Can environmental activist Dr. Evie O'Halloran and government investigator Merritt Shepherd set aside their conflicting ideas about saving the planet and risk their hearts enough to save their love? (978-1-63679-257-6)

The Forever Factor by Melissa Brayden. When Bethany and Reid confront their past, they give new meaning to letting go, forgiveness, and a future worth fighting for. (978-1-63679-357-3)